00 401 058 625

KU-393-537

B144 17/5

SPECIAL MESSAGE TO READERS

THE ULVERSCROFT FOUNDATION
(registered UK charity number 264873)
was established in 1972 to provide funds for research, diagnosis and treatment of eye diseases. Examples of major projects funded by the Ulverscroft Foundation are:-

- The Children's Eye Unit at Moorfields Eye Hospital, London
- The Ulverscroft Children's Eye Unit at Great Ormond Street Hospital for Sick Children
- Funding research into eye diseases and treatment at the Department of Ophthalmology, University of Leicester
- The Ulverscroft Vision Research Group, Institute of Child Health
- Twin operating theatres at the Western Ophthalmic Hospital, London
- The Chair of Ophthalmology at the Royal Australian College of Ophthalmologists

You can help further the work of the Foundation by making a donation or leaving a legacy. Every contribution is gratefully received. If you would like to help support the Foundation or require further information, please contact:

THE ULVERSCROFT FOUNDATION
The Green, Bradgate Road, Anstey
Leicester LE7 7FU, England
Tel: (0116) 236 4325

website: www.foundation.ulverscroft.com

Renée Knight worked as a documentary-maker for the BBC before turning to writing. *Disclaimer* is her first novel. She is married with two children.

DISCLAIMER

This is a work of fiction. Names and characters are the product of the author's imagination and any resemblance to actual persons, living or dead, is purely coincidental.*

*Everything you have just read is a lie.

What if you realised the book you were reading was all about you? When an intriguing novel appears on Catherine's bedside table, she curls up in bed and begins to read. But as she turns the pages, she is sickened to realise the story will reveal her darkest secret. A secret she thought no one else knew . . .

RENÉE KNIGHT

DISCLAIMER

Complete and Unabridged

CHARNWOOD
Leicester

First published in Great Britain in 2015 by
Doubleday
an imprint of
Transworld Publishers
London

First Charnwood Edition
published 2016
by arrangement with
Transworld Publishers
A Random House Group Company
London

The moral right of the author has been asserted

This book is a work of fiction and any resemblance to actual persons, living or dead, is purely coincidental.

Copyright © 2015 by Renée Knight
All rights reserved

A catalogue record for this book is available from the British Library.

ISBN 978–1–4448–2815–3

Published by
F. A. Thorpe (Publishing)
Anstey, Leicestershire

Set by Words & Graphics Ltd.
Anstey, Leicestershire
Printed and bound in Great Britain by
T. J. International Ltd., Padstow, Cornwall

Northamptonshire
Libraries

E

This book is printed on acid-free paper

To Greg, George, Betty and
my mother, Jocelyn

1

Spring 2013

Catherine braces herself, but there is nothing left to come up. She grips the cold enamel and raises her head to look in the mirror. The face that looks back at her is not the one she went to bed with. She has seen this face before and hoped never to see it again. She studies herself in this new harsh light and wets a flannel, wiping her mouth then pressing it against her eyes as if she can extinguish the fear in them.

'Are you OK?'

Her husband's voice startles her. She hoped he would stay asleep. Leave her alone.

'Better now,' she lies, switching off the light. Then she lies again. 'Must have been last night's takeaway.' She turns to him, a shadow in the dead-hour light.

'Go back to bed. I'm fine,' she whispers. He is more asleep than awake, yet still he reaches out and puts his hand on her shoulder.

'You sure?'

'I'm sure,' she says. All she is sure about is that she needs to be alone.

'Robert. Honestly. I'll be there in a minute.'

His fingers linger on her arm for a moment, then he does as she asks. She waits until she is certain he is asleep before returning to their bedroom.

She looks at it lying there face down and still open where she left it. The book she trusted. Its first few chapters had lulled her into complacency, made her feel at ease with just the hint of a mild thrill to come, a little something to keep her reading, but no clue to what was lying in wait. It beckoned her on, lured her into its pages, further and further until she realized she was trapped. Then words ricocheted around her brain and slammed into her chest, one after another. It was as if a queue of people had jumped in front of a train and she, the helpless driver, was powerless to prevent the fatal collision. It was too late to put the brakes on. There was no going back. Catherine had unwittingly stumbled across herself tucked into the pages of the book.

Any resemblance to persons living or dead . . . The disclaimer has a neat, red line through it. A message she failed to notice when she opened the book. There is no mistaking the resemblance to her. She is a key character, a main player. Though the names may have been changed, the details are unmistakable, right down to what she was wearing that afternoon. A chunk of her life she has kept hidden. A secret she has told no one, not even her husband and son — two people who think they know her better than anyone else. No living soul can have conjured up what Catherine has just read. Yet there it is in printer's ink for anyone to see. She thought she had laid it to rest. That it was finished. But now it has resurfaced. In her bedroom. In her head.

She tries to dislodge it with thoughts of the previous evening. The contentment of settling

2

into their new home: of wine and supper; curling up on the sofa; dozing in front of the TV and then she and Robert melting into bed. A quiet happiness she had taken for granted: but it is too quiet to bring her comfort. She cannot sleep so gets out of bed and goes downstairs.

They still have a downstairs, just about. A maisonette, not a house any more. They moved from the house three weeks ago. Two bedrooms instead of four. Two bedrooms are a better fit for her and Robert. One for them. One spare. They've gone for open-plan too. No doors. They don't need to shut doors now Nicholas has left. She turns on the kitchen light and takes a glass from the cupboard and fills it. No tap. Cool water on command from the new fridge. It's more like a wardrobe than a fridge. Dread slicks her palms. She is hot, almost feverish, and is thankful for the coolness of the newly laid limestone floor. The water helps a little. As she gulps it down she looks out of the vast glass windows running along the back of this new, alien home. Only black out there. Nothing to see. She hasn't got round to blinds yet. She is exposed. Looked at. They can see her, but she can't see them.

2

Two years earlier

I did feel sorry about what happened, I really did. He was only a child after all: seven years old. And I was, I suppose, in loco parentis, although I jolly well knew that none of the parents would have wanted me being loco anything. By then I had sunk pretty low: Stephen Brigstocke, the most loathed teacher in the school. Certainly I think the children thought so, and the parents, though not all of them: I hope some of them remembered me from before, when I had taught their older children. Anyway, I wasn't surprised when Justin called me into his office. I'd been waiting for it. It took him rather longer than I'd expected, but that's private schools for you. They are their own little fiefdoms. The parents might think they're in control because they're paying, but of course they're not. I mean, look at me — I was barely interviewed for the job. Justin and I had been at Cambridge together and he knew I needed the money, and I knew he needed a head of English. You see, private schools pay more than state and I had had years of experience teaching in a state comprehensive. Poor Justin, it must have been very difficult for him to remove me. Awkward, you know. And it was a removal, rather than a sacking. It was decent of him, I

4

appreciate that. I couldn't afford to lose my pension, and I was around retirement age anyway, so he merely hastened the process. In fact, we were both due for retirement but Justin's departure was quite different to mine. I heard that some of the pupils even shed a tear. Not for me though. Well, why should they? I didn't deserve those kinds of tears.

I don't want to give the wrong impression: I'm not a paedophile. I didn't fiddle with the child. I didn't even touch him. No, no, I never, ever touched the children. The thing is, I found them so bloody boring. Is that a terrible thing to say about seven-year-olds? I suppose it is for a teacher. I got sick of reading their tedious stories, which I'm sure some of them laboured over, but even so, it was that sense they had of themselves, that at seven, for crying out loud, they had anything to say that I might be interested in. And then one evening I had just had enough. The catharsis of the red pen no longer worked and when I got to this particular boy's essay, I don't remember his name, I gave him a very detailed critique of why I couldn't really give a shit about his family holiday to Southern India where they'd stayed with local villagers. Well, how bloody marvellous for them. Of course it upset him. Of course it did and I'm sorry for that. And of course he told his parents. I'm not sorry about that. It helped speed up my exit and there's no doubt I needed to go for my own sake as well as theirs.

So there I was, at home with a lot of time on my hands. A retired English teacher from a second-rate private school. A widower. I worry that perhaps I am being too honest — that what I have said so far might be a little off-putting. It might make me appear cruel. And what I did to that boy was cruel, I accept that. But as a rule, I'm not a cruel person. Since Nancy died though, I have allowed things to slide a little. Well, OK, a lot.

It is hard to believe that, once upon a time, I was voted Most Popular Teacher in the Year. Not by the pupils at the private school, but by those at the comprehensive I'd taught at before. And it wasn't a one-off, it happened several years running. One year, I think it was 1982, my wife, Nancy, and I both achieved this prize from our respective schools.

I had followed Nancy into teaching. She had followed our son when he began at infants'. She'd taught the five- to six-year-olds at Jonathan's school and I was assigned the fourteen- to fifteen-year-olds at the comp up the road. I know some teachers find that age group a struggle, but I liked it. Adolescence isn't much fun and so my view was, give the poor buggers a break. I never forced them to read a book if they didn't want to. A story is a story after all. It doesn't just have to be read in a book. A film, a piece of television, a play — there's still a narrative to follow, interpret, enjoy. Back then I was committed. I cared. But that was then. I'm not a teacher any more. I'm retired. I'm a widower.

3

Spring 2013

Catherine stumbles, blaming her high heels, but knowing it's because she's had too much to drink. Robert reaches his hand to grab her elbow, in time to stop her falling backwards down the concrete steps. His other hand turns the key and pushes open the front door, his grip on her arm still firm as he leads her inside. She kicks off her shoes, and tries to inject some dignity into her walk as she heads for the kitchen.

'I'm so proud of you,' he says, coming from behind and folding his arms around her. He kisses the skin where neck curves into shoulder. Her head stretches back.

'Thank you,' she says, closing her eyes. But then this moment of happiness melts away. It is night. They are home. And she doesn't want to go to bed even though she is desperately tired. She knows she won't sleep. Hasn't slept properly for a week. Robert doesn't know this. She pretends all is well, managing to conceal it from him. Pretending to be asleep, lying next to him, alone in her head. She will have to invent an excuse to explain why she's not going to follow him straight to bed.

'You go up,' she says. 'I'll be there in a minute.

I want to check some emails.' She smiles encouragement, but he doesn't need much. He has to be up early the next morning, which is why Catherine appreciates even more the real pleasure he seems to have got from an evening where she has been the centre of attention and he the silent, smiling partner. Not once did he hint that maybe it was time to go. No, he had allowed her to shine and enjoy the moment. Of course, she has done this for him on many occasions; still, Robert had played his part with grace.

'I'll take up some water for you,' he says.

They have just returned from a party, the aftermath of a television awards ceremony. Serious television. No soaps. No drama. Factual. Catherine had won an award for a documentary she had made about the grooming of children for sex. Children who should have been protected but weren't because nobody had cared enough; nobody had taken the trouble to look out for them. The jury had described her film as brave. She had been described as brave. They have no idea. They have no idea what I'm really like. It wasn't bravery. It was single-minded determination. Then again, maybe she had been a little bit brave. Secret filming. Predatory men. Not now though. Not now she is at home. Even with the new blinds, she fears she is being watched.

Her evenings have become a series of distractions to stop herself thinking about the inevitable time when she will be lying in the dark, awake. She has managed to fool Robert, she thinks. Even the sweating, which comes on as bedtime

8

gets closer, she has laughed off as the menopause. She has other signs of that, sure, but not this sweating. Though she had wanted him to go to bed, as soon as he has, she wishes he was with her. She wishes she was brave enough to tell him. She wishes she had been brave enough to tell him back then. But she wasn't. And now it is too late. It was twenty years ago. If she told him now he would never understand. He would be blinded by the fact that, for all this time, she has kept a secret from him. She has withheld something that he would feel he had a right to know. He is *our* son, for Christ's sake, she hears him say.

She doesn't need a fucking book to tell her what happened. She hasn't forgotten any of it. Her son had nearly died. She has been protecting Nicholas all these years. Protecting him from knowing. She has enabled him to live in blissful ignorance. He doesn't know that he almost didn't make it into adulthood. And if he *had* held on to some memory of what happened? Would things be different? Would he be different? Would their relationship be different? But she is absolutely sure that he remembers nothing. At least, nothing that would bring him close to the reality of it. For Nicholas, it is simply an afternoon that has merged in with many others from his childhood. He might even remember it as a happy one, she thinks.

If Robert had been there, it might have been different. Well of course it would have been different. It wouldn't have happened. Except Robert wasn't there. So she didn't tell him because she didn't need to — he would never find out. And it was better that way. It *is* better that way.

She opens her laptop and googles the author's name. Almost a ritual, this. She has done it before, hoping there'll be something there. A clue. But there is nothing. Simply a name: *E. J. Preston.* Made up, probably. 'The Perfect Stranger *is E. J. Preston's first and possibly last book.*' No clue as to gender even. Not *his* or *her* first book. It is published by Rhamnousia; when she looked that up it had confirmed what she had already suspected, that the book is self-published. She hadn't known what Rhamnousia meant. Now she does. The goddess of revenge, aka Nemesis.

That's a clue, isn't it? About gender, at least. But that's impossible. It can't be. And no one else knew those details. No one still living. There were others, though — anonymous others. But this has been written by someone who really cares. This is personal. She looks to see if there have been any reviews. There are none. Perhaps she is the only one to have read it. And even if others do, they will never know that she is the woman at its heart. Someone does, though. Someone knows.

How the fuck did this book get into her home? She has no memory of buying it. It just seemed to appear on the pile of books by her bed. But then everything has been so chaotic with the move. Boxes and boxes full of books still waiting to be unpacked. Perhaps she put it there herself. Took it from a box, attracted to the cover. It could be Robert's. He has countless books she has never read and might not recognize. Books from years ago. She pictures him trawling through Amazon, taking a fancy to the title, to the cover, and ordering it online. A fluke. A sick coincidence.

But what she settles on and begins to believe is that someone else put it there. Someone else came into their home, this place that doesn't yet feel like home. Came into their bedroom. Someone she doesn't know laid the book down on the shelf next to her bed. Carefully. Not disturbing anything. On her side of the bed. Knowing which side she slept on. Making it look as if she had put it there herself. Her thoughts pile up, crashing into each other until they are twisted and jagged. Wine and anxiety, a dangerous combination. She should know by now not to mix her poisons. She grips her aching head. Always aching these days. She closes her eyes and sees the burning white dot of sun on the book's cover. How the fuck did this book get into her home?

4

Two years earlier

It had been seven years since Nancy died and yet I still hadn't got round to sorting through her things. Her clothes hung in the wardrobe. Her shoes, her handbags. She had tiny feet. Size three. Her papers, letters, still lay on the desk and in drawers. I liked coming across them. I liked picking up letters to her, even if they were from British Gas. I liked seeing her name and our shared address written down officially. I had no excuse once I'd retired though. Just get on with it, Stephen, she would have said. So I did.

I started with her clothes, unhooking them from hangers, taking them out of drawers, laying them out on the bed, ready for their journey out of the house. All done, I'd thought, until I saw a cardigan that had slipped off its hanger, and was hiding in a corner of the wardrobe. It is the colour of heather. Lots of colours, actually. Blue, pink, purple, grey, but the impression is of heather. We had bought it in Scotland before we were married. Nancy used to wear it like a shawl: the sleeves, empty of her arms, hanging limply at her sides. I have kept it; I'm holding it now. It is cashmere. The moths have got at it and there is a small hole on the cuff that I can fit my little finger through. She hung on to it for over forty

12

years. It has outlived her and I suspect that it will outlive me too. If I continue to shrink, as I undoubtedly will, then I might soon be able to fit into it.

I remember Nancy wearing it in the middle of the night when she'd get up to feed Jonathan. Her nightgown would be unbuttoned with Jonathan's tiny mouth around her nipple and this cardigan draped around her shoulders, keeping her warm. If she saw me watching from the bed she would smile and I would get up and make tea for us both. She always tried not to wake me, she said she wanted me to sleep and that she didn't mind being up. She was happy. We both were. The joy and surprise of a child delivered in middle age when we had all but given up hope. We didn't bicker about who should get up or who was stealing whose sleep. I'm not going to claim it was fifty-fifty. I would have done more, but the truth is that it was Nancy who Jonathan needed most of, not me.

Even before those midnight feasts, that cardigan was a favourite of hers. She wore it when she was writing: over a summer frock; over a blouse; over her nightdress. I'd glance over from my desk and watch her at hers, striking out at her typewriter, the limp sleeves quivering at her sides. Yes, before we became teachers Nancy and I were both writers. Nancy stopped soon after Jonathan was born. She said she'd lost her appetite for it, and when Jonathan started at the infants' school she decided to get a job teaching there. But I'm repeating myself.

Neither Nancy nor I had much success as

writers, although we both had the odd story published. On reflection, I would say that Nancy had more success than I, yet it was she who insisted I carry on when she gave up. She believed in me. She was so sure that one day it would happen, that I'd break through. Well, maybe she was right. It has always been Nancy's faith which has driven me on. She was the better writer though. I never lost sight of that, even if she didn't acknowledge it. She supported me for years as I produced word after word, chapter after chapter, and one or two books. All rejected. Until, thank God, she finally understood that I didn't want to write any more. I'd had enough. It just felt wrong. It was hard to get her to believe me when I said it was a relief to stop. But I meant it. It was a relief. You see I'd always enjoyed reading far more than writing. To be a writer, to be a good writer, you need courage. You need to be prepared to expose yourself. You must be brave, and I have always been a coward. Nancy was the brave one. So, that's when I started teaching.

It did take courage though to clear out my wife's things. I folded her clothes and put them in carrier bags. Her shoes and handbags I put into boxes that had once held bottles of wine. No inkling, when that wine came into the house, that the boxes it arrived in would leave containing my dead wife's accessories. It took me a week to pack everything up, longer to remove it from the house.

I couldn't bear to let everything go at once and so I staggered my trips to the charity shop. I got to know the two women at All Aboard quite well. I told them the clothes had belonged to my wife and after that, when I dropped by, they would stop what they were doing and make time for me. If I happened to turn up when they were having coffee, they'd make me a cup too. It became strangely comforting, that shop full of dead people's clothes.

I worried that, once I finished the job of sorting through Nancy's things, I would fall back into the lethargy I'd been in since I'd retired, but I didn't. As sad as it was, I knew I had done something Nancy would have approved of and I made a decision: from then on I would do my utmost to behave in a way that, if Nancy were to walk into the room, she would feel love for me and not shame. She would be my editor, invisible, objective, with my best interests at heart.

One morning, not long after that clear-out period, I was on my way to the Underground station. I had woken with a real sense of purpose: got up, washed, shaved, dressed, breakfasted and was ready to leave the house by nine. I was in a good mood, anticipating a day spent in the British Library. I had been thinking about writing again. Not fiction; something more solid, factual. Nancy and I had sometimes holidayed on the East Anglian coast and one summer we had rented a Martello tower. I had always wanted to find out more about the place, but every book I'd found on the subject had been so dry, so lifeless. Nancy had tried too, for various birthdays of mine, but all she had come

15

up with were dull volumes full of dates and statistics. Anyway, that's what I settled on as my writing project: I would bring that marvellous place to life. Those walls had been soaked in the breath of others over hundreds of years and I was determined to find out who had spent time there from then until now. So that morning I had set off with quite the spring in my step. And then I saw a ghost.

I didn't have a clear view of her. There were people between us. A woman pushing her child in a pram. Two youths ambling. Smoking. I knew it was her, though. I would know her anywhere. She was walking quickly, with purpose, and I tried to keep up but she was younger than me, her legs stronger, and my heart raced with the effort and I was forced to stop for a moment. The distance between us grew and by the time I was able to move again she had disappeared into the Underground. I followed, fumbling to get through the barrier, fearful that she would get on a train and I would miss her. The stairs were steep, too steep, and I feared I might fall in my rush to join her on the platform. I gripped the rail and cursed my feebleness. She was still there. I smiled as I walked up to her. I thought she had waited for me. And she turned and looked right at me. There was no smile returning mine. Her expression was anxious, perhaps even scared. Of course it wasn't a ghost. It was a young woman, maybe thirty. She was wearing Nancy's coat, the one I had given to the charity shop. She had the same colour hair as Nancy had had at that age. Or at least, that's what I had seen. When I

16

got up close I realized the colour of this young woman's hair was nothing like Nancy's. Brown yes, but fake, flat, dead-brown. It didn't have the vibrant, living shades of Nancy's hair. I could see that my smile had alarmed her so I turned away, hoping she would understand I hadn't meant any harm, that it was a mistake. When the train came, I let it go and waited for the next one, not wanting her to think I was following her.

I didn't fully recover until halfway through that morning. The quiet of the library, the beauty of the place and the comforting tasks of reading, making notes, making progress got me back to the place I had been when I started my day. By the time I got home in the early evening, I was quite myself again. I'd picked up one of those Marks and Spencer meals as a treat, an easy supper. I opened a bottle of wine, but drank only one glass. I don't drink much these days: I prefer to have control over my thoughts. Too much alcohol sends them haring off in the wrong direction, like out-of-control toddlers.

I was keen to go through my notes before bed, so I went to my desk to make a start. Nancy's papers were still littering the desktop. I flicked through circulars and old bills, knowing already that I'd find nothing of real importance. If there had been, wouldn't it have made its presence felt by now? I tipped the lot into the waste-paper basket, then took my typewriter from the cupboard and set it down in the centre of the cleared desk, ready to start work the following morning.

When Nancy had been writing she had had

her own desk, a small oak one which now sits in Jonathan's flat. When she stopped, we agreed that she might as well share mine. She had the right-hand drawers, I the left. She kept her manuscripts in the bottom drawer and although there were others stacked on the bookcase, the three in the desk were the ones she had had most hope for. Even though I knew they were there, it gave me a shock to see them. 'A View of the Sea', 'Out of Winter' and 'A Special Kind of Friend', all unpublished. I picked up 'A Special Kind of Friend' and took it to bed with me.

It must have been nearly forty years since I had read those words. She had written the novel the summer before Jonathan was born. It was as if Nancy was in bed with me. I could hear her voice clearly: Nancy as a young woman, not yet a mother. There was energy in it, fearlessness, and it threw me back to a time when the future had excited us; when things that hadn't happened yet thrilled rather than frightened. I was happy when I went to sleep that night, appreciating that, even though she was no longer with me, I had been lucky to have had Nancy in my life. We had opened ourselves up to each other. We had shared everything. I thought we knew all there was to know about each other.

5

Spring 2013

'Wait — I'll come out with you,' Catherine calls from the top of the stairs.

Robert turns at the front door and looks up at her.

'I'm sorry, sweetheart, did I wake you?'

She knows how hard he had tried not to; he kept his shower short, tiptoed around while dressing. Catherine, however, had been awake the whole time. Lying there. Eyes half closed. Watching him and loving him for being so considerate. She had waited as long as she could. As soon as he left the room she had scrambled out of bed, dressed, then chased down after him. She couldn't be alone yet. Later maybe, but not yet.

She sits on the bottom stair, cramming her feet into trainers.

'I've got a stinker of a head. Best thing to do is get out there and clear it,' she says, tying her laces with shaky fingers. She hears herself, sounding so normal, so plausible. Shaky fingers could be a hangover. She has taken the week off work to unpack and settle them in — to turn their new place into a home — but this morning she cannot face it. And it's true, she does have a stinker of a head. It has nothing to do with last night's celebrations though.

19

She sees Robert check his watch. He has to be in early.

'I'll be quick, I'll be quick,' she says, running into the kitchen, filling a bottle of water, grabbing her iPod before running back to him. They slam the door shut, double-lock and walk together to the Tube. She reaches for his hand and holds it, and he looks at her and smiles.

'That was fun last night,' he says. 'Did you get lots of nice emails?'

'A few,' she says, although she hadn't bothered to check. It had been the last thing on her mind. She'll have a look later, when she's home, when her head is clearer. He pecks her on the cheek, tells her he shouldn't be late home, hopes her head feels better and then disappears into the Underground. She turns round as soon as he has gone, sticking in her ear-buds and running up the road. Back the way they'd come, towards the only green space in the area. Her feet slap in time to the music.

She passes the top of their road and keeps going. Her heart is thumping, sweat is already running down between her shoulder blades. She is not fit. She should be doing a fast walk, not a run, but she needs the discomfort. She reaches the high, wrought-iron gates of the cemetery and runs through. She manages one circuit then stops, panting for breath, bending down and resting her hands on her knees. She should stretch out, but she feels too self-conscious. She is not an athlete, merely a woman on the run.

Keep going, keep going. She straightens up and sets off again, a gentle jog, not punishing,

20

allowing thoughts to stir. As she reaches the halfway point she slows to a walk, keeping it brisk, wanting her heart to stay strong, to keep pumping. Names float out to her from the grave-stones: Gladys, Albert, Eleanor, names from long ago of people long dead. But it's the children she notices. The children whose stones she stops to read. The beginnings and ends of their short lives. Doesn't everyone do that? Stop at the graves of the children tucked up for ever in their grassy beds? They take up less space than their grown-up neighbours and yet their presence is impossible to ignore, crying out to be looked at. Please stop for a moment. And she does. And she imagines a stone that could have been there, but isn't.

Nicholas Ravenscroft
Born 14 January 1988, taken from us on
14 August 1993
Beloved son of Robert and Catherine

And she imagines how she would have been the one who would have had to tell Robert that Nicholas had died. And she hears his questions: Where were you? How could that have happened? How was it possible? And she would have burst open, poured everything out on to him and he would have sunk under the weight of it. She sees him struggle, pushing against it, trying to raise his head above the deluge, gasping for air but never quite getting enough to make a full recovery.

Nicholas didn't die though. He is alive, and she didn't have to tell Robert. They have all survived intact.

6

Two years earlier

I woke the morning after reading 'A Special Kind of Friend' refreshed. I was eager to start work and had planned to look through my notes before typing them up. I knew there was some paper in the dresser cupboard: everything seemed to end up either on or in our dresser. I could picture the sheaf of paper sitting beneath the games of Scrabble and Backgammon, but when I tried to pull it out, it wouldn't come. It was trapped in the back of the dresser. A panel had been pushed in and I pressed against it, trying to release the paper; still it wouldn't budge. Something was stuck between the dresser and the wall. I put my hand around the back and touched something soft. It was an old handbag of Nancy's: a cunning one that had managed to evade the trip to the charity shop.

I leaned against the wall, stretching my legs in front of me with the handbag on my lap. It was black suede with two pearl drops clasped around each other. I dusted it down and looked inside. There was a set of keys to Jonathan's flat, a lipstick and a handkerchief still pressed in a square where it had been ironed. I took the top off the lipstick and sniffed it. It had lost its scent yet kept its angled shape from the years it had stroked Nancy's lips. I held the hanky to my nose, and its perfume conjured up memories of evenings at the theatre. What I hadn't expected to find was the yellow envelope of photographs with Kodak in thick black lettering on the front. This was a precious find and I wanted to make an occasion of it.

I made myself some coffee and settled down on the sofa, anticipating a flood of happy memories. I assumed the pictures were holiday snaps. I think I even hoped there might be a few of the Martello tower: that finding the handbag was Nancy's way of helping me on with my project. In a way it was, but not the one I had had in mind that morning.

My head, which had been so clear at the start of the day, felt as if the contents of someone else's had been dumped into it. I could no longer tell which thoughts were mine and which were theirs; which ones were true and which were lies. My coffee had gone cold; the pictures were spread out on my lap. I had expected images I recognized, but I had never seen these pictures before.

She was looking straight into the camera. Flirting? I think so. Yes, she was flirting. They were colour photos. Some were taken on a beach. She was lying there, a smiling sweetheart on holiday in a red bikini. Her breasts were pushed up as if she was some sort of pin-up girl and she certainly looked as if she thought herself a very desirable woman. Confident. Yes, that's what it was. Sexual confidence. Others were taken in a hotel room. They were shameless. She was shameless. I couldn't look away though. I could not stop looking. I went through them again and again, tormenting myself, and the more I looked, the angrier I became because the more I looked, the more I understood.

What chewed at my heart was that I knew who had taken these pictures. I knew the handsome face behind the camera even though I couldn't find him. I looked and looked, but no matter how many times I went through them, all I could see was his shadow caught on the edge of frame in one shot. I even went through the negatives, holding them up to the light in case there was one of him that hadn't been developed. There were more negatives than prints and I hoped one of these might reveal him, but they were blurred, out of focus, useless.

How could Nancy have brought those photographs into our house? Hiding them from me, allowing them to sit and fester in our home. They must have been there for years. Did she forget about them? Or did she take a risk, knowing that I might come across them one day? But it was too late. By the time I did, she was dead. I would never be able to talk to her about them. She should have destroyed them. If she wasn't going to tell me, she should have destroyed them. Instead she had left me to find them when I was a pathetic old man; long after the event; long after a time when I could have done anything about it.

One of the things I had most prized about Nancy was her honesty. How many times did she look through those pictures in private? And hide them again? I imagined her waiting for me to go out before looking through them; hiding them when I came home. Every time I took something out of the dresser, every time we played Scrabble, she knew they were there and didn't say a word. I had always trusted her, but now I worried what else she might have hidden.

It is extraordinary how much strength anger gives one. I turned the house upside down searching for more secrets. I attacked our home as if it was the enemy. I went from room to room, ripping, spilling, tipping, making a godawful mess, but I found nothing else. The whole experience left me with the sensation that I had reached down into a blocked drain and was groping around in the sewage trying to clear it. Except there was nothing solid to get hold of. All I felt was soft filth, and it got into my skin and under my fingernails, and its stink invaded my nostrils, clinging to the hairs, soaking up into the tiny blood vessels and polluting my entire system.

7

Spring 2013

A speck of dust lands on the pillow. No one else would hear it. Catherine does. She hears everything — her ears are wide open. She sees everything too. Even in the pitch-black. Her eyes have become accustomed to it. If Robert woke now he would be blind; Catherine isn't. She watches his closed eyes: the twitching lids, the flickering lashes, and she wonders what is going on behind them. Is he hiding anything from her? Is he as good at it as she is? He is closer to her than anyone else and yet she has managed, over all these years, to keep him in the dark. It doesn't matter how intimate they are, he just can't see it and she finds that thought frightening. And by keeping everything locked up for so long she has made the secret too big to let out; like a baby that has grown too large to be delivered naturally, it will have to be cut out. The act of keeping the secret a secret has almost become bigger than the secret itself.

Robert rolls on to his back and starts to snore so Catherine gently propels him on to his other side so his back is to her. Careful not to wake him — she cannot risk a conversation this deep in the night — she moves close enough so she can smell him.

She remembers the moment, twenty years ago, when he put his arm around her and said: 'Are you OK?' She was not OK, but she hadn't wanted him to notice because she couldn't tell him why and she wasn't as good then as she is now at covering up. She had said, 'No, not really,' and though she had felt tears behind her eyes she stopped them from falling because she knew if they fell they would be followed by a torrent of words. If she had cried she wouldn't have been able to stop everything else coming out. So she didn't cry, she made a confession, but it was a false one.

'I want to go back to work. I feel bad even saying it. I know I'm lucky having a choice to stay home, you're earning enough for both of us, but . . . I'm lonely. I'm depressed . . . ' It was the beginning of her digging a tunnel of escape from herself — and from Nicholas too. Her son was a constant reminder, though she couldn't tell Robert that. She couldn't say that being on her own with Nicholas was sending her mad; that his presence threw up memories she wanted to wipe out.

'Do you understand?' she asked. And she remembers looking up into Robert's eyes and wondering whether he could see through her.

'Of course I do,' he said, pulling her close to kiss her. Nevertheless she felt his disappointment. He tried to hide it with his kiss; he tried to cover up his regret that she had confessed herself unable to be the kind of mother he wanted for their son. He never said this, he never voiced his disappointment, all the same she knew it was there, unspoken, between them.

There was a moment when she nearly told him the truth. Instead she lied again and said that she was going to stay with an old schoolfriend for the weekend. It was a friend he didn't know well, a friend who lived outside London; he would never find out. She told him it was an emergency — that the friend was having a breakdown. She packed a bag and left straight from work on Friday, leaving the new nanny to pick up Nicholas from school and getting away before Robert got home from work. She took a taxi, not the Tube — she didn't want to risk bumping into anyone she knew.

When she came home on Sunday evening, Nicholas was already in bed. Robert told her she looked pale and she said it had been a pretty ghastly weekend and that she was exhausted. That was all true.

'I need an early night, that's all,' she said and immediately changed the subject, asking him about the new nanny.

'Seemed to go well. Nick was in a chirpy mood when I got home on Friday.'

'That's good,' she said.

And the following morning she made sure she was fine. There was a little colour in her cheeks, and she had to get Nick ready for school before going to work so there was no time to talk, for him to notice that she was distracted. Work too was hectic. She was up to her eyes and that's what she wanted. To be so busy that there was no room left in her head for remembering. And she succeeded in emptying her mind of the past.

That was the point. That was what drove her. Now the past has elbowed its way back in, shoving everything else aside — standing there, chest puffed out, demanding her attention.

The book still lies on the table next to the bed. She can't finish reading it. Each time she has tried, she retreats like a coward, rereading the same words, over and over — trapped in its middle. She peels away from Robert and slides out of bed, picking up the book and creeping downstairs like a burglar.

She thumps it down on the kitchen table and turns her back on it, a feeble act of rebellion. Today is Sunday, a day of rest, but not for her. She makes tea, takes it up to the spare room and sits on the floor. There are five boxes here waiting to be unpacked: two have Nicholas's name on them; three are marked *Spare Room*. She can't remember what's in them. She feels light-headed from lack of sleep and her hands are shaking as she pulls things out, tearing and ripping at newspaper, unwrapping knick-knack after knick-knack, all pointless, useless things. She'd hoped for a clue — a note, an envelope, anything that might be connected to the book and help her trace its route into her home — there is nothing. She tries another box. Book after book after book, which she dumps on the empty shelves, not bothering to stand them up, allowing them to slip and slide against each other, leaving some to tumble to the floor with a thump.

She eyes Nicholas's boxes. He was supposed to have come a week ago to sort through them but he hadn't, and she had wanted to do it for him, but Robert had stopped her. They were Nick's things, not hers. And Catherine had been frustrated because she damn well knew that Nicholas wouldn't do it properly. And the point was he didn't have a bedroom here any more. What they had now was a spare room. For guests. Nicholas could come over whenever he liked. Of course he could. And if he ever wanted to spend the night, then of course he could do that too. In the spare room. He has his own flat now. Pays his own rent. And that's good. He is twenty-five years old. He has done better than they had ever dared hope. He has a job. A routine. Independence. And that's what Catherine wants for him. A chance to be the best he possibly can be. The rush of thoughts leaves her breathless, as if she has spoken each one out loud.

'Darling?' Robert's voice is gentle, yet still it makes her jump. She looks up at him from her nest of torn newspaper, her hands black from it. It is nine o'clock and she has already been up for four hours. She sees concern on his face. She looks a wreck. At forty-nine, you can't get away with not sleeping and think it won't show. Of course he notices her pale, dark-ringed face.

'I wanted to make a start before Nicholas comes. To make it easier for him,' she lies, and looks around at the chaos.

'It can wait. There's no rush. Let him do it.' He puts a hand on her shoulder. 'Scrambled eggs?'

She nods. She is starving. She always is now

30

she doesn't sleep. She follows him downstairs and slumps into a chair at the kitchen table, a dead weight in the room.

'Shall I do lunch?' he suggests. Nicholas is coming for Sunday roast and she has bought a chicken.

'No, no, I'd like to,' she says. She knows it will make her feel better if she can play her proper role and disguise herself in the smell of roasting meat juices.

She can see the book at the far end of the kitchen table. She had hoped that removing it from their bedroom would give her some peace. Robert is watching her, nursing questions in his head. Is she depressed? Is it the move? He is about to speak, but Catherine gets in first. She has been nursing her own question, preoccupied, playing with it, and so doesn't notice Robert's intake of breath, his preparation for speech. If she had, she might not have plucked up the courage to ask:

'Is that your book?'

She makes sure her mouth is full so she appears casual as she nods to the end of the table. Robert glances over and reaches for the book, sliding it towards him. He takes a while to answer. When it comes, his answer is dismissive: a shake of the head.

'Any good?' He picks it up, turning it over, reading the blurb on the back.

She swallows. 'Not really. Bit slow.' She watches him turn it over again and look at the cover.

'*The Perfect Stranger*,' he reads. 'What's it about?'

She shrugs. 'Oh, it's nonsense. Weak plot. Implausible.'

And he tosses it aside. Carelessly. No thought. Treating it in a way she wishes she could.

'Why?'

'I thought it might be yours,' she ventures.

'Thanks,' he says, but she misses the smile in his voice.

'I don't remember buying it, that's all. I wondered where it came from . . . ' Her voice trails off as she stands and takes her plate to the dishwasher. Robert shrugs at the book, wondering why she's so interested in it, thinking it's merely a diversion from the thing that is really worrying her. He is convinced that she is trying to make conversation and this concerns him. They're not that kind of couple. They don't need to 'make conversation'. They are close — closer now than they've been in years. He recognizes the signs: Catherine at home with too much time on her hands; too much time looking inwards; thinking about herself.

'Cath. You've done a great job on the house — it already feels like home. But I know you too well. You're itching to get back to work, aren't you?'

She looks at him. He honestly believes that.

'I love that you're not a domestic goddess. You should be off making another film, not stuck here, unpacking boxes and dressing the house.'

Her eyes fill with tears, confirmation to Robert that he is right. He is her rock. She lets him believe it. 'You're right, I know I've been distracted — '

He cuts in. 'So go back — there was no need to take two weeks off. Most of it's done anyway and the rest we can do together in the evenings, weekends. There are only a few boxes left. Why not?'

'Yes, why not.' She manages a smile. And then her brain sparks to life. She remembers. She remembers how the book came to be in their home. It's seeing it sitting on the table. An image she remembers. It was soon after they moved. The table had been littered with stuff. A box full of glasses half unpacked, screwed-up scraps of newspaper tickling the book's cover as it sat there patiently, waiting for her to pick it up. A pile of unopened post and a jiffy bag, its grey fluff exposed where she'd ripped it open. And from which she had taken the book. The envelope had been forwarded on to them. She remembers the thick red ink which had crossed out their old address and written on the new. She can feel Robert's eyes on her as she clears away the rest of the breakfast things; her renewed energy confirms to him that he was right. He knows her so well.

Thoughts fizz through her head: the book was sent to their old address, so whoever sent it doesn't know where she is now. They did not come into her home, into her bedroom. She will telephone the family who moved into their old house. She will ask them not to forward on anything else. It's too much trouble, she'll say. She's happy to come and collect anything. Perhaps she will go further. Perhaps she will say that they've had a couple of nuisance letters,

33

nothing too serious but they'd rather not have anything else forwarded on. And if anyone asks for their address, please would they say that they don't have it? Or their phone number, no they mustn't give out the phone number. She decides all this while kissing Robert on the forehead and going upstairs to have a shower. She will do all this tomorrow though, not today. Today she will concentrate on Nicholas, on her family. On having a proper Sunday together.

8

Two years earlier

I hoped that working on a book about eighteenth-century monoliths would keep my head clear — that it would divert my mind from dwelling on Nancy's betrayal. That's how I thought of it then. I thought of her secret as a betrayal. I tried not to. I tried very hard to concentrate on writing about the Martello tower. I had propped a photograph of one on the dresser shelf above the collection of postcards Jonathan sent from his travels. It squatted there, lumpen and grey, so I took it down again. How could I concentrate? There was a sliver of metal rattling around in my head. A tiny shaft of silver taunting me from my desktop. Attached to the spare keys to Jonathan's flat which I had found in Nancy's bag was another smaller key. Too small for a front door but a key to something else, a key to something that was in his home, not mine. It caught the light and winked at me every time I tried to focus on my work. Who did I think I was? A man with ten-foot walls to protect him from the past? I wasn't built like a Martello tower. I was a man with thin, crêpey skin who needed to find out what else his wife might have hidden. I was human, at least. That slip of a key had burned a hole in my head and I knew I wouldn't be able to write anything until I had unlocked its secret.

Jonathan's flat is at the top of a mansion block, pre-war, built in the thirties. There is no lift but someone has thought about those of us who might struggle to reach the top and they have put a chair on each landing. I sat in every one. Onwards and upwards. I dragged myself up the last flight and then looked down, through the beautiful wrought-iron balustrade which curved and fell to the cold stone floor. A softly curving funnel through which a human might swallow-dive, not touching the sides, slipping through until they ended in a bloody mess at the bottom. I had a feeling that I shouldn't have come, that I had no right to intrude. This was Jonathan's place.

The plant outside his front door was dead. It hadn't been watered for some time. I put the key in the lock. There was probably a knack to it, but I didn't have it and it seemed to take for ever to get in, and all the time I was expecting someone to tap me on the shoulder and ask what I was doing there.

Once inside I was struck by the most terrible smell. Putrefying. Something rotten, something dying or dead. I went straight into the kitchen, assuming it must have been in the bin, but that was empty. On the kitchen table was a vase of flowers. Dead, dried, crisp, just a green line around the vase where the water had once been. I hesitated, not sure it was my place to throw them out. I went into the sitting room and sat on Jonathan's sofa and looked around. I could see the unmistakable signs of femininity. More flowers on the small table by the window. Lifeless, ugly, their parched stems desiccated sticks crying to be put out of their misery. A woman's touch. I left them where they were. I hadn't put them there. They were nothing to do with me.

When I walked into Jonathan's bedroom I gagged from the smell. His bed was unmade, the duvet mussed and falling off. The cover was dark blue, the bottom sheet maroon. It reminded me of school uniform: good dark colours that didn't show the dirt. The smell came from the corner near Nancy's desk. I approached it, hand clamped over my nose and mouth, and there it was. A body. Rotting. Neck broken, mouth open, teeth bared, giving off that inside-out stench of putrefaction. I should have known. Death. Always leaving its predatory stench like a lusty tom-cat, long after it has left the scene. I found a plastic bag in the kitchen and, wearing it like a glove, picked up the whole thing, trap and mouse, and disposed of it in the kitchen bin.

I returned to the bedroom and sat at Nancy's desk. It's smaller than mine and the tops of my legs rubbed against its underside. It would have been even more of a squeeze for Jonathan, and I imagined his six-foot frame and his strong legs squished into what had been his mother's space. I was pleased to see it had been taken care of. No rotting flowers there. No water rings from cups, or glasses of water, just an undisturbed film of dust. There were pieces of paper neatly stacked on it and a photograph of Nancy and me. Mum and Dad. Husband and wife. Two people in love. Two people who were loved.

I clicked the switch on the desk light, but the bulb had gone. And then I began my invasion. I pulled at the first drawer and looked inside: empty, apart from the odd pencil stub and leaky biro. I went through the others and found the same. The last drawer was the smallest. Tucked under the desktop, it ran between the two pedestals, a slender hidey-hole. It was locked. I put in the key, turned it then slid the chair aside and pulled open the drawer. And what an industrious place it was. Pens, pencil sharpener, pencils, a box of paper-clips, three notebooks. They were the type Nancy used: blue-lined reporter's pads, nothing special. She'd always carried one with her when she was writing, filling it with thoughts or sights that struck her, overheard conversations — that sort of thing. I flicked through one, but didn't give it much attention. It was the manuscript underneath the notebooks that interested me. I picked it up. 'Untitled'. Someone else's work, I presumed, because Nancy always came up with her titles first, and it was dated long after I knew she had stopped writing. Was it Jonathan's? I turned the page. But no, this manuscript was dedicated to Jonathan. He hadn't written it. *To my son, Jonathan*, I read, and then my wife's name typed at the bottom of the page: my wife proclaiming her authorship. A book, written in secret and locked away from my prying eyes.

Sticks and stones, I told myself, yet I feared the words on those pages might actually break me. I wasn't ready for them. There were other objects rattling around in that drawer, cuddling up to my wife's manuscript: a Swiss army knife; a half-empty pack of cigarettes and a can of deodorant with a cheap, erotic name. I grabbed the deodorant and marched around the flat like a crazed pest controller, shooting *Wildcat!* into the air, covering up the stench of dead animal and everything else that offended my senses. When I was calmer, I put the can back and picked up Nancy's untitled work, holding it against my chest as if it was a small, trembling creature. I shouldn't have taken it, it wasn't mine to take, it was Jonathan's. But I did take it. I left the notebooks and took the manuscript. Jonathan would never know I'd been there, and I promised myself that I would return it as soon as I had read it.

9

Spring 2013

'Mum, what do you want me to do with this stuff?'

Catherine finishes her glass of wine and closes her eyes in irritation. Drinking at lunchtime is never a good idea but Robert had opened two bottles of their best wine, and she had been determined to join him and Nicholas in drinking it.

'Just take what you want and I'll sort the rest,' she shouts. Silence. She hears the thump of books and files being dumped on the floor of the spare room. She pushes her chair back, the impatient grind of its legs on the stone setting her teeth on edge.

'Coffee?' she hears Robert call to her retreating back.

Nicholas is sitting on the floor in the same position Catherine had been in at dawn.

'I don't know what to take.' He looks bewildered.

'Take whatever you don't want thrown out. We haven't got the space any more, Nick.' He nods, as if understanding, but she can tell he doesn't quite get it.

'Don't you want any of it?' And she hears the hurt in his voice. She has done it again. She has hurt him with her impatience and her brisk efficiency.

'Well,' she says gently, sitting down next to him, 'let's see.' She picks up a large manila envelope and peers inside. It's full of Nicholas's primary-school reports, bound together with an elastic band. Should she take one out and read it? Would he like that? Nicholas's school reports had always left her with a sinking feeling. What does it matter now though? He is twenty-five. Maybe now they can laugh about it, and she overcomes her resistance and reads a comment from Miss Charles. How well she remembers the permed head and thin lips of Nicholas's form teacher. It was his last year at primary school and Catherine chooses the comment carefully.

'Nicholas is a popular member of the class, with both sexes,' she smiles, leaving out the end of Miss Charles's sentence: ' . . . but he struggles to settle down to his tasks and his work suffers as a result.' For years, always the same story. Disappointing; more effort needed; he struggles to stay focused. Still, at least in those days he had friends. There seem to have been fewer and fewer of them as the years have gone by.

'I'll keep these.' She smiles, gathering up the envelope and hugging the reports to her chest as if she is fond of them. 'How's the flat?'

He shrugs. 'All right.'

'Flatmates OK?'

He shrugs again. 'Bit nerdy.'

'What, all of them?'

He shrugs again.

'Oh dear.' Catherine makes an effort to sound

41

as if she is giving Nicholas the benefit of the doubt, but she imagines his flatmates are bright, engaged, focused. They probably read, and that's what makes them nerdy in his eyes.

'They're all students,' he says.

'You're still enjoying work though?' She struggles to cover the awkwardness between them.

'It's fine.' He shrugs. 'You know.'

She doesn't know. How can she know if he doesn't tell her? Nicholas is working in the electrical department at John Lewis — it's not quite what she and Robert had imagined for their son, but considering he left school at sixteen with a handful of GCSEs it seems a godsend. There was a time when they were unable to imagine him ever being able to commit to any kind of job. She remembers how hurt she had been by the phone calls from other mothers, even close friends, who couldn't wait to tell her about their children's results, asking the cursory question about Nicholas and all the while knowing damn well he'd be lucky to come away with any passes. It was a long time ago, yet she's never quite forgiven them. It wasn't sisterly — it was cruel. Anyway, Nicholas has stuck it out at John Lewis, so there must be something he likes about it.

'I'll take this with me,' he says, and pulls out a mobile. Aeroplanes. Delicately made from balsa wood and paper, wings a little torn, strings tangled.

'And Sandy?' He shakes his head at the balding dog Catherine holds in her hand. Her turn to be hurt now. She is trying to coax him back to boyhood memories: to the time when he couldn't sleep without his cheek resting on Sandy; when he couldn't sleep without her tucking him in. It's so bloody complicated. She wants him to be a grown-up but she also wants him to remember how much he loved her once. How much he needed her. She is nervous too that he still needs her more than is good for him and it makes her tougher and it makes her relieved, in the end, that he is leaving Sandy behind. She stops at the door and turns to him.

'You do understand, Nick, don't you?'

He has hooked the mobile on the corner of a shelf, and is trying to untangle the strings.

'What?'

'About us moving. You know. We just didn't need such a big place any more.'

He doesn't answer, and she knows she should resist pushing it, yet she can't.

'Don't you want to be independent? We're here if you're ever in real trouble, but it's time, Nick. Isn't it?'

He shrugs. 'If that's what you want to tell yourself, Mum.'

'The match is about to start,' Robert calls from the sitting room and Nicholas brushes past her to join his father, leaving her with the sting of his words.

Catherine returns to the kitchen and pours the rest of the bottle into her glass and slides open the door on to the terrace. She lights a cigarette, alternating between dragging on it and slugging wine from her glass. She thinks it calms her

43

down. It doesn't. It jangles her nerves. Makes her twitchy. She wants to punish herself. The cigarette is part of that, a slow self-destruction, and the book is another. She returns to the kitchen and takes it out from under the Sunday papers, where she had buried it earlier, and opens the first page. No, there's not a hint here of what is to come. It is gentle. Soft. She flicks ahead to the part she knows will hurt her. She is lost in it, sinking beneath its weight. Its injustice. Her eyes close, the words washing over her, to the sound of a roar from the TV. A goal. Silence.

She must have fallen asleep. She doesn't know how long for. It's getting dark outside. She is groggy. The TV has been turned off and she hears whispering in the hallway, by the front door. Then footsteps coming into the kitchen.

'I'm off.' Nicholas raises his hand in goodbye and comes towards her. He's going to kiss her, and she leans forward, standing up to meet him halfway. His lips brush past her ear. 'Oh, I've read that.' Her heart stops. Her throat closes. 'I enjoyed it.' Sweat pricks her top lip.

Robert smiles: 'Your mum's struggling with it.'

'Really? Not like you, Mum,' and she feels the book leaving her hand and moving into her son's. He misreads her face. 'Yes, I did finish it. I do read, you know.'

'No, no I didn't . . . Is this your copy? Did you send it to me?'

'No.'

'Maybe you left it here?'

'No. I didn't. Mine's in the flat.'

'How come you've read it?'

44

'Catherine — ' Robert thinks she's being unnecessarily provocative.

'No, no, I only meant it's a weird coincidence. It was sent to me when we moved and I'm not sure who — '

'Well mine was a present.'

'A present? Who from?' She cracks. He looks at her, surprised, shrugging. 'A grateful customer. Someone I helped, I think. I can't remember — they left it at the till with my name on it. No big deal.'

'Who was it?' she asks again.

'I don't know, Mum. I told you. What's the problem? Why does it matter?'

She turns away, frightened of what he might read in her face, and mumbles her reply: 'It doesn't. No, it's fine.' She can't let go though. 'So, you liked it?' she says.

'Yeah, I did. Don't want to spoil it for you though.'

She waits. 'It's OK, I probably won't finish it.'

'Well, I'll see you. I'll call you during the week.' He makes his way to the front door with Robert at his heels. She follows them.

'So what happens?' She is desperate. 'I probably won't finish it,' she repeats. He opens the front door and turns round.

'She dies. Sticky end. She deserves it though.' And then he hugs his father and with a grin wiggles his fingers in farewell to his mother.

10

Eighteen months earlier

The words in Nancy's manuscript did not break me. They made my heart race, they stirred me up, yet they did not break me. When I'd read 'A Special Kind of Friend', written by the young Nancy, I had heard her voice so clearly and it had made me weep. Now, with this later work, her last work, I heard her just as clearly, but as the mature woman I had been married to for over forty years. As the woman I had cared for when she was dying: washed, read to, fed, comforted as best I could. I had not expected to find this woman in print, yet there she was. I had given up on writing, but she had not. And, after spending time with her book, after reading it over and over, her words, which at first had unsettled me, gradually settled down within me, finding little nooks and crannies where they made themselves comfortable, until I trusted them, and they trusted me.

I came to understand that Nancy wanted me to find her manuscript, just as she had wanted me to find the photographs. She had hidden them in places where she knew, eventually, I would come across them. She could have destroyed them, but she chose not to. She was waiting until I was ready — and I hadn't been ready during her lifetime. I needed time with them on my own. Nancy's manuscript churned me up, shook me about and sparked some life into me. It reminded me of something Nancy and I had always agreed on: fiction is the best way to clear one's head.

It had been such a long time since I had put words down on paper and this was the first time I had done it without Nancy being there — she had always been my motivation. Doubts I'd had in the past, questions I'd tormented myself with, vanished because I knew why this book had to be written and I was in no doubt who it was for.

I turned my desk towards the window so I could look out on to the house opposite and watch the comings and goings of the young family who lived there. Off to school in the morning, Mum coming home in the afternoon with the children. Their day was a useful shape for me, it reflected the shape I'd had all those years ago when Nancy would leave for school with Jonathan and return with him at teatime, and I would finish my last sentence of the day.

I had put the photographs out of sight in my desk drawer, but they were at the heart of the story so I took them out and pinned them to the window frame. They formed a collage of sex and deceit: a kind of mood board. Every time I watched that young family coming in or out of their house I was reminded, by the frame through which I viewed them, of how innocence is so easily corrupted. It kept me focused.

I didn't rush it; I spent months copying out Nancy's manuscript into my own hand. I wanted to know how she had felt when she constructed those sentences; I wanted to get into her head, to see what she had seen when the words appeared on the page. I wrote by hand because I needed to feel the shape of each letter; for my skin to make contact with the paper and feel its smoothness as my hand moved from left to right, slithering across the page.

There could be no distance between me and it. Skin, pen, paper, skin — I wanted them to become one. I took as long as I could and enjoyed the rhythm of the words, digesting every one. There were moments when I felt a sentence could be improved on, but I didn't stop to make corrections at this point; I pressed on, telling myself that only when I had reached the end would I allow myself to look back, like a climber approaching the summit. Don't look down.

I remembered how Nancy and I had laughed at writers who made the preposterous claim that they had been possessed by their characters; that it had felt to them as if their book had written itself. For me, at least, this was true. I saw the characters leap from the page, alive, fully formed. Fleshed out and breathing. My hand, slippery yet firm, ejaculating the words as they flowed from Nancy into me.

The experience was life-giving, opening the door for Nancy to come back to me; her gentle, loving presence returning to our home. At the end of each day's writing, when my hand ached from it, I made myself tea and toast and read aloud to her, as if she was sitting in her old chair opposite me.

And then, when I was finally satisfied, I typed it up. Bang, bang, bang went my fingers, nailing each word to the page. Finally it was done. How long did it take? From beginning to end? I spent a year with Nancy's manuscript, copying it out, but the real beginning of course was years ago, I just hadn't recognized it at the time. I felt Nancy smiling at me, encouraging me on. She always said that one day my writing would break through.

11

Spring 2013

As soon as the front door closes behind
Nicholas, Catherine locks herself in the downstairs loo. The weapon being used to torment her
had been practically placed in her son's hand,
although so far Nicholas doesn't seem to realize
that he has a direct connection to the book. She
hears Robert outside the door and picks up a
magazine, rustling the pages to let him know
she'll be some time. She looks down at her
knickers hanging around her ankles and is
suddenly awash with self-pity. She doesn't
deserve this. Why torment her? And why now?
She begins to cry, almost wanting Robert to hear
and comfort her. He is standing on the other
side of the door.

'Are you OK?'

'Fine, yes.' She rustles the magazine again
then gets to her feet, pulling up her knickers and
blowing her nose under the sound of the flushing
toilet. She checks herself in the mirror. She looks
like shit, but it's Sunday, that's allowed. Pull
yourself together, you stupid cow. Read the rest
of the book, stop putting it off. Face it. Then you
will know what to do, what you are up against.
She smiles at her reflection, and almost laughs at
the madness of it.

* ★ ★

It is three in the morning and Robert is asleep. She had managed to get through their evening together, and when they were in bed had gone through the ritual of lying next to him, feigning sleep, waiting for him to doze off. The moment he did, she had crept downstairs and locked herself in the loo again. Now she is reading a description of her own death. Of how someone else has imagined it. Of how it will end for her. And it is merciless. It is messy. And she sees what she would not be able to see if she was dead. The image others would see when they looked down at her. Her skull crushed, leaking brains. Her tongue severed by her own teeth. Her nose, sliced off, wedged under a cheekbone. That's what the train would do to her after she'd jumped in front of it. Only Catherine would know, as she fell, that in fact she hadn't jumped at all. She had been pushed. Very gently, nudged. Tipped over on to the track as the train came into the station. It is busy. There are crowds of people. Such a terrible accident. This is the price she must pay for living the past twenty years as if everything is absolutely fine.

Fear this intense is a distant memory for Catherine. She had forgotten what it was like. She is middle-aged, an age where death sidles up and plays on the mind more frequently, but she has always succeeded in marching onwards, shrugging the pinchy fingers of fear that might snag her progress. Only now she is caught in their grip. The hatred directed at her is

51

undiluted. It's the sort of hate she imagines being directed at sadistic murderers and child molesters, and she is neither of these. The author has twisted her into something vile. Defaced her character. He or she wants her to explain herself. Why should she? She shouldn't have to. That is not the role she should be cast in.

Catherine is the one who teases the truth from people. She has made a career out of it. It is what she is good at. She is persuasive, one of the best. Seducing the truth from people, opening them up, filleting out the delicate secrets they'd rather not reveal, then laying them out on a slab for others to look at and learn from; and all done in a perfectly charming way, never ever giving anything of herself away. And she will not open herself up for examination now. She will hunt out the hunter, the one who twisted this story. But who is this? Someone she has never met? Yes, someone she doesn't know. She reads the last sentence again: *Such a pity she hadn't realized that doing nothing would be such a deadly omission.*

She wants to screw up this book but its two hundred pages are stronger than her. She will destroy it though. She will not be passive. She rises up from her seat, dressing gown flowing, and strides into the kitchen. She finds the matches — long, elegant matches whose only purpose to date has been to light fig-scented candles — and strikes one, holding the flame against the cover of the book. It is slow to burn, the laminated cover resistant, at first only issuing a toxic smell. At last the pages begin to catch, the edges blacken and produce a sliver of red, followed by a blue-and-yellow glow as the fire takes. She holds the book for as long as she can before burning her fingers, and then drops the fiery bundle into the sink, turning on the tap and extinguishing the fire she had started.

'What are you doing?' She doesn't move. Robert thunders towards her and stares down into the blackened mess. They both study it, this thing which, despite all her efforts, is still recognizable as a book. He is standing next to her, searching her face for an explanation. Catherine sidles away from him, pulling her dressing gown tighter.

'Catherine?'

She shakes her head. Caught. She has been caught. Perhaps she wanted to be. Perhaps it is for the best. Between finger and thumb Robert lifts the sodden pulp and holds it up: *Perfect*, the only distinguishable word left on the jacket.

'It's about me.' She might as well have said, 'I've lost my mind.' She wishes she could suck the words back, but they are out. Is this what she wants? To tell him? Now?

'Darling.' She hears confusion and anguish wrapped in the word as Robert drops the book back into the sink. She grabs at it with both hands, rushing it to the bin as if it is still on fire, and tosses it in. She pulls out the black bag and ties it up. All this done at speed, as if someone has pressed *Fast-forward*. She runs the bag to the front door and out of the flat, dropping it into the dust-bin outside and banging down the metal lid. Slower now, she walks up the steps into the hall and closes the door behind her.

She can see Robert in the kitchen, watching her. He doesn't move and neither does she. The length of the hall stands between them, a ten-foot space swimming with unspoken words. Catherine struggles to work out which ones to swallow, which ones to use. And once chosen, which order they should be in. She is the first to move, travelling through the hall towards Robert, her mouth open, gathering up words as she goes.

'It was sent to our old address. To me. It's about something that happened, years ago.' She falters. 'They're trying to punish me.'

'Punish you? Who's trying to punish you?'

'Whoever wrote the book.'

'Punish you for what? Is it to do with a film you made? If it is, we should get the police involved . . . '

'No, it's nothing like that.'

'Well, what then?' He sounds impatient. He is tired. 'Who sent it?'

'I don't know.'

'What makes you think it's about you?' There is scorn in his question.

'I recognized myself.'

'Do they name you?'

She grabs his hand, hoping it will give her strength to carry on.

'No, they don't name me, but they describe me and — '

'Describe you? What — blonde? Middle-aged? For God's sake, Catherine!'

He takes his hand out of hers and sits down. She feels the words slip down her throat and anger rise up. She is angry with his ignorance. Blames him for not knowing. For not being there. For making it so hard for her to tell him. And now the moment has gone. She cannot tell him, not like this, and her speechlessness makes her weep. She sits down, and collapses, face on arms.

'Oh, Catherine, Catherine. You shouldn't have let things get this bad.' His tone is softer and she feels his hand on her hair. 'What is it about that book? Nick read it, didn't he? That seemed to bother you. Why?'

He waits for an answer and she forces herself to look up at him, her face soggy and flushed.

'It frightened me . . . I saw something in it that . . . ' She pushes herself on, trying to tell him some truth. 'It made me hate myself. I'm sorry, I'm so sorry . . . ' She falters; she can't do it, so she tells him something she knows he will believe. 'I'm being paranoid . . . it's in my head, I can't explain . . . '

A moment's silence, then he fills it.

'Oh, Catherine, you don't have to explain to me. I'm the one who should be sorry. I didn't mean to get angry, it's just that I worry about you.' He takes her hands in his. 'I know it's not been easy between you and Nick. It's hard for you. You know he loves you though, don't you? He and I find it easier to talk, that's all.' He puts his arms around her to soften his words, but they still make her flinch. 'He can be tricky, I know that. I'm not blaming you. That book's obviously triggered something . . . connected with you. What's it about? Guilt? A mother and son?' He

55

waits for her assent and reads it in her silence. 'You have nothing to feel guilty about, Catherine. Nick is twenty-five and it's about time he moved into his own place. He can always come home to us if he needs to. We've still got a spare room.' He takes her face in his hands and forces her to look at him.

'The only one who's punishing you, Catherine, is you.' His voice is gentle. 'You must stop it. Promise me?'

She nods.

'We've been here before, Cath. Let's deal with it quickly this time — there's no need for you to torment yourself. Go and see the GP. Talk to her. And why don't you ask her for something to help you sleep?' He smiles. 'I know you too well. You've tried to hide it, but I can tell. And you look bloody awful.' He kisses her. She nods again.

'I'm sorry, you must be exhausted,' she says. 'And you've got to be up early tomorrow.'

'It's fine,' he says. 'Promise me you'll go and see the doctor.'

'Yes, I will. I promise.'

'You know you can tell me anything. You know that, don't you.' It is not a question. He takes her hand and leads her upstairs. 'Just talk to me, Catherine. When you feel like this, talk to me.' His words — kind, caring — conflict with the backdrop in her head: her face, the one her husband is stroking, smashed beyond recognition on a railway line.

12

End of winter–spring 2013

A sharpened pencil in the right hands can be a lethal weapon. At the very least it can take out an eye, at the worst push through the socket into the brain. I had sharpened mine to perfection. But a lethal weapon is useless unless it hits its target.

I knew who my target was; I had known her name for years. All I needed was to reach her.

I took advice from a local man, the printer who had produced the Order of Service cards for Nancy's funeral. It was he who suggested I cut out the middle man and publish the novel myself: 'Go direct to the reader,' he said. Music to my ears, but 'online'? Well, there he had lost me. I was not 'online'. I didn't even possess a computer. There aren't many advantages to being old and lonely, but in that instance I managed to make the most of my pitiful situation. I needed help, and that kind man gave it to me. 'A laptop,' he suggested. Yes, I liked the sound of a laptop and he helped me buy one, guiding me through the bewildering process, and then he set me up online. I would never have managed it without him. Such a patient man, so obliging. He gave me a freedom I didn't even know I lacked — set me off on a voyage into a boundless universe; me, an elderly man, free to roam wherever I wanted.

My first port of call was her name. I typed it in, and up it all came. Photographs, a short biography and all her credits, everything she'd ever worked on. A few imposters came up too, but I recognized the real thing when I saw her. Even though we'd never met, I had no doubt which Catherine Ravenscroft was mine. And there was her husband too. Robert. Robert and Catherine. In one photo he had his arm round her. Her hair was windswept and she was smiling. To my amazement, I discovered that when I clicked on this photo I could find out the exact spot where it had been taken: GPS coordinates. I looked them up on a map, and there it was. Fowey in Cornwall. A holiday in a smart hotel, I imagined. The photo taken on a mobile phone. Perhaps her son had taken it. Her little boy, a young man now. Nicholas. Nicholas Ravenscroft. Here he is. No university education? A drop-out? Surely not. A salesman? I'd expected more from the offspring of such an ambitious and successful couple. Oh, happy days. So many missing years, and yet it took me no time at all to catch up and find out what she and her family had been up to. What a full, rich life she'd been leading, and how well she'd been rewarded for it. It showed in her teeth — straight and white — a sign of prosperity for sure, rather like a tan was in the sixties. Her hair was expensive too, well cut, and the grey hairs (surely she would have had some by now) ingeniously blended with blonde. Yes, she was thriving all right.

I became quite the intrepid traveller. There were other paths I was drawn to, and I confess that at times I grew distracted. One led me to a former pupil. He'd been a favourite, this young man, except he wasn't so young any more — he was approaching middle age. I'd thought of him over the years, wondering what he'd made of himself, and now I could find out. With light fingers I picked my way through his career, his social life. Unmarried, no children. From this distance, it was safe to watch him. No one would know.

Back to business: I needed an address, the bullseye at the centre of my target. I knew where she worked, but it was her home address I was after and that was proving elusive. It was her husband who eventually spilled the beans. I read a profile of him in the business section of a newspaper. Blah, blah, blah and then: *Robert Ravenscroft lives in North-west London with his son and wife, Catherine, a successful documentary film-maker.* Not a whole address, but a clue. In the end it was my fingers which did the walking and found me their listing in the telephone directory. Mr R. Ravenscroft. I noted down the telephone number for future reference.

I was like a child at Christmas when my friend the printer delivered the first copies of my book. In fact Christmas had been and gone — a solitary one for me. A ready-meal of turkey for one, roast potatoes and Brussels sprouts, gravy and cranberry sauce. It smelled better than it tasted — a hint of festive spice in the air when I peeled off the cardboard lid. I had to wait until the end of January for my real Christmas, but when I took that first book out of the box I knew it had been worth waiting for. I'd used an image from one of Jonathan's postcards on the cover. Blue sky, burning sun. Yes, it worked very well: a hot, white sun you could see even when you closed your eyes. My friend was all for sitting me down and guiding me through the process of managing orders online, but I didn't have time for that. I was keen to get on. I reassured him that I'd mastered the Internet universe. I had no intention of waiting for orders online.

When I put that first book into a jiffy bag and wrote her address on it my hands were trembling with anticipation. I took such care, making sure I didn't transpose any letters or numbers on the postcode, only to decide in the end that I would hand-deliver it. Hot off the press, a free gift for a very special person. To keep it a surprise I delivered it in the wee small hours when I was sure I wouldn't be seen. There was a satisfying slap when it landed on the mat: a grenade waiting for someone to pull out the pin. I wanted her to feel its full blast when she was least expecting it, perhaps curled up on the sofa with a glass of wine in her hand. I didn't include a note with the book. I wasn't seeking attention for myself — it was recognition I was after. Not of me, but her. I wanted her to recognize that the woman in the book was her true self, not the one she pretended to be: the real one. I wanted to smack her in the face with the truth.

I suppose the book was like a terrier, my Jack Russell of a novel which would sniff her from her hiding place and chase her out into the open. Its sharp, pointed teeth would expose her, strip away the counterfeit selves she'd assembled. How well she's hidden inside her long, successful marriage, her celebrated career — being a mother, too, we mustn't forget that. Such a useful disguise. Be honest, for fuck's sake. Own yourself. Let's see how you live with yourself after that.

I was tired when I got home so I went to bed for a bit. I woke around lunchtime and made myself a cheese sandwich. It was a sad affair; the cheese was dry and the bread stale. I had a shelf in the larder where I still kept the preserves Nancy had made. I hadn't touched them since she'd died, but that day I picked out a jar of onion chutney, scraped off the mould and spread chutney over the cheese. As I swallowed down the first bite of sandwich something caught at the back of my throat. I stopped chewing, using my tongue to wheedle out the alien body. It wasn't alien though, it was part of Nancy — a long, white hair. I could have chosen any jar, but for some reason it was that one I'd been drawn to — the one which contained a token from my wife. I sucked it clean and laid it on the side of my plate. It was a sign of her approval, I was sure. She was pleased with what I had done so far. It made me think about what else I might do to please her. Be bold, I thought. So I was.

It was a bright, crisp day, the sun sharp and valiant and I enjoyed the feel of it on my face as I sat on the top of the bus. Although it was only a short walk from Oxford Circus, it took longer than it should have to negotiate my way through the dithering pedestrians and reach the electrical department of John Lewis, but lunch had restored my energy. A new vacuum cleaner, that's what I settled on; which one, though? I looked around for help and there he was. The man I was looking for. He *was* helpful at first, the suited young salesman with his slip-on shoes and his name badge. He seemed to understand exactly what I needed. Something light for an old boy to manage up and down the stairs. He was sympathetic when I told him that my wife, sadly deceased, had taken care of most of the household duties. He suggested a Dyson, something I could pull behind me, with a handle to make it easier to get up the stairs. Attachments and a super-suck, nothing stronger on the market. Oh, but I did feel nostalgic for an upright. I felt I would be more comfortable with something that resembled our old model. I couldn't help noticing the smell of tobacco on him. Just back from a sneaky fag, no doubt. The upright proved even heavier than the Dyson — I wasn't sure I had the strength to manage it. Perhaps something non-electrical might be better? A Bissell? Isn't that what they're called? Something with rollers that catch the dust as they move over the carpet? What about that? He cocked his head and looked as if I had asked him to conjugate his Latin verbs. Then he fired off his own questions: how thick was my pile? Carpet or rugs? Bare floors? He struggled on as best he could and we went backwards and forwards until he could no longer hide his impatience. Was I taking up too much of his time? Was I eating into his tea break? I could see the tension in his jaw, the gritting of his teeth, the glancing over to a colleague and the rolling of his eyes. I'm sure if his manager had seen that, he would have been taken to task. What would you do, if you were me? I asked. The Dyson, he said. You're the expert, I replied and he took down the box and told me 'it won't disappoint'. Well worth the money. Never knowingly undersold. He carried it to the cash desk, at which point I had a change of heart. How to break it to him? It was a lot of money for someone on a pension. I couldn't go through with it, I said. I hoped I hadn't wasted his time.

I'd wanted to give him a chance. Surely he would have a go at persuading me to buy something I didn't need. But he was hopeless. A complete waste of space. I doubt he would be considered the right material for the management training scheme. A couple of days later I returned with a thank-you gift for him and left it with the girl at the cash desk. Tell him it's from an appreciative customer, I said.

Having delivered my first two books, I had to wait, frequently checking my laptop for a review, a message — anything. I wasn't surprised there was nothing from him, but I had anticipated some feedback from her. Heartless bitch. I had wanted to remain anonymous for as long as possible and to tease her out, but now I felt compelled to go back to her house and see what the hell was going on.

Such a nice house. Recently painted, front

garden well planted. This was a home. A nice home, yet a home into which I would not be welcome. I had been standing there for about an hour. It was cold, a bitter spring day. At last a car pulled up. The rear doors burst open and children piled out. Three of them in varying sizes. That wasn't right. Followed by a woman. The mother. The wrong mother. Perhaps it was the wrong car too. Just because it had stopped outside the right house, didn't make it the right car. The wrong mother walked up the path of the right house and unlocked the front door and went inside. I crossed over. This was the house where I had dropped my grenade, but it had fallen into the wrong hands.

I took a step on to the path, and saw a face looking at me from a downstairs window. Another joined it. Two small faces looking at me. Then a third, trying to get in on the act. I smiled at them and they shot away from their post, the curtain swinging back into place. I kept smiling as I walked up to the front door and rang the bell. I could hear their squeally voices inside, excited, I suppose, by the idea of a stranger at their door. The three little pigs.

It was the mother who opened the door. It was teatime, but she had the chain across. It wasn't midnight, for goodness' sake, it was teatime. Broad daylight. And I was smiling at her. I wouldn't be smiling if I meant them any harm.

'Good afternoon. I'm so sorry to bother you . . . ' Pause for emphasis. To demonstrate I really was sorry. 'I'm trying to get in touch with an old friend — Catherine Ravenscroft. She used to live here, I believe . . . ' Blink. Refresh smile. 'I popped a birthday present through the door a few weeks ago, but haven't heard anything and . . . well, that's not like her.'

'They moved,' she said. Not returning my smile even slightly.

'Aah, that explains it. It's been a while since I've seen her and the family. I wonder . . . ' Pause again. Don't want to appear pushy. 'Do you have an address for her?' Another blink. I am old, frail. And it's cold out here. Be kind to me.

She shook her head.

'No,' and she began to close the door. The bloody cheek of it. Quick as a flash my foot went in.

'Please,' I said. 'I don't want to be a pest, but it is important I get in touch with her.'

The three little pigs were now twitching behind their mother.

'Get your foot out of my house,' she said. And she meant it. Cold as you like. Of course I withdrew my foot immediately. And apologized. And she slammed the door on me. I hadn't intended to frighten her — that was the last thing I wanted. Frankly, it was counter-productive. I couldn't just leave it there, though. I needed to know whether she had forwarded on my package. So I settled down on her doorstep, on my aching knees and pushed my fingers through her letterbox.

'Please. At least tell me whether you forwarded on my gift.' And then a stroke of genius. 'I'm her godfather, you see. I'd hate her to think I hadn't remembered her birthday.'

'Muuuuuum,' an appeal from one of the piglets. Actually, I've always been fond of pigs. Intelligent, loyal creatures. Mummy wasn't being very kind to this old man.

'Yes, I sent on a package. Now go away. They asked us not to give out their address. Go away or I'll call the police.'

Up I got again. A creak, an ache, but all was not lost.

'Thank you so much,' I murmured as I moved up past the letterbox. I'd got the wrong house, and my little missile had taken a more circuitous route than I would have liked, but it sounded as if it might have gone off after all.

I continued to check for reviews, but still nothing. I kept track of her with the help of my laptop. I'd become addicted, needing an 'online' fix every few hours. Occasionally I was rewarded with something new. Moving pictures with sound. A talky. Goody goody. There she was with her husband. What a comfortable-looking man. They were all dressed up on a night out. Clever girl. She'd won an award: *Catherine Ravenscroft's brave documentary exposing the grooming of young girls* . . . Oh, the delicious irony. I couldn't wait to hear her voice. I closed my eyes and let the sound wash over me: '*I would like to thank the brave children who spoke out, who trusted me, because without their courage, without their willingness to tell the truth about what happened to them* . . . ' God, she was convincing. Yes, those children were brave indeed. She would have sacrificed them without hesitation for her own glorification. They really had no idea what she was like, did they, those people who'd rewarded her? I wanted to silence her, I couldn't bear to hear her voice. I would make her disappear. A cross in a red box. Click. Exit. Now you see her, now you don't. Simple.

13

Spring 2013

Buried beneath the earth, deep underground, at least thirty feet between her and natural light. Catherine isn't alone: there are scores of others like her. But are they really? Is he here? Is she here? She clutches her bag to her stomach and snatches a look behind her, to her right, to her left. Eyes meet hers then flick away.

> *. . . she felt a gentle stroke across her back and turned around. A sea of faces met hers, but she wasn't interested in any of them. She glanced up at the platform indicator and saw the train would be arriving in three minutes — what she didn't know was that it was also announcing how long she had left to live . . .*

She begins to panic. This was a mistake. A foot treads on her. Someone trying to trip her? She pulls her own foot away and glares at the owner of the trainer, who mumbles an apology and stares ahead, eyes on the prize, wanting to beat her on to the train, not to push her under it. Breath on her neck, the smell of aftershave to her left; she holds her breath, can't breathe in that nauseating smell. Steals a look. A man, taller than her, leers down. Shit. She should have taken the bus. Fuck it, when she'd left the house she'd been determined not to let that book cripple her, and the bus meant three changes, too long to get to work. Too difficult. Catherine the brave, that's who she is, not a whimpering coward. She is trying to be Robert's Catherine. Since her late-night book-burning he has started to believe in her again. He has been so careful around her, so considerate. She kept her promise and made an appointment with the doctor and Robert has seen the small yellow pills that sit beside her bed. They help her sleep a little, and help him believe she is getting back to her old self.

They are pushing her and she cannot allow herself to be pushed closer to the oncoming train. She has inched forward each time a train has passed, moving a little closer, ready for the next one, but not too close. She has discovered a new respect for the yellow line. Her body twitches with the fear that a psychopath will pick her out at random and push her on to the track. It has happened to people before, and she believes it could happen to her too. Except it wouldn't be random. She would be chosen. It would look like an accident and Catherine knows how easy it is for accidents to happen.

She fixes her eyes on the track, and sees parts of herself splattered on to it. The train arrives, she stands her ground and pushes forward. Her turn to go over the top. She makes it. The doors close. No seat, but for once she is grateful for the bodies pressed around her, keeping her upright. Eight stops and she will be there.

Eight stops and she gets off and up out into the street. She keeps walking, doesn't look back. Onward to work, onward to the desk which she needs to get behind. The closer she gets to it, the safer she feels. She almost forgets that, a short while before, she had suspected perfect strangers of watching her, waiting to push her. Not now though. Now she is safe. She swipes her pass, goes through security and joins the few already waiting for the lift. They know her here. And she knows them.

'Hey, how was the move?'

Catherine smiles at Kim, lovely Kim, lovely, young and vibrant Kim. She dumps her bag on the desk with a thump and takes out the ugly metal lump she'd won and holds it up in self-mocking triumph, placing it on the shelf behind her. It's open-plan here too, just like home.

'Went well,' she says and settles into her chair. This is a place where she is in control, where she can manage things, start them, stop them even, if she wants.

'Isn't it hideous?' Catherine says, looking at her award.

'Useful blunt instrument though. We'll be glad of it when Simon comes in,' Kim quips.

'Yes, and so easy to clean off the blood with one of these handy wipes . . . ' Catherine whips out a screen cloth and cleans the dust from her computer, surprised at how easy it has been to join in with Kim's murderous banter.

'Coffee?' ask Kim.

'Please.' Catherine smiles.

Others start arriving: producers, researchers,

70

production people. There are hellos, congratulations, general goodwill towards her and her towards them. Even Simon, who breezes in bursting with entitlement, is almost tolerable. Simon is her contemporary — another documentary director — who came from the newsroom so sees himself as a serious heavyweight, but this morning Catherine doesn't care. It's the contrast between how she has been feeling and how she feels now. Almost normal.

'Well done, by the way.' Simon winks, giving Catherine's award the once-over.

She ignores him and opens a new notebook.

'So what next?' he says. Oh, chirpy, chirpy, irritating man.

'Someone's interested in turning my documentary into a feature film,' she lies, and enjoys seeing him struggle to keep the smile on his face.

'That's great,' he says.

'Isn't it,' she replies, her eyes locking on his.

'Well, if you want to talk about it, let me know — I've had a bit of experience with some of those film guys,' he smirks.

'Oh, I will, Simon.' She gives him a wink then turns her back and picks up a pen, drumming it on her notebook. A list, that's what she needs to do. A list is always a useful starting point.

The book: The Perfect Stranger.
The author: Friend of . . . Relative of . . . Witness of . . . ?

Catherine stabs at her list with the pen and remembers when she met Nancy Brigstocke. It was 1998. It had been just the two of them and they'd met only once. Nancy had got in touch with Catherine. She remembers the stab of guilt she'd felt when she received her letter, knowing that Nancy may have been waiting for Catherine to initiate a meeting. It would have been easy for her to track Nancy down, but it couldn't have been that hard for Nancy to find her. Who would have the heart to refuse passing on her details? The letter was written in fountain pen, blue-black ink. She can still see the slant of the script, the loop of the capital letters at the beginning of each sentence. The note had left its mark. Catherine had felt compelled to meet her.

It had been a Friday afternoon in October. The sky was white, the air was muggy. Muggy in October? It couldn't have been muggy in October, but that was how it had felt to Catherine. Suffocating. She remembers taking her hat off and stuffing it into her pocket. She'd put it on when she'd left work, thinking it would be cold; instead she'd felt hot. The heat had built up in her head until it felt as if her brain was being slowly cooked, turning her thoughts into a mushy stew. She'd pulled off her hat and undone her coat. Nancy Brigstocke had kept her coat buttoned up. It swamped her. She was a tiny woman. She wore gloves; no hat. Catherine remembers looking down and seeing the pink of her scalp through her thin white hair. She had guessed that she would be about her own mother's age, but she looked older. She had cancer. That's what she had written in her note, and she had looked like a woman losing a battle.

She'd told Catherine that she had lost her husband recently — another reason Catherine had agreed to meet her. What if Nancy Brigstocke hadn't died? Could she still be alive? Living with cancer? She adds her name to the list.

Their meeting had been strained. There was so much Catherine had wanted to say but couldn't, so she had let Nancy speak. She had heard the hunger in her voice — probing, trying to nudge Catherine into opening up. She wouldn't. She couldn't. 'There is nothing I can say that will help you,' she'd said. And then Nancy had asked to meet Nicholas, and Catherine had had to say no. She'd tried to make her refusal gentle, saying she couldn't allow it, he was too young. Catherine had taken the frail woman's hand and she is sure she had felt death in it. She had seen it in the woman's eyes, too, as they looked up at her; Catherine had turned her head, unable to face it. She said goodbye and walked away, and she had kept on walking, not looking back. She didn't want Nancy to see that she was crying. She didn't want her to misunderstand her tears. She was crying for all the things she hadn't said and for this tiny woman, shrunken inside her smart, herringbone tweed coat. Her leather gloves. Her thin, combed hair, her comfortable shoes. The effort she had made with her appearance was heartbreaking. The effort she'd made to appear stronger than she was. But perhaps Catherine had underestimated her strength and she had triumphed over death and was now marching on Catherine too. Perhaps it hadn't been death at all in her eyes, but something else, something equally cold. Was Nancy Brigstocke capable of producing the poison in the book?

'Anything you need doing?' Kim is looking over her shoulder. Catherine shuts her notebook.

'Not really. I've scribbled down a few thoughts, but why don't you come up with a list of possible stories and we'll go over them in the morning?'

Kim agrees. Kim would do anything for her. Catherine is her chance for advancement — the only one who gives her the opportunity to be more than just an efficient assistant.

'Actually, I did have a few ideas while you were away. I'll bash them out. See what you think.'

'Great!' Catherine smiles. That's what she loves about Kim. She is motivated, proactive. She doesn't need to be asked twice, not by Catherine. She wonders what Kim would think if she read *The Perfect Stranger*.

★ ★ ★

Catherine leaves work early. She knows she kept Nancy's note. There are a couple of boxes still in her bedroom full of things she doesn't know what to do with. She remembers putting the note in a folder, along with miscellaneous photographs and letters from her mother and old friends. When they'd packed up to move from the old house she'd thought about throwing it out, but had decided to keep it. Her hand grazes the faded pink of the file and pulls it out. She flicks through and yes, there it is. Pale-blue

74

notepaper and blue-black ink. And there is an address in the top right-hand corner. No phone number, only the address. The chances of Nancy still being alive and living at the same address are slim, but it's worth a try. Her heart races, a shot of adrenalin: the right kind — fight not flight. Face to face, that's how Catherine prefers things. Whose face she will confront is uncertain, but someone must answer for what she's being put through. She checks her watch. Four o'clock. Time to get there and back before Robert comes home.

Catherine makes her way up the last flight of stairs and tries to imagine how a woman dying of cancer could have managed them. And if Nancy Brigstocke is alive, how would she manage them now? She knows her own mother would not be able to. She punches the light on the last landing: it doesn't work. She tries again. Nothing. Some-one has neglected to change the bulb. And someone has neglected to water the plant in the pot by the front door. Dead, dried-out and brittle. A mean pinch of light comes through a small, dirty window in the roof, barely enough for her to see the numbers on the two front doors. She stands in front of Nancy Brigstocke's last known address and presses the bell. There's no sound. She knocks, two sharp raps with bare knuckles, and, hitching her bag over her shoulder, waits. Nothing. No one there. She crouches down and peers through the letterbox. Green carpet, legs of dark wood furniture, no movement.

She sits on the top stair and opens her bag, burrowing inside for her pad and pen. She must word her note with care. *Dear Mrs Brigstocke,* she begins. She mustn't be aggressive or defensive. She mustn't seem angry. She thinks she succeeds in being persuasive and fair. She tears her note from the pad, folds it in half and pushes it through the door. This is mad. The chances of Nancy Brigstocke still being alive and finding her note are less than slim. She rests her head on the door for a moment, and is aware of someone standing behind her. She can hear their laboured breathing from the effort of climbing the stairs. Catherine turns round. A woman with long, white hair is watching her, bags of shopping hanging from her arms, her breath coming in short gasps.

'Mrs Brigstocke?' Catherine asks. Could it be Nancy after years of illness, neglect, hair unwashed, too long, thick socks oozing through fraying sandals? Surely this woman is too tall? All the same . . . Catherine takes a step forward, peering into her face, searching yet not recognizing. The woman pushes past her, shuffling towards the other flat. She puts down her shopping and fumbles a key in the lock.

'I was looking for Nancy Brigstocke. Do you know if she still lives here?'

The woman mumbles her reply: 'She hasn't lived here for years.'

'Do you know if she is . . . where she might be living?' Catherine hears herself stutter. 'We lost touch — I haven't seen her for a while . . . the last time we met she was ill . . . '

The woman is inside her flat now, the door ajar as she keeps an eye on Catherine, looking

76

her up and down, a rude stare that grazes her skin. A stare full of suspicion.

'I'm a friend of the family — we lost touch . . . ' Catherine tries and the eyes drill into her, detecting her lie, making a silent judgement. *Some friend.*

'Are you from social services?' the woman asks.

'No, it's nothing like that . . . I lost her address and . . . then I found it . . . I wanted to talk to — '

'Has someone been claiming her pension?'

'I'm not from social services, really . . . I just wanted to see her again.'

'Well, you're too late. She was dying when they took her off . . . and that was years ago. Poor soul — all sorts of gubbins she was strapped up to. She'll be dead now, I'm sure.'

'I'm sorry,' Catherine mumbles, turning away. She should have known. Of course Nancy is dead. She walks towards the stairs.

'He might get it, though — whatever it was you stuck through the letterbox.'

Blood thumps in Catherine's ears. She turns round.

'Who? Who might get it?'

The woman assesses her, takes her time to decide whether to answer.

'Who might get it?' Catherine repeats, a wisp of fatal panic in her voice. The woman frowns at the question, which doesn't sound quite right coming from someone who is supposed to be a friend. She begins to close her door and Catherine rushes forward, putting her hand out

77

to stop her, desperate.

'Please . . . '

A cat mews from inside the flat — hungry and vying with Catherine for the woman's attention.

'Please . . . ' Catherine tries again.

'Mr Brigstocke — he comes by from time to time.'

'Mr Brigstocke?'

'Her husband.'

'But her husband's dead.'

'I thought you said you were a friend of the family?' The woman's eyes narrow, seeing Catherine for what she is. A liar.

'Of hers. I knew Nancy Brigstocke. She told me her husband was dead.'

'Maybe she didn't trust you.'

The words startle Catherine; they could be true.

'We were friends,' she tries again. They were not friends. They had never been friends. They barely knew each other and her lie squirms in the air. 'We lost contact with each other . . . I'm trying to understand what happened . . . ' There are tears in Catherine's eyes now and perhaps it is these which make the woman relent.

'Haven't seen him for a while, but he comes by now and again. It was sad at the end. The place was beginning to stink, but she wouldn't open up, she wouldn't answer the door, so someone from the Residents' Association had to phone him and get him over. He had a key, you see. Must have been a terrible state in there. And then the ambulance came and they took her away. That was the last time I saw her.'

'Didn't he live here with her?'

'No. It's the son's flat. She moved in while he was off on one of his trips — always off somewhere, he was. That's what she said. Her husband never lived here, although he looked after her in the end. He was holding her hand the whole time when they took her away. He told her he'd come to take her home so he could look after her. I heard him. I was here watching — in case they needed anything. I like to think they were together at the end.'

'Do you have his number? Or address?'

The woman tuts. Enough questions. She shakes her head and closes the door. Catherine stands on the other side, knocks, desperate for more.

'What about his first name? Can you tell me that at least?' She waits. Knocks again. 'Please.'

The door stays shut. Eventually Catherine makes her way down the stairs, gripping the cold metal of the banister with a slippery hand. She is shaken by how much she didn't know and she thinks of her note lying on the other side of the door, written to a woman who is probably long dead. And then she remembers her mobile number written in the middle of it. Shit. How long before he calls her? What will he say? What does he really want? The 'dead' husband. And she begins to wonder whether Nancy left the flat willingly. Or was she too weak to resist? Did he force her? Did he make her go home with him? Nancy told her he was dead. Why? Was she scared of what he might do?

'Stephen . . . ' The name echoes down the

stairs. Catherine looks up at the dark shape leaning over the balustrade. 'His name is Stephen.'

She continues on down, images from the book flickering through her head. He'd got some things right. The details of what she'd been wearing. How would he know? And then she hears a sound echo from the past: click, click, click.

14

Late spring 2013

So, she and Nancy met. Secretly, without me
knowing. I found her note when I went to the
flat to return the manuscript. I had to read it
several times before I trusted that I had
understood it correctly. And when I did, it
winded me: a sharp blow to the stomach,
twisting my gut and leaving me breathless.
Discovering they'd met hurt, but not as much
as the discovery that Nancy had told her I
was dead. That phrase sucked the life out of
me: . . . *when we met, you had recently lost your
husband.* She had been *struck* by Nancy's
dignity. It had *stayed with her.* She could not
believe that *you could possibly be the author of
the book which has found its way into my home.*
She even wondered whether Nancy was aware of
its existence? Well, of course not. She's dead, you
stupid bitch.

What a self-satisfied, smug fool she is. Her
tone is respectful, though, I'll give her that. She
described my wife as a woman of *integrity,* a
woman with *great depth of understanding.* She's
right about that. Nancy really did understand
people. She said she thought she and Nancy
should meet up and talk and she thoughtfully
left her telephone number.

It's my own fault I was taken by surprise. If I hadn't dismissed Nancy's notebooks as idle scribbling and taken them when I took her manuscript, I would have known about their meeting a while ago, because it's all in there. The notebooks weren't merely filled with ideas for a novel, they were much more than that. It was only after I'd read the note that I turned to the notebooks, and there it all was, the detail of their meeting: the date, the time, the place, even the weather. And Nancy's delicious description of CR: *I recognized her from the moment she walked towards me, and the sight sickened me. She had no idea I had seen her before. She was cold, as if things washed over her without leaving a mark — as if she has been Scotchgarded. Nothing seems to stick to her. She's wiped herself clean — not a trace of dirt on her . . .* Nancy saw right through her, and she hadn't liked what she'd seen.

I took those notebooks home with me and read and re-read them, finding much to comfort me. I am grateful she kept them. Like the photographs, they are pieces of a puzzle. I have sucked up every word in them; I have tasted the ink on their pages; I take them to bed with me and sleep with them under my pillow, dreaming that the words swim off the page into my head so that Nancy's most private thoughts are absorbed into mine. I have eaten those pages and swallowed them down. She is in me now, my darling girl. Now we are one. She has given me strength: the outside world can't touch me, but I can touch it whenever I choose.

It is surprisingly hot. April had been bitter but May is a scorcher. I don't want to open the windows even though the air would cool the atmosphere. I prefer them closed and the curtains drawn. I have sealed myself in, bricked myself up. It is midday. My only concession to the heat is that I have removed my socks, my bare feet tucked under my desk, where I don't have to look at them. They are not a pretty sight. I have been rather lax with my hygiene lately and my toenails have grown long. They are curling at the ends, confused about which direction they should be going in. Hard, like bone. I bite my fingernails to keep them short, spitting them out and leaving them where they stick, brittle and sharp around my desk. I am not a bloody circus performer, though: I can't do the same with my toenails. Besides, I suspect my teeth wouldn't be up to the job.

A knock on the door. I am not expecting anyone. I get up from the desk and peer through the window. It is my printer friend, Geoff. I let the curtain fall. Shall I let him in? The house is a mess. I take my time. If he leaves before I get there, so be it.

He is still there when I open the door.

'Wondered how you were you doing,' he says.

'I'm all right,' I reply.

He is holding up my book.

'I read it, he says. 'Not what I was expecting at all, to be honest.'

I raise an eyebrow, but he smiles and so I risk it. I stand aside and let him in. He walks through and I watch him look round in surprise. I still haven't cleaned up properly after my tantrum at finding the photographs.

'I had a break-in,' I say.

'Oh God, Stephen, I'm so sorry.'

I shrug. 'They made a mess, but they missed the valuables,' I say, nodding towards my laptop safe and sound on the desk. I offer him tea and he accepts, following me into the kitchen. I am aware of the scratch of my nails on the linoleum as I walk. Does he notice? My slippers are under the kitchen table and I stop on my way to the kettle and pop my feet into them.

'So how's it been going?' he asks again.

He is nervous, his tone over-cheerful. I wait to finish filling the kettle before I answer.

'I'm doing all right,' I say, and glance over my shoulder at him.

'And with the book? How are sales?'

'Ah, well, slow but steady,' I reply. I'm not interested in sales, although he doesn't know that. I wait for the kettle to boil then warm the pot. I wonder whether he knows I have shifted only two copies, but am sure that I alone am privy to that information.

'Thing is, if you're going to sell online you've really got to get a profile — start a blog or something, you know . . . and I wasn't sure you'd be up for all that. I could help you, if — '

'So what did you think of it?' I interrupt. I keep my back to him, nervous as a schoolboy. 'You said you read it. What did you think?'

'I really enjoyed it,' he says, and I turn, hungry for more.

'To be honest, it's not the sort of book I'd

84

usually go for, but it hooked me. I think you could get a real publisher, if you wanted.'

'That's very kind, but surely my little book wouldn't interest a professional.' I empty the teapot and pop in three teabags, pour in boiling water, put on a cosy and bring the pot to the table.

'Well, I think it could — it's as good as a lot of the stuff out there that gets published.'

I search the cupboard for two clean cups and am careful to give them a wipe with a cloth, just to make sure. I settle down opposite him.

'Milk and sugar?'

'Milk, two sugars,' he says.

I like Geoff. He doesn't tell me much about himself, and he doesn't ask about me. We talk about books and music, and there's something in his careless appearance that I find comforting. His nose hairs are not trimmed, they shiver like spiders' legs when he blows on his tea. He is ungroomed — a sign of sound mind, in my opinion. At the same time, he is respectful, not deliberately scruffy. He has shaved, though I can see his razor has lost its edge; he wears a shirt not a T-shirt, but it's too tight round his tummy, the buttons straining round his middle and more hair sprouting through the gap, and his top button is missing, not undone. I feel a fondness towards him, and I think he does me, too. Perhaps he lost his father or perhaps he fears he will end up like me. Whatever the reason, he has been kind without condescending. And he likes my book, he genuinely likes it.

'Stephen, I know you want to manage it all

85

yourself, but, I hope you don't mind, once I read your book I thought . . . well, it deserved a bit of help, so I've taken a few copies round to the local bookshop and they said they'd put them out. See how it goes. They're keen to promote local authors, and when I told them about you, they were really interested.'

I was stunned.

'It's in a bookshop? The one on the high street?'

'Yes. Have I done the wrong thing?'

Do I look unhappy? I am surprised, that's all. 'No, no. It's just that I would never have thought of doing that. Thank you.' I am touched.

'I don't think you realize how good it is.'

Oh, but I do, I really do.

'Well, you know — no one likes to blow their own trumpet.'

My mind races. Is she ever likely to travel up to these parts and wander into my local bookshop? For a moment my mind runs away with thoughts of a book-signing and her queuing up and having me sign her copy. Geoff is smiling at me and I realize I am smiling too, smiling with this little fantasy.

'I was quite surprised by some of it.' He raises an eyebrow. 'Pretty explicit.'

My smile has gone. He is worried that he has stepped over a line. I lift my chin, then resume my smile. I feel his relief.

'Life in the old dog,' I say, and look at him over my mug as I sip my tea.

I want to tell him it's true. I want to tell him it should be on the non-fiction shelf. I don't want to scare him though, and for the moment the end is still wishful thinking — a work of fiction not yet realized.

'What did you think of her?' I ask instead. 'Do you think she got what she deserved?'

He mulls this over.

'Well, I don't know. It's a hard one, that. I mean, she was a manipulative cow, but I guess she seized the chance to get away with it, didn't she?'

I feel my heart clench. How easy for him to say. He is not sitting here, suffering the consequences of what she did and didn't do.

'You didn't answer the question,' I manage. 'Did she deserve it?'

'Well, I wasn't sorry when it happened,' he says, 'so I guess I think she did. Great description.'

That's better. I nod, sip my tea and begin to enjoy the opportunity that has landed in my lap. I feel a busy afternoon ahead of me, surfing for bookshops in her neighbourhood. Why not? Get it out there, nothing to lose. I'll have to spruce myself up — or perhaps Geoff would be a more presentable ambassador. Dear Geoff, my innocent accomplice.

'Do you think there's hope? Do you think other bookshops might be interested?'

'Well, yes, they could be. See how it goes at Hillside Books first and take it from there.'

'So, if it goes well, would you be willing to help me spread the word?'

'Happy to, Stephen. Happy to.'

I think there might be tears in my eyes.

'I can't tell you how much it means to me to have your support. It's a lonely road, Geoff, and to know that there's someone else who believes in me, well . . . ' I falter.

And he smiles. You know, I think I've made his day.

15

Late spring 2013

Second day back at work and Catherine has regained focus. That's what it looks like to her colleagues. The familiar sight of Catherine, upright in her chair, tapping at her computer, twisting her finger in a curl at the back of her head as she reads and makes notes. She is pulling something together, drawing threads into a story. Kim hovers over Catherine, but Catherine is absorbed in what she's doing and Kim knows better than to disturb her when she's like that. Instead she places a cup of coffee on the desk and moves away.

Catherine has found confirmation of Nancy Brigstocke's death. Cancer. Dead ten years now. Her husband is alive though. Stephen Brigstocke, BA. He is no longer dead husband with a question mark. He is retired teacher. Why the hell hadn't she checked that before? Why hadn't she used the same rigour she would use on any other story, on her own? It hadn't occurred to her that Nancy would lie about the death of her husband. She knows now. And she knows what he looks like too.

She's had a phone call from the woman who bought their old home. She was angry. She accused Catherine of being duplicitous, of not warning her that some creepy old man was going to turn up on her doorstep. Catherine had been full of apologies and told her that he was indeed her godfather, but that she'd had no idea he would show up like that. She assured her that there was nothing sinister going on and that, no, there would be no more unwanted visitors. Not to her anyway, Catherine thinks.

The call left her shaky. It is spreading. Oozing out. Ripples on a pond. She must get to him before he can do any real harm. Because he hasn't harmed her yet. He has rattled her. And he has shown his malevolence in his extended poison pen letter, and by sending it to her son he has made it clear that he wants his poison to spread beyond her. What is at stake, for now, is her reputation, her integrity. She is a woman who is liked, admired, trusted and loved by a few. That is what he threatens, because once it is out there, once it has been said, there will be no taking it back. She will never again be the person they thought she was. He will have distorted their view. Nicholas has read it, although he didn't recognize her in it. Nothing chimed with him. Of course it didn't. The woman in the book is not the mother he knows. And Nancy is dead. So who is to say that this perverted account of events is true? It is the product of a sick mind; the mind of a bitter old man. But the mind of a killer? Surely not. No, it is her reputation, not her life, which she fears for most.

'Kim? Have you a minute? There's something I'd like you to look into.'

Kim scoots her chair across, parking it next to

Catherine's, pen and pad in hand.

'Stephen Brigstocke. Retired teacher. Early seventies. London-based. Probably taught in North London. Would you track down his last places of employment? Don't make contact, I just want to know where he's been over the last few years. And a home address, if you can get it, and telephone number. Start with the teaching unions.' Catherine watches her write down the name *Stephen Brigstocke*, then hesitate before adding the word *paedophile* in brackets with a question mark. Catherine doesn't correct her. Why should she? She watches Kim scoot back to her desk and pick up the phone, zealous in her pursuit of a suspected child molester.

It takes less than an hour for Kim to come up with the school where Stephen Brigstocke last taught. Rathbone College. Catherine recognizes the name. A private school in North London. One they almost sent Nicholas to. One where some of their friends sent their children. Before that, Sunnymeade Comprehensive. Many years there. Why the move from state to private? Catherine tries to read between the lines. Loss of principles? Cash-driven? Retired in 2004 on a full pension.

'A bit old to still be teaching, wasn't he?' Kim reads over Catherine's shoulder. Catherine glances up the page: *Born 1938*.

'I suppose, although private schools work by their own rules,' she says. 'Have you got anywhere in finding contact details for him?'

'Not yet. I'm waiting to hear. I'll keep on it.'

'Great. Thanks.'

'So what's the story?' It's a perfectly reasonable question.

Catherine hesitates. 'I'm not sure yet. It may be nothing. But you know . . . ' and she entices her assistant with a smile to make her believe she will be the first to hear if Catherine comes up with anything concrete. She has no intention of letting Kim find out too much about this investigation. Still, she is grateful for her help.

'Coffee?' Catherine asks, reversing their roles for good measure and neatly ending the conversation by taking their cups into the kitchen.

★ ★ ★

An hour later, and two cups of coffee down, Catherine has established that the present head of Rathbone College is distinctly uncomfortable when the subject of Stephen Brigstocke is raised. The previous head had retired soon after the former English teacher, and the current one's reluctance to talk about him indicates to Catherine that there was something fishy about Brigstocke's departure.

Brief calls to a couple of friends — quite a skill, this, to make contact with long-neglected friends, keeping the niceties short without causing offence, yet still managing to get what you want from the call — and she finds her way to someone who is more than happy to open up on the subject of Stephen Brigstocke. A mother whose little boy was taught by him. A mother who prides herself on having led the campaign to remove him from the school.

A nasty man. A teacher who hated children. And what's more, the school knew about it. They tried to cover up his inadequacies: shunting him down to where they thought he could do least harm; away from the GCSE pupils, letting him loose on the youngest children in the school. There is no stopping this mother. She is still angry. All they were interested in was protecting their results and they gave no thought to the damage he would inflict on the minds and self-esteem of seven-year-old boys. Disgusting. Altogether disgusting.

This mother remembers the first time she met Stephen Brigstocke, sitting on the other side of a table from him at a parents' evening. He actually looked bored when he talked about her son. He was a man who didn't seem to care what anyone thought or how he came across. Simply didn't care. And that struck her as a dangerous thing. To simply not care. Well, it is, isn't it? It's more than just bad manners. Most people care, don't they, on some level, about what other people think? Not him. Catherine agrees that it must have been very unsettling. And the mother was sure he had been drinking. She and her husband could smell it on him. Not just the usual small glass of white, but something stronger. Spirits. He gave all the signs of being a heavy drinker. There was something rotten in him, definitely rotten.

Of course the school did their best to protect him. When the first question marks arose about his teaching, they sent him on extended sick leave. They hinted at bereavement. His wife had died, and of course everyone tried to be understanding. And then he came back. He must have had some special relationship with the old head because, well, they should have got rid of him long before they did. When she read the filthy things he wrote on her son's essay, she was absolutely horrified. And her son wasn't his only victim. He had violated other children too.

'Violated?' Catherine cuts in. Oh yes. This mother is clear in her view that what her son suffered at the hands of Stephen Brigstocke was nothing less than a violation.

'He was not the sort of man you would want to leave your child alone with, of that I am perfectly sure.'

'Did he ever physically harm any of the children?' Catherine presses her.

There's a pause.

'Well . . . I did hear that the reason he left his previous school was that he became too attached to one of the boys. Let's put it like that.'

'What do you mean?' Catherine needs more than this dainty word *attached*.

'It was a former pupil. Apparently he took an unhealthy interest in him once he'd left the school. I heard he was threatened with a restraining order. I only found out about it after he'd retired. To be honest, it didn't surprise me.'

'So this was a pupil at his previous school: Sunnymeade Comprehensive?'

'Yes, that's right.'

'And how did you hear about it?'

The mother tries to remember. 'A friend of mine. Her children went to Sunnymeade.'

'Do you know the name of this pupil? I'd like to talk to him.'

'Well, no. I'm sure I could find out though.'

'That would be incredibly helpful. Thank you. And thank you for taking the time to talk to me.' Well of course she took the time. Catherine has a reputation, a string of socially conscious credits to her name. She is a woman of sound credentials, a woman who can be trusted to do the right thing. For the first time in weeks her head feels clear, uncluttered by shame. She is working up a story, gathering information, getting to know her enemy.

16

Late spring 2013

I have her telephone number, I have her address and I have seen her in the flesh. She is no longer just a figment on my laptop. I've taken to haunting the Underground station where she changes trains on her journey to work. Right now, I'm standing behind her.

There are a few people between me and her, and she is taller than me, but I can see her through the gaps between their shoulders, their necks. If I reach forward, I'll be able to touch her. Her hair is caught in the back of her collar and she flicks it out, then shifts her shoulder to hitch her bag up. She's twitchy. I like that. But her fingernails are painted. I don't like that. They make me want to weep. They are a sign that she doesn't care. That she is carrying on as if nothing has happened. I don't want to see that. She must not be allowed the comfort of amnesia. That cannot happen. She should not be able to paint her nails, do her hair. She should not care about herself. She knows what she has done and yet she still thinks she is worth preserving. I want to see her nails chewed and bleeding. I want to see a sign that she feels something.

There's a surge forward as the train pulls in and I allow myself to be carried behind her. I am walking on air. She is being pushed too, but not by me. I haven't touched her. She glances round, misses me; I'm not in her sight-line, she is head and shoulders above me. We're not ready yet, Nancy and I. I've brought Nancy with me. Her arms are over mine, my chest is where hers was. I have taken to wearing her cardigan most days. The doors open. She gets on. She doesn't mind the gap, and trips on her way. Have I missed my moment? Then the doors close and I watch her move off. Does she heave a sigh of relief? I can't be sure, but she ought to. Not this time. Not yet. But we know her route now. We know where and when to find her.

And I am capable of great patience. I was a fisherman years ago. Amateur, of course. I fished from the rocks by the Martello tower. This is like fishing. I have thrown in the bait and now I must wait. Just wait. It will come.

Geoff is on standby too, to throw in more bait as soon as I give the word. There are two bookshops in her neck of the woods, and he will move in at my command. Good old obliging Geoff. And there will be a bite, I know it, and when it comes I will haul in my catch. Well, not haul exactly, it will hardly be a netful, so not a haul. One bite, that's all I need, one bite from one slippery fish. I anticipate how my hand will tingle when I feel the tug on my line. I want to see the hook caught in the throat. To see my catch gasping for breath. Its fate in my hands. A simple crack on the head with a blunt instrument. Or will it be enough to have removed it from the depths and watch it gasp for air, its eyes wide and staring in panic? There is something extremely satisfying in that idea. A fish out of water. A fish rudely introduced to a hostile environment. Will it survive? Unlikely. The sudden exposure will probably kill it. They drown, don't they, fish? If they're left too long out of water. So, exposure first, and then perhaps I'll put it out of its misery.

17

Late spring 2013

It is not the 'boy' but his mother who Catherine speaks to. She is a more hesitant informant than the previous mother. Though it takes Catherine a while to coax it out of her, she opens her up in the end. Yes, it had been a very upsetting time. And for her son, Jamie, who is now thirty-seven, well it had been frightening. Catherine is patient, understanding. She really doesn't want to push her. They can easily speak another day. Perhaps she would prefer Catherine to come and see her? No, she'd rather do it now, over the phone.

Stephen Brigstocke had taught Jamie in his GCSE year and then taken him through his A levels. He was a good teacher and Jamie had liked him. He'd taken an interest in him, given him extra help if he needed it, and they had been grateful. If it wasn't for Mr Brigstocke, he might not have done so well and got a place at Bristol University. It was a big thing for all of them — Jamie was the first person in the family to go to university. She remembers driving him up there with his stuff and then leaving on the Sunday night. She'd cried, leaving her boy there. It was the first time he'd been away from home for more than one night, and her husband had told her she was being silly, that he'd be fine.

They both thought university was the safest place for him to start living independently.

'Anyway, that first week Jamie saw Mr Brigstocke on the campus. He was wandering around and Jamie thought it was just coincidence — that he had some work to do there or knew someone. Then he saw him again. He was outside one of his lecture halls, but when Jamie went up to talk to him he hurried off as if he hadn't seen him. Pretending he hadn't seen him. He started following Jamie. He'd be in the pub, hanging around campus, outside his lectures, always keeping his distance, never talking to Jamie, never coming up to him, just watching him. And it really freaked Jamie out. He said it was like Mr Brigstocke thought he couldn't see him — like he thought he was invisible. We told Jamie to tell someone, but he didn't want to make a fuss. Then one day he went back to his room and Brigstocke was sitting there, on his bed. He'd told one of the other students he was his uncle. Jamie said he kept repeating the same thing over and over — that he should make the most of university, he shouldn't waste his time. Over and over. It scared Jamie. He was bonkers, off his head. In the end, Jamie had to pretend he was meeting someone — that was the only way he could get rid of him. There were lots of things that we found out later — not from Jamie, from one of his friends. Jamie would never talk to us about it. The friend told us that Jamie suspected Brigstocke of going through his stuff when he'd been in his room. You know, his personal stuff. That things had been moved about. We didn't know about it till much later. If we had . . . well, my husband would have gone up there straight away and sorted him out.'

'What did you do?'

'We wanted to inform the police, only Jamie wouldn't let us. My husband spoke to the university and they said they'd keep an eye. For a while, nothing happened. Then one night when Jamie was in bed, Brigstocke turned up. Started banging on his door, wanting to be let in. Said he'd missed his last train and he wanted to sleep on Jamie's floor. I mean, he was a bloody nutcase. Another student, Jamie's mate, helped get him out of there.'

'And did the police get involved that time?'

'No, no, Jamie wouldn't call them and he wouldn't let us when we found out. But his mate said that he'd sorted Brigstocke out. He didn't come back after that. We went up there as soon as we could. Jamie's friend told us Brigstocke had been sobbing at Jamie's door, banging and banging for Jamie to let him in, and he'd had to drag him away. Jamie was too upset. It was his mate who got Brigstocke out of there. Bashed him about a bit — well, he had to. He said he was a nutter, crying like a baby. Jamie never told us any of that. Thing is, he'd really liked Mr Brigstocke, looked up to him.'

'Thank you, Mrs Rossi, thank you so much. Do you think Jamie would talk to me?'

'God no. He'd be furious if he knew I'd been talking to you. Even now. He completely clammed up about it — never talks about it. Sometimes I wonder whether, you know,

101

anything had happened before he went up to uni. I mean Brigstocke was obsessed with Jamie.'

'What do you mean? Did you ever suspect anything while Brigstocke was teaching Jamie?'

'I don't know. I don't know . . . No, no, not really. I'm not sure. Jamie trusted Mr Brigstocke. It was Mr Brigstocke got him through those exams. They spent a lot of time together.'

'Listen, let me leave you my number and if you think Jamie might want to talk, please give me a call. It's possible he's not the only one Stephen Brigstocke took an interest in.'

It's been a good day's work. Productive. Catherine is building up a picture of Stephen Brigstocke, and it is not a pretty one. That makes her feel better, a little safer. She is not the only one who is hiding things. She is about to leave when Kim hands her a piece of paper with the address and phone number she's been waiting for.

★ ★ ★

She is in no rush to get home. Robert had said he'd be late, so she takes her time, gets off at an earlier Tube stop and decides to walk the rest of the way. It's a nice evening. She passes her local bookshop, stopping to look in the window. It is full of temptation — full of things to cleanse her palate. She is stepping over the threshold when she hears her name called from across the street. She wants to ignore it — she feels the bookshop sucking her in, dragging her to its shelves — but the voice calls again, closer now, at her shoulder.

102

'Catherine!'

She turns and is met with a wide smile from a friend she hasn't seen for a while.

'How are you?'

'I'm fine, I'm fine. How are you?'

'Good. I'm good. What are you doing?'

'Well, I was about to go and buy a book — need to find a birthday present.' Why is she lying?

'Oh, come and have a drink. Come on, a quick glass of wine . . . '

The friend is beguiling. The sun is shining. Robert will be home late. They can sit outside, have a glass of wine, smoke a cigarette. She gives in, allows herself to be led away.

★ ★ ★

It is still light when she gets home. Even so, she pulls down the blinds and turns on the lights. Robert will be another hour. The silence in the house invites Stephen Brigstocke back into her head. He had been held at bay for a while: the company of her friend, a glass of wine, had helped push him away, but now he has slipped in again. The piece of paper with his telephone number is in her purse. She takes it out and looks at it, then presses the number into her phone. Her finger hovers over the word *Call*. What will she say? Her mouth is dry. What if she makes it worse by phoning? She doesn't know what to say. What does he want? Why hasn't he called her? Maybe he hasn't been back to that flat since she put her note through the letterbox.

103

Maybe he doesn't have her number. Or maybe he does, and is choosing not to use it. Perhaps he doesn't want to speak to her. Then what does he want? He sent her the book — he wrote the book — so she would read it. And she has. She must let him know. But he sent it to Nicholas too. Was that to get at her? There was no note to Nicholas — a note could have made everything clear to him, but he didn't do that. It was a warning to her: to let her know that he knows who her son is; where he is; a threat. He needs to know that she has read the book. She can do that. But does he want an apology too? For her to say sorry? An admission of guilt? That is too much to ask. She can give him something though. She can put her hand out at least, if it means he will leave her alone. Yes, she is prepared to go some way to meet him. It would be better to write, not speak. She can't trust herself on the phone. He wouldn't believe her anyway — better to compose some words and send them to him. She deletes his number and puts the piece of paper back in her purse.

She opens her laptop and finds the site for *The Perfect Stranger*. She has lost count of the number of times she has studied that page. Nothing ever changes on it. She clicks *Review*. Careful now. Be very careful. His wife told her he was dead. His own wife denied his existence. She didn't trust him. Catherine must be careful. He is sick, this man. He has shown how twisted his mind is. She tiptoes out the words: '*There is a pain at the heart of this book which is undeniable. It is rare for a work of fiction to* create such powerful feelings in its reader.' Should she give her name? No, too risky. No one must connect her to this book, and it could come up in the future, if someone googled her. Still, he needs to know that it is her, so she signs herself Charlotte, the name he has given her in the book, and then presses *Submit*.

18

Early summer 2013

I sleep during the day now and stay awake at night. I like the dark. I am not alone. Nancy is with me and I have my laptop too. It is my pet — I use it to do my shopping, like sending the dog out to bring in the newspaper: groceries delivered to my door. What a clever chap. It's mainly canned stuff. Like the war. Meat in tins. Chunky chicken. But it doesn't matter what I eat, it all tastes the same because another flavour overpowers everything; even when I've brushed my teeth until the gums bleed, I can't get the taste out of my mouth. It makes everything sour. And tonight it is particularly bad.

I have read a review. Is it a nibble? By now she must know that Nancy is dead so it is me she is talking to. I feel the twitch on my line. *There is a pain at the heart of this book which is undeniable. It is rare for a work of fiction to create such powerful feelings in its reader.* She's called herself Charlotte. Is that an acceptance of her guilt? But the more I read it, the more I see it for what it is; *such powerful feelings* — she doesn't say what those 'feelings' are. Powerful revulsion? Powerful loathing? I want precision, not vague feelings. I want shame, fear, terror, remorse, a confession. Is that really too much to ask? This little review has got right up my nose. It is so very carefully written: careful not to apologize, careful not to accept responsibility. I should have known that she would try to slither her way out of it. How dare she presume that her empty words, so nimbly crafted, will be enough? Even after all these years, Mrs Catherine Ravenscroft, award-winning documentary-maker, mother of Nicholas the vacuum-cleaner salesman, continues to twist the knife with her painted nails and her sly review. She has made a mistake in thinking that her pithy little missive will satisfy me. It has provoked me. It is an insult. I'm not interested in her acknowledgement of my pain. It's too late for that. She needs to feel it, to know what it's like. Only then will I get through to her. She needs to suffer as I have.

19

Early summer 2013

Catherine wakes. She hadn't remembered falling asleep, but her head tells her she has slept for some time. Her eyes are sticky with it. The bed is empty and light squeezes through the bottom of the blind. She allows her head to sink back on the pillow. The sun warms the room. It must be a nice day out there. It is after ten. Robert left hours ago. She thinks how pleased he will have been to see her so sound asleep.

He told her last night he'd have to be in early this morning. It was the first time in ages he'd even mentioned work. She's been so self-absorbed, but last night Robert unburdened himself: he had let things pile up at work, he was feeling swamped. Catherine knew how he hated not being on top of things; he needed to be one step ahead so that he could feel in control. If he wasn't, it made him . . . well, not quite panic, but certainly become very anxious. He was a lawyer — people relied on him to get things right.

Last night they'd sat up late chatting and she felt, for the first time in ages, that she was actually present. She was shocked when he told her the charity he worked for was about to come in for a grilling by the Parliamentary Treasury Select Committee. They were suspicious of the way government aid had been channelled through some of the charity's projects.

'Is it dodgy?' she asked.

'No, no, just incompetent,' he said.

'Will you have to appear?'

He shook his head. 'It would be easier if I did though. Somehow I have to make sure none of the directors look like criminals rather than incompetent, well-meaning buffoons.'

'They're lucky to have you,' she said, and took his hand.

When they'd met, Robert had been a lawyer working for the Home Office. He was nearly thirty and she was twenty-two, but he was shy and it had made him seem younger than he was. Catherine was working for a newspaper — her first job. She was ambitious; so was he. They were both determined to get ahead and both of them were doing well. She remembers how surprised she'd been by his openness — he was so unguarded that it had made her feel protective towards him. The first time they'd met he told her he had *political ambitions*. Those were the words he'd used — a little coy, apologetic. She'd encouraged him to talk. It was the first of many 'off-the-record' chats they had in a pub in Stoke Newington: neutral territory, where no one from either of their workplaces would be likely to come. Robert had been a member of the Labour Party since he was a student; so had she, only she'd let her membership lapse, whereas Robert never had. He'd hoped to be selected as a parliamentary candidate — he would have been one of the youngest ever. It had never happened, but she knew it was a desire he still nursed. They'd talked about it last night. He'd smiled, pleased that she'd brought it up, but he'd shaken his head.

'Nah, not now,' he said.

'I'd support you, you know, if that's what you want.' It was a relief to think about someone other than herself. She sees it as a sign of her recovery and sits up, leaning against the pillows.

It has been nearly a week since she sent the review and her instincts tell her it was the right thing to do. Stephen Brigstocke needed her acknowledgement. Now he knows that she recognizes what he has been through. It has helped her too, she thinks. Perhaps that's another reason why she is sleeping better. Writing those words forced her to think about his pain, not just hers. She cannot accept responsibility for it, but she can begin to understand why it has driven him to such an act of studied hatred. Yes, it has been good for her to think about that. Perhaps some balance has been restored for both of them in different ways.

She gets out of bed and pulls up the blind. It is glorious out there. She doesn't want to go to work — she'll call and tell them she's working from home. She goes downstairs and makes tea then sits at the table with her laptop. She opens the page for *The Perfect Stranger*. Her review is still up there but nothing else has been added. An image of the book's cover hovers in the corner of the screen, producing a throb of anger in her gut at the memory of its invasion. She exits the page. She will never look at it again.

20

Early summer 2013

It's morning. I have been up all night. I don't feel like breakfast. It is ten a.m. according to my lapdog and I am stiff from sitting in my chair so long. I need to move. I suppose I have become a little 'stir crazy'. Too much time in front of a screen. Not something that usually afflicts someone of my age. Three paces to the window and I open the curtains. It is a stunning day. I had no idea. It leaves me blinking as if I have run out in front of a car in the dead of night. It is the right kind of day to leave the house.

I have had duplicates made of the photographs, sending off the same negatives Nancy had sent off all those years ago. I half expected a nasty note to come back from the lab, but it didn't, just a fresh set of glossy prints. I slip on my lightweight summer jacket, then pop the envelope with the prints into the pocket. Yes, this is the right kind of day to leave the house.

Whenever I step into one of London's beautiful squares I regret that I haven't made an effort to do it more often. It is so invigorating. And Berkeley Square is a gem. There's nothing hidden about it, it is well aware of its value and shows it off shamelessly. This is where to come if you are in the market for a Rolls-Royce. Which of course I am not, and neither, by the look of them, are the fellows sharing the square with me this lunchtime. I close my eyes and raise my face to the sun and for the briefest of moments feel glad to be alive. I am still here, alive and ready to kick. But first I finish my sandwich, enjoying being part of this al fresco lunching club. I feel a comradely spirit between myself and the other diners, a few of us on benches, others lying on the grass or sitting on jackets. None of us knowing each other, yet relaxed nevertheless in each other's company: privileged to be sharing this luscious green space along with the ancient plane trees, the only living things older than I in the square. I scrunch up the paper from my sandwich and drop it into a bin, appreciating its presence, appreciating the security that it is still there and hasn't been removed for fear of a bomb being left in it. This is a safe place. As I cross the square I take the envelope from my pocket, checking the address again. No. 54 Berkeley Square.

The front of No. 54 has been partially torn out and replaced with glass, oversized slabs of glass, as if the building's mouth has been forced open and these glinting tombstones shoved in to prevent it from ever closing again. A building permanently trying not to gag. It's a humiliating expression for this once noble façade. I walk through its gaping orifice and present myself to a young woman behind the reception desk and hand her the envelope with a smile.

21

Early summer 2013

Catherine decides to spend the day in domestic bliss. She texts Robert and tells him she's taking the day off work and asks how his day is going. *Well*, he texts. *Home by 7.* She sends him three kisses. Tonight she will make a decent supper. They will have a bottle of crisp, white wine; they will have food flavoured with fresh herbs and they will have each other. She still enjoys Robert's company more than anyone else's; there is no one she would rather spend an evening with; no one whose opinion she respects more than his. She thinks back to the night a few weeks ago when she almost told him everything. Thank God she hadn't. Robert thinks he is the strong one, but he isn't really and marriage is delicate, not just theirs, but all marriages. There is a balance to maintain, and she thinks she has succeeded in keeping theirs on course.

Robert hates any kind of confrontation. She has hardly ever seen him angry, even with Nicholas; even when he was at his most challenging. It was always Catherine who raised her voice, never Robert. He was the one who smoothed things over. Although at times this upset her, made her feel like the cuckoo in the nest, she can see why he did it. If Nick couldn't or wouldn't talk to her, he at least knew he could talk to his father.

Robert had grown up an only child between warring parents and become expert in mediation. It hurt her to think that she and Nicholas needed a mediator, but at times they did. Her fault, she admits. She hadn't been able to reach him in the way she wanted to. He seemed to misread her voice, her tone, her facial expressions. It would take nothing for him to become angry with her and after a while she became self-conscious with him. Nothing felt natural. It hadn't always been like that, but certainly was from adolescence onwards. She has never doubted her love for Nicholas, yet the bond they'd had seems to have been eroded. Perhaps if she and Robert had had another child, things would have been different.

It is hard for Catherine to think about these things; she normally pushes them away, but she allows herself to hope that now Nicholas has moved out, the distance and space might help them see each other with a better perspective.

She can't remember ever looking forward to going to a supermarket, but she does today. It is good to be able to concentrate on the mechanics of ordinary life and she wallows in the experience. She picks up a bunch of flat-leaf parsley, its long stems flopping in her hand, and puts it in her trolley. She buys fresh food; things that, if they are not eaten, will rot and smell and remind her she is losing control again.

The dull task of putting away the shopping gives her as much pleasure as the supermarket.

Something so ordinary and thankless is such a luxury when you have been feeling the way Catherine has been feeling. She savours the simple pleasure of taking the food from the bags and putting it away: everything has its place and she is the one making sure it gets there.

It's only four o'clock — hours before she needs to start cooking. She goes into the sitting room and lies on the sofa. She is like a cat, languishing in the one sun spot in the room. She closes her eyes, though she is not tired, merely relaxed. Then she does something she has not done for weeks. She picks up a book and starts to read. It is a safe book — one she has read before — and she lies back on the sofa and disappears into it.

At six o'clock she pours herself a glass of wine and phones her mother. She never misses this weekly call, although recently they have been hurried, careless conversations and her mum deserves more than that.

'Mum? How are you? How's your week been?'

'Lovely, darling. Quiet, you know . . . but very nice. When did you get back from holiday?'

Catherine hesitates, not sure whether to correct her; they haven't been on holiday since last summer. Recently her mum has started getting confused about dates and times.

'We've been back ages, Mum — you know, I've seen you lots since then.' She tries to be gentle and not alarm her. There is nothing to be alarmed about, not yet. Her mother shrinks time but she remembers other things very well. Catherine gets her on track again: 'So did you go and see

Emma's new baby?' Catherine's younger cousin has just had her third child.

'Yes, they came and picked me up. They're so kind. Lovely little thing. All smiles. And how's Nick? Is he still enjoying his job?'

'Yes, he likes it, he really does.'

'That's super, he's such a clever boy.'

Nick and his grandma have always been close. When he was born, Catherine's mother moved in for a few weeks to help. It had given Catherine a new respect for her. She helped care for Nicholas, but she cared for Catherine and Robert too. She made meals, babysat, allowed them to have naps in the afternoon, whatever she felt they needed. She was never a martyr about it, never told Catherine how she should do things, she simply offered her support and love.

'Sorry I haven't been over recently, Mum. It's been a bit hectic, what with the move and all. Let's organize a Sunday lunch and I'll get Nick over too. I'll come and pick you up.'

'You don't have to pick me up, Catherine, I can pop on the bus.'

'Well, we'll see, Mum.' The last time Catherine's mother tried to take the bus she panicked about where to get off and stayed on until it returned to the bus station. She knows she is tiptoeing around her mother's gentle decline, not yet named but gradually making itself visible. Catherine has organized a helper to come in twice a week to lend a hand with cleaning and shopping. It is good to know that someone else is keeping an eye on her too.

'Well, I'd better get on with supper, Mum.

Speak soon, lots of love.'

'And to you, darling, take care of yourself.'

At seven, she texts Robert to let him know supper will be ready for seven fifteen. She puts on some music; allows herself to turn it up loud; allows herself another glass of wine; allows herself to feel at home.

By nine o'clock Robert is still not back. Catherine is worried. He has not replied to her calls or texts. It is not like him to be so utterly thoughtless. To simply not show up. A knot twists in her gut. She leaves a message for Nicholas, asking him to call her if he hears from his dad, but she hears nothing from him either. She is beginning to rehearse what she will say to the police when Robert finally texts her. He is stuck at work. No apology. No kiss. Fucking hell. She is hurt. Bugger. Fuck. He hasn't given her any thought.

22

Early summer 2013

Catherine is wrong. Robert has done nothing but think of her. For hours. Unmoving. Sitting at his desk when everyone else has gone home, his head on fire with thoughts of his wife. The package had sat unopened on his desk all afternoon and then, when he was about to leave, he had picked it up.

He had his jacket half on, ready to go home to Catherine, when he tore it open. He had, like her, been looking forward to an evening together, and that's what he was thinking of when he opened the envelope. He had frowned and slipped out a fan of photographs, thoughtless, not really registering what he was looking at. A quick glimpse. There was something else in the package too. A book. The book Catherine had burned. *The Perfect Stranger* by E. J. Preston. He opened it to the first page: *Any resemblance to persons living or dead is entirely coincidental . . .*

And then he had sat down and taken his jacket off.

He went through the photographs again, this time giving them his full attention, studying them one after the other. There were thirty-four in all. He picked up the manila envelope they'd arrived in and studied that too. The handwriting on the front. He didn't recognize it. *Delivered by hand*, it said in the corner, with Robert's name written in fountain pen; not a biro, a fountain pen loaded with royal-blue ink. Then he had stood up to catch his assistant before she left.

'Where did this come from?' he had asked. She had been surprised by his tone, stopped what she was doing.

'Someone left it in reception.'

'Who?'

'I'll find out,' she said, and picked up the phone with Robert standing over her. She turned to him.

'It was a man. An old man. Lucy said he handed her the envelope and told her it was for you. He didn't say anything else. She said he looked a bit . . . well, rough. She thought he was a tramp, but he was polite and he didn't hang around, just left the envelope and walked out.'

'Thanks, I'll see you in the morning,' and he'd dismissed her.

He is still sitting at his desk, the photographs spread before him like a Hockney collage: small images pieced together to reveal a bigger picture. Yet Robert cannot see what that bigger picture is. What he sees is Catherine. Catherine on a beach fingering the ties at the side of her red bikini with Nicholas near by, smiling at the camera. Catherine asleep, peaceful. Another with her propped up on one arm, her breasts pushed together, beautiful, spilling over the top of her bikini, her smiling face resting on her hand. Who is she smiling at? Catherine and Nicholas sitting in the shallows, Nicholas looking out to sea,

Catherine looking directly at the camera. She looks sexy, swelling with it, and their little boy, five at the time, sitting at her feet.

The photographs have been taken over a series of days; not one day but several. More than several? He tries to remember. Nicholas is in most of the beach scenes. There are other photographs too, where Nicholas does not appear. Was he there, in the background? He must have been near by. Was he in the same room? Was he in the next room? Alone? Was he asleep? What did he see? What did he hear? In these other photographs Catherine is wearing underwear, not a bikini. Knickers and bra. Definitely not a bikini. Lace. Straps that slip off shoulders. Nipples seen, sharp, through the lace. Knickers, not bikini bottoms. Nothing as robust as that. Tiny, fragile. Nothing that would stay on underwater. He should know — he had bought them for her, for their holiday. And her hand is down the front of her knickers and her head is back as if she is looking at something on the ceiling, but she is clearly not looking at anything. She has taken herself away somewhere else; she has reached a place which has parted her lips and closed her eyes. Lost in her own exquisite space. Not quite alone though, because someone else is there. A silent, appreciative witness. Invisible. Except in one photograph. One slip-up. A shadow on the edge of the frame.

Robert is grateful he is alone; grateful that no one is there to witness his tears. The initial shock at seeing the pictures has given way to an ache that runs through him like a steel blade slicing down from the crown of his head to his stomach. He feels his insides leaking from the gash. His fingers had been shaking when he'd texted Catherine to say he was stuck at work. A text was all he could manage. He couldn't speak to her, not yet. He was not capable of having the conversation he knew they would have to have at some point, but not now.

He wants to believe that it is a mistake, yet he cannot deny what he is looking at. It is her. In full colour; in close-up. He can almost smell her body coming off the shiny prints. The images speak for themselves; images that are new to him, and yet flashes of which he recognizes. The underwear. He had chosen it, and the red bikini. Her face is the same — younger, but the same — and yet her expression is not one he quite recognizes. And that is so, so painful. He has never seen that absolute abandon on Catherine's face. It is Catherine and yet it is not his wife. The location he recognizes too. Spain in . . . when was it — '91? '92? A small Spanish seaside town. A summer holiday for the three of them. And then his anger rises, and he is grateful for it — allowing it to overwhelm the pain for a moment. He remembers he had missed part of that holiday. He had flown home early, leaving Catherine and Nicholas behind. A case had come up, something which must have felt important at the time but now is lost in the more important fact that it took him away from his wife and child.

Catherine may not look like his wife in the photographs, but Nicholas is absolutely recognizable as his son. His smile. His slender body, baby fat gone, very much a little boy, no longer an infant. All angles, knobbly knees, sharp elbows. A constantly moving flash of a boy, electric with curiosity. Looking at this little boy fuels his anger. What did Nicholas witness? How much did he see? How much did he understand? The poor little mite would have had no choice. He couldn't catch a flight home. He couldn't ask Daddy to come and fetch him.

Robert pushes his mind back to when Catherine and Nicholas came home from that holiday. It was soon afterwards that Catherine announced she wanted to return to work full-time. He remembers it well. It had come out of the blue. He had assumed she would stay at home a while longer, then go part-time. It wasn't the money; he'd been earning more than her — enough for both of them. It had upset him, yet he hadn't said anything; he'd covered up what he felt because he put her needs before his. He had kept his disappointment to himself.

He swallows down the phlegm that has gathered at the back of his throat. She'd told him she was depressed, that she missed her work. She didn't say it, but he could tell that being a mother was not enough for her; she put her own needs before their child's. As had he. He had put Catherine's needs before Nick's. So it hadn't been about work — it had been about her affair on holiday.

She was depressed about their marriage, not about being at home. He looks at the photos spread out on his desk. She found something more exciting on that holiday. Fucking hell, he's been such an idiot. He should have pushed her the other night when he caught her burning the book. She was about to tell him and she would have, if he'd insisted. But of course he didn't. He played right into her hands, as always. That's why she hasn't been sleeping; that's why she's so fucking caught up with herself: she's been found out. It wasn't about Nick moving out, or her guilt — she doesn't give a fuck for Nick or him. No, she's been found out, that's what this is about. Found out about an affair she had years ago. An affair she had under their son's nose. Jesus Christ.

Poor Nicholas, trapped in Spain with his mother and who else? Who was there with them? His mother with a stranger and him, a five-year-old witnessing God knows what. The perfect stranger? He rakes through his memory to see if he can retrieve any conversation he might have had with Catherine when she came home, something that might give him a clue. All he comes up with though are innocuous phrases: *We missed you . . . It wasn't the same once you'd left.* Well, that's for fucking sure.

And what about Nicholas? Did he say anything that Robert could have picked up on? Should have picked up on? Did his behaviour change? Was he withdrawn? Robert can't remember Nicholas saying anything at all. Surely he would have said something like, *Mummy's friend did this . . .* or *We met this nice man . . .* or *Mummy made a friend?* He can't remember his son saying anything, ever, about the time when he was alone with Mummy on

123

holiday. And a stranger. Was it a stranger? Or did he know him? It worries him that Nicholas said nothing. It is not normal for a child to simply say nothing. A child only says nothing when they are hiding something, something that is unsayable.

His phone beeps. A text from Catherine: *Wish you'd let me know earlier*. No kiss this time. He doesn't respond. He doesn't want to talk to her, text her even. But his son he must talk to. He must see him. Remembering the Nicholas in the photographs and knowing how he is now as a young man, he is struck by the discrepancy. That crash-bang-wallop of a child is nowhere to be seen in the plodding, rather aimless, twenty-five-year-old Nicholas. That child was snuffed out by adolescence — smoked out — and never quite recovered. He'd always asked himself why. Why did he drop out? Why was he so unmotivated? And his mother had said nothing. Well, maybe this is why. Maybe little Nick saw, heard things he shouldn't have. Perhaps now Robert has the key to unlock whatever it is that knocked the fizz out of his son.

'Nick? Hi, it's Dad.'

'Hello.' His voice is flat.

'Listen, have you eaten?' Robert infuses his voice with enthusiasm.

'Er, no.'

'Well, I'm going to swing by and take you out to supper. I've had to work late and I'm starving . . . ' Nicholas hesitates, but Robert is determined: 'Just a quickie, we can grab something in the pub near you. It's on my way home.'

'Mum's trying to get hold of you, by the way.'

124

'I've spoken to her, don't worry,' he lies. 'I'll see you in fifteen minutes.'

★ ★ ★

There are four bells on Nicholas's front door, three with scribbled names, one without. Robert rings the top, nameless bell. He hasn't been here since he and Catherine helped Nicholas move in three months ago. He pictures him making his way down the four flights. When he finally opens the door he looks exhausted.

'Shall we go?' Robert beams, over-compensating for his son's lack of enthusiasm.

'I'm not quite ready.'

'That's fine. I'll come up and wait.' Robert follows him, holding back his strides to fit his son's heavy tread; taking in Nicholas's bare feet, the dirty soles; the post littering the hall floor; the stained, cigarette-burned carpet. Robert waits in the sitting room, peering into the kitchen, taking in the sink full of dirty plates, the blackened frying pan on the hob, the bin that needs empty-ing — juice and milk cartons, scraps of food spilling from the black bag. What you'd expect from a flat full of students, he tells himself. Except Nick is the only one who isn't a student. His flatmates are out and the place reeks of dope. He hopes that it's from them, not Nick. Please don't let him be back on weed again. But he doesn't want to risk annoying his son, so says nothing.

'Ready?' Robert pushes open the bedroom door and his stomach dips again. Pants, plates, jeans, cups, all dumped in their own filth. The duvet has a yellowish tinge to the edge where Nicholas's face has rubbed against it. He is sitting on the bed, putting on his socks. Robert watches him push his feet into the pair of black slip-on shoes he wears for work and feels another surge of anger towards Catherine. This is her fault. She pushed Nicholas away. She persuaded Robert that it would be good for him to be independent. There's not even a lampshade on the ceiling light. His throat catches. He sees the mobile Nicholas had had as a little boy hanging from a hook intended for something else: the fragile paper wings of the planes crashing against the wall, not enough space for them to float freely.

'Come on, mate, let's get going.' He gives his son an encouraging smile. He is determined to get through the evening without breaking down.

★ ★ ★

Father and son. A bottle of red wine. Steak and chips. Robert had persuaded the kitchen to serve them late. A loving father who wishes he had done this before. Wishes he had made a habit of it. He asks Nicholas about work, but only half listens as he answers. Being a trainee salesman for John Lewis isn't the career Robert and Catherine had wanted for their son, nevertheless Nicholas seems to have enough to say about it to convince his father he's all right. He's perked up now he has eaten. He was ravenous. He tells Robert about training days and staff benefits.

But is this really what he wants to do with his life? Is it enough? Does he enjoy living in such squalor?

'So, how you finding it? The flat?' Robert asks.

Nicholas shrugs, but then a smile tickles his mouth.

'Haven't actually been there much recently,' he says, sticking his fork into Robert's chips.

'Oh?'

'There's a girl I've met. I've been spending quite a lot of time at her place.'

'So tell me about her.' This is good news.

'Not much to tell. Don't think she'd be Mum's cup of tea — '

'Well, it's nothing to do with her, is it?'

His tone makes Nicholas look up in surprise.

'So what's she like?' Robert moves on.

'Nice. We're hoping to go away this summer, if we can get the money together.'

'Really? Where?'

'Somewhere cheap. Maybe Spain. Or Majorca.' He grins.

'Spain.' Perfect. 'D'you remember that holiday we went on when you were little? To Spain?'

Nicholas looks irritated by the change of subject. 'No, I don't.'

'You were about five. I had to go home halfway through because of work. You and Mum were there on your own.' He scrutinizes Nicholas's face for a sign, but there is nothing. A blank, revealing surely that something must have been erased.

'Vaguely. Not really.'

'It was only for a few days.' He wants to nudge

his son into remembering without causing alarm. 'I felt bad about it at the time. I shouldn't have left you. On your own. With Mum.'

Nicholas looks at him, shrugs. 'I don't really remember, Dad. Don't feel bad about it.'

Robert searches his face again for any flicker of pain, but detects none. Whatever he experienced back then has been buried deep.

'You should take your girlfriend somewhere nice. I'll help you out. It must be hard on your salary, with the rent and everything.'

Nicholas is thrown. This is surely against the rules, Mum's rules, but he's happy to take anything he can get from his father.

'Thanks,' he says.

★ ★ ★

After Robert has dropped Nicholas back at the flat, he drives around until he is sure Catherine will be asleep. He parks outside the building and looks up at their bedroom window. The light is off. He takes the book from his bag and, lighting the first page with his phone, reads: *Victoria station on a grey, wet, Thursday afternoon. The perfect day on which to escape . . .*

He is too tired tonight to face what it might tell him, and it is the photographs which have seared his heart. He will read the book tomorrow. He googles *The Perfect Stranger* from his phone, and finds the site for the book. Like Catherine, he finds nothing to tell him who the author might be — male, female, young, old. He presumes male, of his age. He reads the review and wonders who wrote it. He gets out of the car, shuts the door and lets himself into the flat. He listens for a moment, then goes up to the spare room, taking care to be silent.

23

Early summer 2013

This is the second night running that Catherine has gone to bed alone. She had tried to stay awake last night, waiting for Robert to come home, but she couldn't. When she woke the following morning there was no sign that he had been to bed at all. It was only when she heard the front door close and ran downstairs that she realized that he had, and then he had left again without wanting to wake her.

He must be really snowed under at work to come home so late and leave so early in the morning. She had wanted to talk to him, ask him why he hadn't called her and let her know what was going on, why he wasn't home for supper. He is a thoughtful man. Yes, thoughtful. So thoughtful that he'd slept in the spare room so as not to wake her. He is pleased she is sleeping again and didn't want to disturb her. And then again in the morning he must have made sure she wouldn't wake. She should have been grateful, but she wasn't. She was uneasy. And her unease had grown during the day when her calls went unanswered and her texts received replies which were slow to come and terse in tone.

And now, on this second night alone, she lies in bed, listening out for him again. It is just before midnight. She hears the rumble of a train, the hiss of cars on the wet road, the grumble of a taxi pulling up. The slamming of a door. She sits up. This could be him. She listens for a key in the front door, but hears nothing except the distant chime of the church bell ringing midnight. She gets up and goes to the top of the stairs. Then she hears the sound of keys being laid on the hall table, so quietly that if she hadn't been listening, she would have missed it. If she had been lying in bed, as she guessed Robert thought she was, she wouldn't have known that he had come in and was downstairs. What she really heard was the effort he'd put into hiding his return. She waits for him to come upstairs. When he doesn't, she makes her way down, tightening the cord on her dressing gown, trying to strangle the churning in her stomach.

Robert looks at Catherine, but says nothing. His eyes stay on her as she comes closer and pulls out a chair, joining him at the kitchen table. He drinks from a glass of whisky he has poured himself, his eyes still fixed on her.

'Robert,' she says softly. His name is all she can find to say.

He puts down his glass, reaches into his jacket pocket and takes out an envelope. He tips the photographs on to the table and spreads them out with his fingers, as if he is about to perform a card trick. She looks at them, confused at first, as he had been when he first saw them. Then it hits her. She sees the images. Hears the sound. Click, click, click.

'Oh God,' she says as she is dragged back, an

131

unwilling time traveller. She doesn't touch them, just looks.

He grabs her wrist and makes her pick them up. 'Look at them. Look at them closely. Look at yourself.' And she does. Tears come to her eyes, her throat closes, dry, choking. She wipes her sleeve across her eyes. She cannot cry — if she cries she will never stop, it will go on and on and she will drown. They will both drown. Is this the worst moment? She knows it is not.

'I said, look at them.' She has never heard him so cold, never felt this chill his voice sends through her. He doesn't shout, but love has been stripped out, leaving only fury.

'Look at all of them.'

And she is forced to go through them, one by one.

He stops her hand when she gets to a photograph of her masturbating. There is more than one and he will not allow her to flick through them. She must look at them slowly. Then he snatches them from her and lays three down side by side: a triptych of his shameless wife. His wife spread out in glossy colour on their kitchen table, her fingers sticky, tucked into herself. Light, nimble fingers. And then Robert begins to cry, and it breaks her heart.

'Oh, Robert, I'm so sorry . . . I should have told you . . . ' She moves towards him, wanting to put her arms around him, to pull him closer, but he pushes back his chair. He doesn't want her touching him. He snatches up a photograph of Nicholas on the beach with her.

'What the fuck went on?' That voice again.

132

There is more anger than pain in him.

'I should have told you . . . but . . . Nicholas didn't know anything. Really. He didn't know . . . it was so long ago . . . I — '

'I know exactly when it fucking was,' he interrupts. 'It doesn't matter how long ago it was. You did this — ' and he grabs up the photographs and throws them in her face.

The shock of it makes her gasp. Most of them fall to the floor, a couple settle on her lap. She brushes them off, leaving them where they lie.

'And Nicholas?' he says. 'What did he see? It's one thing doing it to me, but to him? How could you? I didn't think you were capable of . . . '

He can't say it and she waits for him as he struggles to order his thoughts. Yet it is dangerous to wait. She should step in before he says too much, but she is lost. She is lost back then, remembering.

'Who was it? I want to know who the fuck it was. Did it carry on? Or was it some fucking Spanish waiter — a holiday fling, like you were some teenage slut who had a holiday shag. An easy lay. Those fucking English cunts — bit of sunshine and sangria and they're anyone's. Of course they don't usually have their fucking kids with them. Were you bored? Had to get a bit of attention for yourself?'

'No, no, it wasn't like that . . . ' It feels as if a stranger has walked into their home. This is not Robert.

'Well, how was it then? He was taking pictures of our son. So tell me? How was it?'

'Stop shouting at me!' Because he is shouting

and she cannot think if he shouts. He is no longer cold; his anger has warmed him up. 'Please. Stop. I will tell you, if you listen . . . just try and listen . . . ' She grabs his whisky and finishes it. She prepares to say it out loud, to confess why she has never told him. 'I didn't want you to leave us there. Do you remember that? I asked you not to go, not to go back to work, to stay with us . . . ' She stalls, building up to it, but he doesn't let her. He snatches control again, unable to contain his fury.

'You are unbelievable. You're saying that it's my fault? That because I left early it justifies you fucking a stranger under our son's nose? Exposing him to that? You really think you can justify anything you do, don't you? That you are always right. That right is always on your side. Saint fucking Catherine.'

She is stunned. He hates her in that moment, she can see it. So quickly he has turned from love to hate. He is hurt, she tells herself, yet she fears it is more than that. Clogging, dark resentment bubbles out of his mouth. She watches him, his mouth opening, stuff coming out.

'You couldn't do without me for four days? You couldn't manage without sex for four days? As I remember it, we were barely having sex then anyway. That was why I bought you that fucking underwear!' He kicks at one of the photographs. 'So how long did it go on? Did you have little reunions? Meet up over a glass of Rioja back in England? Oh, maybe all those fucking *work* trips. Did you take him with you?'

What had she expected? Not this. She looks at

134

the photographs on the floor and bends down to pick them up.

'Where did you get them?'

Robert ignores her, opening his bag and slapping *The Perfect Stranger* down on to the table.

'So it *is* about you.'

Sweat soaks into her dressing gown.

'Yes, but it wasn't like that — not like it is in there . . . ' It feels as if he has jammed his fist down her throat and she can't get her words out.

'Really? So why were you so worried? Why did you try and burn it? And you've just said that Nicholas knew nothing about it, but he was sent this book too, wasn't he — so he must have been involved — '

'Yes, but not . . . ' she starts and then stops.

'You haven't read it?'

'No. I haven't had the stomach. These tell me enough.' And he kicks at the photographs again. 'Did *he* write it?'

'No,' she whispers.

'What? I can't hear you.' Scornful. Bullying.

She shakes her head.

'So who then? His wife? Did she find out?'

'His father. I think it's his father.'

'His father? Oh, for fuck's sake! He was young? How young exactly? Don't tell me he was under age.'

And then Catherine raises her voice, but it's more a scream than a shout. Shrill and desperate.

'He's dead! He died — '

She catches the shock on Robert's face. A

135

shock wave that has taken twenty years to travel from her to him, and now has smashed down the defences she had constructed around their life together.

24

Summer 1993

It wasn't the middle of the night, or three in the morning. It was teatime on a bright, sunny day. Nancy and I had been sitting in our garden, reading the newspapers and drinking tea. We had moved our chairs to the corner of the terrace, making the most of that last bit of sun before our north-facing garden was in total shadow. I didn't hear it at first; it was only when I went into the kitchen to refill our cups that I saw two figures through the glass of our front door. And then I heard them. I realized later that they had probably been knocking for a while, because what I heard from the kitchen was no longer a knock but a thump, with a fist. Not aggressive, yet urgent. The teapot was in my hand, ready to pour, and I put it down and glanced through the open kitchen door at Nancy, her hat pulled down, shielding her eyes from the sun, lost in concentration. What was she reading? I don't know exactly, I remember it was the review section so it would probably have been something about a play or a film, or a concert that she might have circled with her pencil and suggest we get tickets for. We never did. We never went to the theatre or listened to music after that.

I left her reading and went to the front door. You just know when something is so wrong. And I wanted to leave her as long as possible in that old world where the Sunday papers could be read and sympathy felt for other people's troubles, not our own.

'Mr Brigstocke?' he asked. And I nodded, not moving from the doorstep, not wanting to let them in.

'Can we come in, sir?' She spoke this time, her eyes determined to hold mine. I hesitated, then stood aside, opening the front door wider, allowing them in.

'Is your wife here, sir?' she asked.

I nodded. 'What's happened? Why are you here?'

'I'm afraid it is bad news, sir. Please go and find your wife.'

And I obeyed. They followed me to the sitting-room door and said they'd wait there. I made the walk through to the kitchen and out of the back door and stood in the shade looking at Nancy, one splash of sun remaining on the edge of her hat.

She looked up.

'What is it?' Her eyes were screwed up, squinting at me in the shadow. 'Stephen?'

'The police are here. In the sitting room.'

And she continued to stare at me, her mouth partially open, knowing, as I did, that we were about to become old before our time. Bowed and buckled under a weight too heavy to bear. She pushed herself up from the depth of the deckchair, the vitality it seemed already having left her. I held out my hand and we walked together into our sitting room and sat in two separate chairs. The police officers had taken the sofa.

'You have a son, Jonathan. Aged nineteen? Travelling in Spain.'

We both nodded. Not dead then, I thought. They used the present tense. Nancy must have thought the same: 'We had a postcard from him yesterday. From Seville.' She actually smiled as she said it, as if this was proof somehow that he was fine; confirmation that he was a good boy who loved his parents; who didn't want them to worry about him.

'We're so sorry — Jonathan died in an accident. Yesterday. We're very sorry.' I nodded, Nancy didn't move. We both sat in our separate chairs and then I stood up and went over to her. I took her hand. It was clammy, unresponsive.

'What sort of accident?' I was thinking road. Something on the road, that's where accidents happen. A car hitting him. Him falling from a motorbike at speed. Being hit by a truck. Something quick and final with no hope of recovery.

'He drowned,' the policeman said, and the policewoman got up and offered to make tea. I pointed to the kitchen.

'It was an accident. The Spanish police are clear about that. Tarifa — the sea is treacherous there. Unpredictable.' He looked at us.

What could we say? What could we do? We needed to be told what to do. He knew that.

'You will have to go to Spain to identify your

139

son,' he told us. 'The Spanish authorities won't release the body until there's formal identification. Unless there's someone else who could do that for you . . . '

'So, you're not sure it's Jonathan? It could be a mistake?' Nancy snatched at hope.

'Mrs Brigstocke, I'm sorry, but there is no mistake. The Spanish police have been through your son's things . . . his bag was on the beach . . . There still has to be a formal identification though.'

'Maybe someone stole his bag?' she pleaded.

'They found his passport. It's definitely Jonathan.'

The female officer returned with the tea — too milky, too sweet.

'The body can't be released until it's been formally identified. After that, you can bring him home,' she said as she put down the tray. 'If there's anyone else who could do that . . . '

'No, there's no one else,' I said.

'No other family?'

I shook my head.

She took this in, then carried on. 'The consulate will help with all the arrangements. They'll look after everything for you.'

The body. Our son. The body. I felt Nancy slip her hand out of mine and wrap it around her teacup.

'Here's the number for the consulate, and I'll give you mine too,' the policewoman said, writing in a small pad. 'In case you have any more questions.' She held the piece of paper out to me, but it was Nancy who took it. She sat

140

down with it, staring at the numbers. She didn't look up when they walked to the door, or when she heard it close behind them.

There were questions, of course, which I hadn't had the presence of mind to ask at the time. How exactly had it happened? What sort of accident? Was there anyone else involved? It was Nancy who found out those details when she telephoned the consulate, and it was Nancy who told me. That is when I first heard the name Ravenscroft. Nancy wanted to get in touch with her, but I persuaded her not to. I'd said it was up to her to contact us, and she'd agreed with me at the time. The fact that Catherine Ravenscroft made no attempt to do so made me even more certain that it had been the right decision. It was only later, after Nancy had developed the film from Jonathan's camera, that she must have changed her mind. But she didn't tell me. She kept it to herself.

When the door closed behind them I saw Nancy was shivering and I took the blanket from the back of the sofa and wrapped it around her shoulders. She still hadn't looked at me.

'Nancy, Nancy,' I whispered. I knelt down and pulled her towards me — I had to pull her, she didn't come willingly. It was shock, she couldn't move. Of course I was shocked too, but in a way I was luckier than she was. I had her to focus on. I had to help her, so I couldn't think about how I felt. I stroked her hair as if she was a child. I said her name again, several times, quietly, as if coaxing her out of sleep. And then she woke up and looked at me, shrugged the blanket from her

141

shoulders and stood up, roughly dislodging me.

'Book a flight, Stephen.' Then she went upstairs and I heard a suitcase being dragged from under our bed.

25

Summer 2013

Robert's neck is stiff, his eyes dry. Catherine's lover is dead. Jesus. That's why she thought she hadn't needed to tell him. She thought she'd got away with it. Her lover was never going to turn up on their doorstep. No wonder she'd been depressed. She was grieving. Had she fallen in love? Not in such a short time, surely. But did it make her think she was missing something? Robert had spent the night in the car, taking the bottle of whisky with him when he stormed out of the flat. She begged him to stay, begged him to listen. She even ran after him.

He only drove up into the next street, he didn't go far. He didn't know where to go, so he parked and sat there, half expecting her to appear at the bottom of the road, having run after him. He kept checking in the rear-view mirror, but she didn't come and so he reclined his seat and drank the whisky.

He should feel sick from it, but he doesn't. It is his wife who conjures up the nausea. Her lies — he doesn't want to hear any more and he ignores all her calls, finally switching his phone off. His anger is solid within him and he clings to it, to stop himself disintegrating. It sickens him to think how she has manipulated him. He should have known. It's the tool of her trade, something he's always admired: her ability to persuade people to do things they'd prefer not to. He never dreamed she'd use that trick on him.

He started reading the book last night while he swigged the whisky. He didn't get far — he was too distracted and couldn't concentrate — but he will read it today, this morning. He'd slept on the back seat, curled up like a baby, his knees tucked into his chest. He is still in the back, sitting upright now, as if he's waiting for his driver. His head aches and his mouth tastes as if he's drunk the contents of the toilet before it's been flushed. He reaches to the front of the car and jams three extra-strength pieces of gum into his mouth. He needs food, he needs coffee and he needs time to sit and read. He can't drive though, he daren't risk it. He must still be over the limit. So he locks the car, straightens his clothes and heads off to the bus stop.

It is five thirty. He has hours before he needs to be at work for his first meeting. He waits for the bus. It is a beautiful day, sunny, quiet. He is the only person waiting, but when the bus pulls up there are a couple of people already on it. People he doesn't normally travel to work with. He guesses that the young African woman is going home after a night shift. He notices the edge of a uniform below her anorak. She looks tired, deep purple rings under her eyes. A hospital worker, perhaps; auxiliary rather than medical. A good woman, he thinks; a woman who works shifts to support herself and her

144

family; a woman without vanity, who has no time for affairs and deceit. He wonders whether his thoughts are racist, and decides they probably are, this presumption of simplicity — the imposition of worthiness to her existence. And the elderly man — Eastern European, he guesses — with a knitted hat even in the summer, and a rucksack with a lunch Robert can smell from two seats away. A builder, he guesses, off to tart up some privileged Londoner's home. A home like his. Where this man, who should have retired by now, will be begrudged cups of coffee and the use of the toilet. On him, Robert imposes a quiet dignity, a silence from where he observes the lives of the people he works for without making judgements on them. When he gets up, ready for his stop, Robert smiles, first at the woman, then the man. Neither of them notices him. Sanctimonious twit is his judgement on himself.

This is a morning of firsts, and he finds a small café, the type he would never normally choose, but it's the only one open at six in the morning around Berkeley Square. He asks for tomatoes on toast. Brown bread, not white. No — toast, please, not fried. And a cup of tea, which when it arrives is the colour of toffee. He has chosen a corner at the back and settles down to read.

He can't resist reading the last line first. He agrees with it. It really is a *pity*, these omissions of his wife's, her *omission* to tell him anything. She only wants to talk now because she's been cornered. He admires the restraint in the language, but can't share it. It's more than a fucking pity. *Deadly?* An idle threat. He feels no need to protect her.

Last night she tried to convince him that the book was not how it had been. It hadn't happened like that. He couldn't listen to her; he couldn't stand the sound of her voice. It was fake. Everything about her felt fake. Of course she would say that. As far as he's concerned, she's lost her chance to give him her version. He can only trust this printed word. She had her chance years ago and now he can't believe anything she says because he knows it will be nuanced. She will try anything to excuse the inexcusable. And it is inexcusable, because of Nicholas. Because he was there.

Less than a week ago it would have been a luxury to have hours to sit in a café and read a book, but now it makes his mouth dry and his fingers shake. He flips back to the first page:

Victoria station on a grey, wet, Thursday afternoon. The perfect day on which to escape. Two young people queued at the ticket office, clutching at each other's hands, then letting go again, but not for long. They couldn't bear not to be connected for more than a couple of minutes . . .

It is not the sort of book Robert would normally read, but he finds it a real page-turner. He can see why it might have attracted Nicholas and why he would have kept reading. It is easy, fluid and light, about a young man, younger than Nicholas, who travels across Europe with his girlfriend. Robert reads of their anticipation and sense of adventure. They have thrown in their jobs to go travelling, determined not to squander their youth. Two people still young enough to travel on a young person's railcard. The smell of trains at night; waking in the morning and arriving in another country; pulling down the window and breathing in Mediterranean skies as they speed through landscapes of freedom. They are in love. They are meant to be together.

What seeps through the airy text, and what Robert imagines had kept Catherine from dismissing the book after the first few chapters, is the slow-coming dark of tragedy. This paradise will be short-lived. All the good things — the smells, the tastes, the heat — are tinged with the threat that this cannot last. By the time Robert has moved from tea to coffee and the couple have arrived in Nice, bad news from home pulls the girlfriend, Sarah, back to England. John, her boyfriend, says he'll return with her, but Sarah will not hear of it. She knows how much this trip means to John; how long he has thought about it, planned for it, saved for it. Sarah is the sort of girl every parent would like their son to be with. There is a tearful farewell at Nice station. John buys a postcard and sits in a café to write to his parents. He buys a pack of Gauloises and smokes one. Sarah doesn't like smoking. Even his parents don't know that he smokes. He buys a stamp, posts his card and continues his journey alone. So now it starts, thinks Robert, and he orders black coffee.

26

Summer 2013

We were definitely the odd ones out at the airport. Perhaps that's just how it felt, and others didn't notice, although I suspect the more perceptive travellers would have spotted the middle-aged couple, red-eyed, looking in desperate need of a holiday, yet apparently dreading getting on the plane. They might have assumed fear of flying. But it was fear of landing that afflicted Nancy and me — the fear of it all becoming real. So far all we had been able to do was imagine. Now we must look at the body of our son, who had gone ahead and experienced something he should have waited for us to do first.

Before we left for the airport, I had taken down from the dresser the three postcards Jonathan had sent us: Paris, Nice, Seville. Glossy and bright. Dashed-off words, which carried little weight when first read but would later be scrutinized over and over. The one from Seville was the last we received: the cathedral bathed in sunshine and tourists being pulled in a horse-drawn carriage in the foreground. How could these tourists know their image would be frozen for ever in our heads? That when that postcard landed on our doorstep, we would see them, then turn them over and read the words

148

which were to become the last words we ever had from our son:

Dear Mum and Dad,
Have spent two days here. Heading to the
    coast tomorrow.
Want to get the ferry to Tangiers.
Love,
J xox

Neither of us spoke Spanish so the consulate in Jerez helped us through the bureaucracy. There was a lot of it. Certificate after certificate that needed to be signed, stamped and handed over to various authorities before we would be allowed to take our boy home.

It had been many years since we had seen Jonathan naked, but he was nearly naked when we looked at him lying there, with only a cloth to cover his genitals. He was perfect. Preserved in death, his eyes closed, and unmistakably our son. The consulate had informed us he would be embalmed — Spanish law insists on it before a body can be transported. I understood the technicalities of the embalming process, we both did, though neither of us wanted to think too much about it.

Jonathan had drowned, but his face wasn't swollen the way I had expected it to be. There was a mark running along the inside of his left arm. I traced it with my fingers, stroking the cold flesh along a purple line which crossed with another. An injury he sustained, we were told, during the accident.

149

I cried, as quietly as I could, but I did cry. Nancy shook. Tremors ran through her whole body, not just her shoulders. She was not shaking with sobs. This was prolonged, lengthy. Something had ruptured inside her, sending wave after wave of shock through her. It was as if she had been plugged in and couldn't be switched off. I put both my arms around her to try and steady her, but I couldn't. And the worst thing about it was her silence. Absolute silence. When I tried to pull her away and get her out of the room, she wouldn't move. She leaned forward and took Jonathan's hand. It was stiff. It wouldn't curl around hers any more. We saw his palm was purple and scuffed, the skin ripped and burned where he had held on to something. He must have held on for dear life. Nancy sank to her knees and kissed his poor hand and I put both mine on her shoulders. The man from the consulate shuffled. There was no doubt this was our son but we still needed to sign a piece of paper to confirm it. He thought it was time for us to leave, I could tell. I must have looked helpless, so he came over.

'Mrs Brigstocke, Mrs Brigstocke, we can go now.'

I was relieved that she ignored him; it left me some space in which to act. I pulled her hand from Jonathan's and put it in mine.

'Nancy, come on, darling.' Finally she let me lead her from the room. The consulate had organized a car to take us to the seaside town where Jonathan had died. I didn't really think about whether we would have to pay for any of

150

it. We did, as it turned out. Jonathan's travel insurance didn't cover it.

We drove in silence from Jerez to Tarifa, sweating in the back of the car. The first thing Nancy wanted to do when we arrived was go to the beach. I asked the driver to wait. It was too hot. Midday. There was no shelter, nowhere to escape the burning sun. It was the largest beach we had ever been to: miles and miles of white sand. It was a desert, except there were crowds of people there. Hordes, cooking, glistening in oil. We were the only ones fully clothed, and our shoes sank into the sand and I wondered whether to take mine off and walk in bare feet, but Nancy marched on so I followed. She headed in a straight line to the sea, her hand holding her hat on to her head. The wind whipped around us and I squinted to stop the sand getting into my eyes. It was a hostile place. It took fifteen minutes for us to reach the edge of the water and then we stood there and stared out. It was like staring into space; I could see no end to it. The wind played on the water, teasing it into white froth, but there were children playing in there and windsurfers helped along by the wind. To them it was a friendly place. The top of my head was burning and I imagined how the skin would blister, then peel in a few days. I couldn't stand it and put a hand on Nancy's arm, but she shook me off. She was not ready to leave. I felt ashamed that I had shown weakness. I looked behind me and wondered which patch of beach Jonathan had lain on. I wondered whether he had tried windsurfing. When I turned, Nancy was taking off her shoes. She hitched up her skirt with one hand and held out her other for my hand. I took off my socks and shoes, rolled up the bottom of my trousers and stepped into the water with her. We stood there for a few moments and I saw her close her eyes, so I closed mine. 'Goodbye, Jonathan,' I said in my head and imagined her doing the same. Then we returned to the car and drove to Jonathan's hotel.

Our driver knew exactly where to go: a cheap hostel for backpackers in a side street about twenty minutes from the beach. I expected kindness from the staff at the hostel, but we didn't receive much. They said they had barely seen Jonathan during his stay. They didn't know him. He was a stranger who happened to die while he was their guest. I found them evasive, almost embarrassed, as if we might turn round and blame them for our son's death. It wasn't their fault. It wasn't anyone's fault, we kept being told. It was an accident. The sea is treacherous, the wind can suddenly come up, as it did that day. Was there a red flag flying? No one seemed to remember.

Jonathan's rucksack was sitting on a chair in the room he had occupied. It was an inhospitable room: a single bed with a sheet and a blanket; a chipped chest of drawers which still held his clothes. The police had returned the bag he had had on the beach. They had found his room key and located his hotel. And there they had found his passport, and that had led them to us.

Nancy took charge of everything. She took his clothes out of drawers and folded them before laying them out on the bed. She wouldn't let me help. It was her domain. While she sorted through Jonathan's things, I sat in a chair at the window and looked out at what Jonathan would have looked out at. He didn't have a sea view — his room was at the back of this cheap hotel. So while I was staring down at two, possibly Scandinavian, backpackers sitting on white plastic chairs at a white plastic table on a yellow-and-pink crazy-paved courtyard, Nancy must have found Jonathan's camera. Did she put it into his rucksack? I don't know. Or did she hide it in her own bag? I will never know, but I wonder when it was that she decided to have the film developed. Was it then, or later, after we'd returned home? I never saw his camera — I always assumed that it had got lost somewhere, or been stolen by someone in the hotel when they knew Jonathan wouldn't be back for it. It was an expensive camera — the most expensive present we had ever bought him. A Nikon, top of the range, with a super-zoom lens. Our gift to him on his eighteenth birthday. If he had lost it, he wouldn't have wanted to tell us.

When I turned away from the window Nancy was holding Jonathan's penknife, Swiss army, another birthday present from us. Was he thirteen? Fourteen? Anyway, it was an age when we felt he could be trusted with it. She found his aftershave, squirted it into the air and sniffed; a last breath of our son's scent. Why was she going through it all now? Pack it up, please. I wanted

153

to get out of there. She held up a pack of cigarettes. Neither of us knew Jonathan smoked. His girlfriend, Sasha, wouldn't have approved. She wasn't the type. Perhaps he picked up the habit once she had left. I wonder where Sasha is now? Middle-aged, married probably. She was perfectly nice, all the same I wouldn't have wanted Jonathan to end up with her. Actually, that's not true. If she hadn't gone home, if she had stayed in Europe with Jonathan, he would probably still be alive. And I would have done anything to have him still alive, even if it meant sacrificing him to marriage with an earnest, slightly humourless woman.

27

Summer 2013

Robert has found Catherine, although she is Charlotte, not Catherine. He glances at his watch. He has half an hour before he must leave to be in time for his first meeting, but he can't stop reading now. He phones ahead and tells them to put it back an hour.

One night in Tarifa, that was all John had planned. One night in the cheapest hotel and then the ferry to Tangiers early the next morning. He was in pursuit of Orwell, Bowles, Kerouac, not love. But he heard her song and he was lost. He was easy prey to a woman of her experience. A woman who was a little bored. A woman who was looking for a bit of light entertainment to fill in a few days before she returned home to her husband. A woman who had a child, but a child who rather cramped her style. He was a useful disguise though, this child — he allowed her to disguise herself as a mother, a woman who no longer put herself first. A good woman. Such a clever disguise. Here I am, she cried from the rocks. Looking after my child. Abandoned by my workaholic husband. I can perform the part very well. See what I'm doing? My voice is gentle when I speak to my little boy. I smile. A lot. I smile a lot. He is such a bundle of energy; a live wire, my little boy. He is happy. Because I am a good mother. Oh, but how tiring he is. He must have my attention all the time, and it is so, so exhausting. I cannot look away for a moment, his voice always calling me: Mummy, look, Mummy, Mummy, Mummy. Look at me. Look at me. And she does look at him, whenever he demands it, and she smiles and her voice is patient, but it is a performance. Her patient voice carries, she makes sure of that, so that those around her in the café will take note of what a lovely mummy she is. Once in a while she glances round to check that her audience is paying attention. Look at me, she is saying, as loudly as her little boy, but she is cleverer than he. And John heard her voice, and he was lost. He couldn't see past the spell she was casting.

He saw her light cotton dress trailing on the ground beneath her chair; her long, tanned leg, a shimmer of gold, stretching out from the split that ran from the top of her thigh — a deliberate split, to allow her to move freely inside her long robe. It was a robe which declared modesty but whispered at the heat beneath.

The image slaps Robert across the face. He has seen it in one of the photographs — a picture of Catherine with her leg stretched out from her beach dress. Sitting in a café with Nicholas. The author really hates her and Robert detects jealousy too, seeping through the pages. He wonders again if it could have been written by a girlfriend, but didn't Catherine say she thought it was the father? He reads on.

Charlotte bought him a beer as a thank-you for helping distract her little boy into eating his supper. Afterwards he walked them back to their hotel; it was getting dark and he had nothing else to do. The little boy was quiet by then, sleepy, holding his mummy's hand, and she and John talked, and he told her that he was leaving the next day to catch the ferry. She told him she was a bit jealous of his freedom, but her jealousy was light-hearted, not really meant. It was still early, and she persuaded him to wait downstairs in the lobby for her while she put her child to bed. It was his bedtime, but not hers yet, and she wanted to buy John a drink as a thank-you, and she would so enjoy some adult company. And he was flattered, at nineteen . . .

Robert's hands are shaking. He holds one up and looks at the jittering fingers in surprise, as if he is holding up a specimen of something he has never seen before. Whatever he is about to read has happened. There is nothing he can do about it, and yet it holds a power over him as if, by reading it, it will happen all over again simply because he is there to see it this time. He reads

157

on, like a teenager desperate to get to the sexy bits.

. . . He was charmed by her shyness, her coy reluctance to let him see her naked. She had lost confidence in her body since becoming a mother, she said, and feared he might recoil at the curve of her stomach with its scar from where she'd been opened up and her son taken out, and that John would be used to younger, firmer flesh. And Sarah was younger, much younger, but he didn't tell Charlotte this. Or that Sarah had been his only lover. Her nervousness emboldened him, and for a moment their roles were reversed, and she allowed him to feel as if he was the one in control, leading the way.

Her son was asleep, on the other side of the door. She had closed it. They were in the room she had shared with her husband. She closed her eyes as he lifted the flimsy cotton over her head, her arms held up as if she was a little girl being undressed for bed. She was wearing her bikini, still sandy from a day on the beach. He pulled the ties at each side of the bottoms and watched them slip to the floor, then he undid the top, a tie at the neck and one across her back, easily undone. She was naked, but he was still clothed. She didn't help him undress, she didn't touch him, she watched him, and he didn't notice the hunger in her eyes. He was beautiful and he was a stranger, and she knew he was in her power. She persuaded

158

him to postpone his trip to Tangiers for a few days, just until she had to leave . . .

'Good book?' Robert is startled. He feels as if he has been caught looking at porn.

'Another tea?' the waitress asks. Robert nods, yes, then no. He doesn't know what he wants, incapable of a decision.

'I'm fine,' he manages, and reads on.

. . . and what John didn't understand was that what she really loved was the game: the secrecy of sneaking him up to her room, so that the hotel staff knew nothing, so that they still smiled and treated her kindly; the secrecy of seeing each other on the beach but pretending they were strangers. Even her son didn't realize that the young man lying on a towel a few feet away from them knew his mother more intimately than he ever would. And John chronicled his passion; it would be something to treasure when he was back at home in the real world. He didn't realize he would never see those photographs, never be able to look back at that time . . .

28

Summer 2013

Catherine had run after Robert, hoping he would stop. She ran out into the middle of the road and stood there in her dressing gown, watching until the lights of his car disappeared round the corner. She stayed out there for some time, waiting for him to reappear — sure that he would change his mind and drive home again. He didn't.

She stayed up all night, hoping that he would at least phone her, but he didn't do that either. She phoned him, leaving messages, which he ignored. She tried to imagine where he was, but she couldn't. She couldn't imagine his location, yet she could picture him reading the book — imagine which part he was reading and how it would make him feel. That was when the fury swelled up inside her at the violence of this attack. She couldn't go to bed, she couldn't even sit down. She couldn't keep still, her body twitching. She paced up and down, boiling the kettle, making tea, swilling it down, then making more; waiting for him. She wanted to make him understand why she hadn't told him. It wasn't for her, it was for them. For Robert, but mainly for Nick. Her silence had been to protect their son and Jonathan's death had sealed it. There had been no need for anyone else to suffer.

But Robert hadn't come home.

It is light now and she is exhausted. Her limbs are heavy, weighted down like ballast, as if all the tea she has consumed has found its way into them, filling them up and making them heavy. She is a squishy, puffy, soggy thing. When she moves she can hear the liquid moving around inside her. Her head is awash too, buffeted by images she can't control and memories that have been dredged up and won't go away.

She wants to close her eyes and never open them again. Not to die, just to sleep for a very long time. She drags herself upstairs, lies on the bed and shuts her eyes. It is almost a relief that Robert knows — about the death, anyway. He has a right to know that much. She should have told him before. She should have told him everything before, but now she is too tired to think. It is lack of sleep, but it is shock too: the shock of Robert's anger and his hatred towards her. She had not expected that and it frightens her to think of it, so she embraces the shock and allows it to numb her and close her down. It is not unpleasant to feel nothing. She will make the most of it while it lasts.

She is in a deep sleep when her phone rings. She grabs it, her eyes still shut, dragging herself back to the present.

'Hello?' She opens her eyes to check the number. No number, only the word *Call*. And no voice either, at the other end.

'Hello?' she tries again. And waits, and listens.

They listen to each other, neither saying a word: he doesn't need to; she knows who he is. He is waiting for her. He doesn't say it, but she can feel it.

29

. . . It was the sort of day where, if you weren't careful, you could get very badly burned. The sun was strong, but a thin layer of cloud masked its ferocity, and the cooling wind lulled the ignorant into exposing their skin without protection. Charlotte was not ignorant. She had covered her own body in protective oil and was now rubbing cream into her little boy. He made quite a song and dance of it, they both did: Charlotte demonstrating what a conscientious mother she was, and her son, Noah, resisting his mother's hands and complaining that the cream was stinging his eyes.

His shrieks were particularly grating that day, because Charlotte had a hangover. She knew she was rubbing harder than she needed to, irritated by her son's wilfulness, and wanting to force him to submit to her own. He had sand on his body so it was as if she was stripping him down with sandpaper, and she was careless too with his face, cream catching on the eyelashes of one eye. She dabbed at it with a towel, but he was crying now and she felt like crying too. She just wanted him to go away. She wished she could enjoy one day, this last day, in the sunlight, with her lover.

John was still asleep in his hotel room, his

cheap hotel. It had been five in the morning when he'd returned there after being with Charlotte in her five-star luxury. They had made love all night, her son asleep in the next-door room. The little boy hadn't heard his mother's sighs as her young lover pleasured her; he hadn't heard the clink of their glasses as they drank together, and then made love over and over.

So while Charlotte wrestled with sun cream on the beach, John slept in. He slept well, like an adolescent. At nineteen, he hadn't quite stopped growing, still exhausted by the demands of his own body, and by those that had been made on it the night before. Charlotte couldn't get enough of him, she'd worked him hard. She knew her time was running out and though she had persuaded him not go to Tangiers, she would soon be flying home to her husband. She made the most of him that night, and she anticipated more the following, their last together.

She tried to play her part of Mother, but her performance that morning was lacklustre. She lay on her stomach trying to sleep while Noah dug with his spade. He chiselled away at the beach, while the wind, along with his excavations, sent gritty sand into Charlotte's face. Enough, she thought, and finally said:

'Ice cream?'

Noah stopped digging. 'Yep, yep,' he yapped.

Charlotte slipped her cotton dress over her bikini, put a T-shirt on Noah and, hand in hand, they left the beach.

As they climbed the steps that led to the shops, John walked towards them. They passed

164

each other, these lovers, and no one would have known they had ever met. His stomach slid with excitement, and hers with desire at the sight of his sleepy eyes and bedded hair. They almost touched, they were so close. They could smell each other and she breathed him in and smiled, but not at John. She was cleverer than that. She directed the smile meant for John at Noah. John knew it was for him though and Noah was taken in, pleased to see that Mummy was happy, and he smiled back, the little innocent. He was so grateful for that gift which wasn't even intended for him.

John recognized Charlotte's towel and placed his own a few feet away, as usual, making sure there were other bodies between them. Far enough away so Noah wouldn't register him, but close enough so he and Charlotte could look at each other. Since that first day in the café, they had been careful about Noah. She didn't want him to recognize John, she didn't want Noah to get friendly with him, 'In case he takes to you,' she'd said, and she couldn't permit that. She couldn't have Noah mentioning anything to his father about the nice man they met on holiday, Mummy's new friend.

John, eyes closed, head down, heard them arriving back on the beach before he saw them. Noah was chatting away at the top of his voice, thrilled about something, so John sneaked a look, intrigued. Noah was pulling an inflatable dinghy behind him, bouncing it along the sand by a rope. He'd been asking his mother for days for a blow-up toy, nagging, and this, their last day on the beach, was the day she chose to indulge him. Any inflatable toy would have done, but she chose the yellow-and-red dinghy, using her charm to persuade the man in the shop to empty his lungs and blow it up. She didn't have the puff, she'd smiled. She'd used up so much of her 'puff' the night before.

The dinghy was a gift for Charlotte as much as Noah. It would distract her son, she hoped, keep him entertained so she could relax with her book, with her thoughts. Noah wasn't very good at amusing himself, but this red-and-yellow plastic boat seemed to do the trick. For the first time in the holiday he seemed happy in his own company, lost in his own little world. He sat in it on the sand, chatting to himself, and his mother stretched out on her front and turned her head to face her lover. John mirrored her, turning his head to her, their eyes locking. There were people between them, but they didn't notice, so absorbed were they in studying each other. She devoured him and he her. Her red bikini, barely covering the parts of her body he had come to know so well. He could visualize every part without even trying. It was as if she lay there naked. Her breasts, her buttocks, her pubic bone. He imagined her smell too, from where he lay, and his erection pressed into the sand.

He was desperate to touch her, desperate to slide under her and into her. And she knew that, she could see it on his face, in his eyes, and she turned on her side, her breasts moving inside her bikini, pushing against her arm as she leaned on it, and she parted her lips and smiled. Then she

166

reached for her book and pretended to read, when really she was posing for him, her lover. Teasing him.

Her arm must have ached after a while, and she sat up. She was restless, bored. She glanced at her son, but he was happy, he didn't need her to entertain him for he was captain of his own ship. She looked up and caught the eye of the mother of the family next to her. Her children were older, adolescents. Charlotte had noticed her smiling at Noah and now Charlotte smiled at her.

'Do you speak English?' she asked.

The woman shrugged and said, 'A little.'

Charlotte mimed a charade of the woman watching Noah while she went to the loo. The mother of the two adolescents was all too pleased to keep an eye on the sweet little English boy. Charlotte was so grateful, she gave the woman her best smile and leaned over to Noah and told him she would only be gone for a moment. She worried he might need to go to the loo too, or make a fuss about her going, but he didn't. He was as good as gold. He didn't even watch as she slipped on her sandals, thin-strapped silver, flat, a thong between her elegant toes, and walked to the toilets. John was watching though. He watched her as she walked towards the toilets at the back of the beach, her hips swaying. He wanted to follow, but he had to wait, make himself decent, so he focused on a leathery-skinned woman, topless, buttocks withering from her thong, until his erection subsided.

Charlotte had stopped off at the showers,

167

raising her face into the water and slicking back her hair, as if she was entirely alone and not on a public beach. She was well aware of John watching her. She turned off the shower and walked into the toilets. John followed. No one else was there and he knew where to find Charlotte: in the changing cubicle at the end of the line of toilets. He tapped on the door and she opened up. Straight away he slipped his hand into her bikini bottoms. He knew that she preferred to keep them on, she'd told him she liked to feel their tautness around her. His fingers searched and found the soft, wet, smoothness she had shown him. He lifted her on to the slatted wooden bench and pushed her bikini bottoms to one side, opening her up gently with his fingers, pushing his tongue up and down her, around her, where she had shown him, just the way he knew she liked it. She had taught him so much. She pushed her arms against the sides of the cubicle, stopping herself from falling, and she was so wet that he couldn't tell what was her and what was his own saliva. The poor boy was drunk with love. Out of his mind with it. Even when they heard someone come in, he couldn't stop, and she wouldn't have stopped him anyway. They heard a bolt slam, they heard a gush of someone else's pee and she pulled down his trunks and pushed herself on to him, wrapping her legs around him and kissing his mouth, taking what had been hers from his mouth into her own and swallowing it back into herself. And he clung to her, and held her, stronger than her and yet not. And when it was over she smiled and took his face in her hands as if he was a little boy. She kissed him on his lips, on his neck and finally on his forehead. A punctuation mark so that he would know that that was all for now.

They waited for the intruder to leave and then Charlotte opened the door and looked out. She went first, he followed a few moments later. She showered again but John kept walking, passing his towel and running straight into the sea, plunging down into a wave.

Little Noah was still in his boat, chatting away to himself. Charlotte had been longer than she thought. The mother had packed up their things, she and her family needed to go. She waved goodbye to Noah and Charlotte thanked her, stroking her son's head as she did so. She watched, on guard again, as he pulled his dinghy closer to the sea. He wasn't in the water, he was on the sand. He was happy. She hugged her knees and looked at him, smiling at his content-ment. She was exhausted and lay down. If she turned her head a little, she could still see Noah. John returned to his towel, rubbing himself down, looking at Charlotte, but she was facing the other way, so he lay on his back and closed his eyes too. He dozed, thinking about the night ahead, a smile on his face as he imagined what they would do to each other.

When he woke, the wind had got up and he put on his T-shirt. Charlotte was asleep. It was then that John noticed Noah. He was still in the boat, but floating now in the shallows, happy being bounced around by the sea. In, out, in, out. Charlotte woke and turned to see what John

169

was looking at. Perhaps she was surprised that something, other than her, had caught his attention. In, out, in, out went the dinghy, and each time the out was a little further and the in a little less. The sea had grown rough and there was a strong undercurrent dragging on the dinghy, pulling it out, a space of choppy water growing between Noah and the shore, where other people swam and played. None of them noticed the little English boy drifting out to sea.

John stood up and looked over to Charlotte. She too was on her feet, but she didn't move. Her feet stayed planted on her towel. She turned to John, fear on her face, then back to Noah. Still she didn't move. She called out to Noah, and then she called out to John. 'Help,' she cried. 'Help me.' And John would do anything for her. He ran immediately to the water's edge, and only then did she move. John led the way and she followed. She called to Noah again and he looked up and waved at her, not a bit frightened. And still no one did anything, and there were no lifeguards on the beach.

John could see that Noah's boat was heading out in the wrong direction. Heading out to sea. Soon he would be a speck in the distance. He ran, kicking sand into sunbathers and dived into the sea. He swam out towards Noah. Strong, a strong young man, a strong swimmer. The current pulled at him, but he went with it, letting the sea use its energy to pull him towards the little boy, so he could conserve his for the swim back. It was a strategy. He knew what he was doing, and he focused on his strokes: clean,

170

powerful. And he reached Noah and he saw how frightened the boy was, calling out to his mother, but she wouldn't have been able to hear him. He must have wondered why she didn't come and get him. Why she hadn't swum out for him. He was trying to stand, but he kept falling — the waves licking the sides of the dinghy and spitting into it. The plastic was too slippery and the boat rocked too much. He was in a blind panic. John tried to calm him down. He told him to sit still and hold on tight to the handles on the boat. But the little boy was frozen, staring towards the beach, hoping that his mother would come and get him. John grabbed the rope and made a fist around it, then began the swim back to shore.

He could see a line of people watching and, at the heart of them, Charlotte in her red bikini. He used every muscle in his body, pushed himself harder than he ever had before. Red, glossy, sinews pulling, stretching, blood pumping. The sea had become his enemy, no longer carrying him but pushing him back instead. And the wind had joined forces with it, whipping the waves, bouncing the boat as if trying to tip Noah out. John called to him to hold tight. When he looked back, Noah was rigid, gripping the handles, still staring beyond John, searching for his mother. Perhaps he thought the boat was making its own way to shore.

John's eyes stung from the salt and his body had gone numb. He had become an automaton, arms and legs propelling him forward. There was no strategy any more. He swam to the rhythm of the blood thumping in his ears. And then two men, two other brave men, broke away from the group and ran, leaping into the sea and swimming towards the young man and boy. One was ahead of the other, a stronger swimmer. He was fast, the sea helping him, sending him towards John and Noah, and he reached them and took the rope from John, pulling the precious cargo towards the beach. No time for niceties, the man turned straight round and swam for shore. John reached out to hold on to the back of the dinghy.

As the man approached the beach, others rushed in to help him, grabbing the boat, taking care of the child. John saw them and he saw that Noah was safe. He saw them on the shore. He was still in the sea — a long way out. He'd lost his grip, but no one had noticed him. He watched as the second rescuer turned back, joining the throng and pulling the little boy to safety. John's hands were white with cold and streaked with red where he had clung on to the rope. He couldn't feel his hand. All he could feel were his lungs. They had grown, become out-sized, no longer room for them in his ribcage. He gasped for breath, but instead he took in a mouthful of water. He had wasted precious time, looking at his hand, thinking about his lungs, when he should have been swimming, and now the sea had pushed him further away and he would have to swim every stroke again in order to get to the point where he had released Noah.

He tried, he really tried. He hoped that some-one would come for him. That someone would remember he was out there. And he wanted his

172

mother. *He wanted his mother to come and carry him out of the water. Like Noah, he yearned for the safety of his mother's arms. He tried to wave to them on the shore, but his arms had lost their power. He couldn't wave. He couldn't swim any more. He pushed down at the sea with his arms, as if he could make it sink and become shallower. He was frightened. They say drowning is one of the better ways to die, but John was scared because he knew no one would come for him. He had spent the last of his strength on her child.*

At last he saw a boat. And he thought for a moment that everything would be fine. But when they reached him he had already gone under two or three times. They threw a rope for him but he couldn't grab it, because he was dead. He was already dead when they reached him. They pulled him in and laid him out in the boat. Someone tried the kiss of life, put their mouth over his. Someone pumped his chest. They drove the boat back to the beach and carried the young man's body, three of them, on to the beach and they kissed him again. Again they tried to revive him. They pumped at his chest, but he had gone.

And at the other end of the beach a small crowd gathered around the little boy and his mother. They were protecting Noah from seeing that the man who had saved him was lying dead, further down the beach. And Charlotte was on her knees, wrapping a towel around her son, shielding him from the sight of her dead lover.

30

Summer 2013

A duck-egg blue Fiat 500 zips across the square. Robert watches it through the window. Catherine's favourite colour. He had thought about buying one for her birthday. He is in the meeting he had turned up late for, even though he had pushed it back an hour. He'd had to shower, shave, change his suit. He always keeps a spare in the office, but it was the suit he had in case he had to go to a function — it was too smart for a day in the office and he'd seen the surprise on their faces, wondering what he was up to later. He is glad to be with them, to have people around him, talking at him. He doesn't have to perform, or speak yet, simply observe, and he can just about manage that. He is grateful for their voices. It is their confidence in him that stops him from falling. Each time he begins to wilt, another word punches through the air and pushes him upright again.

It was only a book. It is only a book. He knows it's just a version of events written by someone who clearly hates her, but can he blame them? And it is a version with enough truth in it for Catherine to have wished for its disappearance. At the very least, she fucked a stranger who then died saving their son's life. It is not her, and yet

174

it is. There is enough of his wife in there for him to recognize. And it has shown him things he had failed to see before. She is a woman who has always got her own way, always done as she pleased.

He remembers the first time he saw her. She'd asked him to meet her for a drink, said she wanted to talk to him off the record. She was young, it was her first job as a journalist. He shouldn't really have gone, he could have lost his job, but she was so persuasive on the phone — she'd made him feel it was the right thing to do. He remembers she was late — even though he was the one doing her a favour — yet she managed to turn it into something charming. He remembers a young, striking blonde walking into the pub, and how he'd hoped it was her. She'd looked round, caught him watching her, and she'd smiled, quite shy. He'd smiled in return and got to his feet. She paid for the drinks, insisted on it, and he gave her everything she asked for, answered all her questions. Off the record, of course, but she had used what he told her. She managed to keep him out of it, but still she didn't hold anything back. She was a good journalist. All the same, he could have lost his job. Even at that first meeting he was ready to do anything for her. She knew what she wanted and how to get it. Fuck the consequences.

The book shows him a mother who put herself before her child. It's true, she has never been a natural mother. Her lover had died and work became her escape. Did she blame Nick for her lover's death? Is that why she couldn't bear to stay at home and look after him? No wonder it has always been so difficult between her and Nick. And Robert has covered up for her, smoothed things over, always been there to support her, tried hard not to make her feel guilty, never criticized her, never judged her. Until now. An image from one of the photographs comes back to him. He tries to push it away and focus on the present, but he sees the past. Catherine showering on the beach, her neck arched, her eyes closed as the water runs down her face and body, a smile on her lips. She is enjoying being looked at. His hand is shaking again and he clenches his fist, pushing it under the table. All the tension he's buried for years, thoughts he's never allowed himself to think before, rise up.

He loved her though. If she'd told him about her affair at the time, he could have forgiven her. But not now. He bites the inside of his cheek to stop himself crying. He would have done anything for her. He'd wanted to have more children, but even that he'd given up without a fight. She never actually refused, she just managed to keep coming up with excuses until it was too late. He'd wanted Nick to have a brother or sister; he thought it would take the pressure off him.

A piece of paper lands on the table in front of him. Information he should be reading; details he should be taking in. He picks it up and hides behind it. He has a vague memory of Nick wanting the dinghy, or something inflatable, and they had agreed it was not a good idea.

Nevertheless she had bought it for him, when Robert had gone home, and she hadn't watched him, she hadn't looked after him, and someone else's son died to save Nicholas. But whose? Who wrote this book? The girlfriend? A parent? The old man who dropped off the photos? That poor old man. A bastard thing to do, but can he really blame him? Should Robert thank him for what his son did? He should be grateful, though he can't manage gratitude yet. If *John*, or whatever the fuck his name was, hadn't been there, *Charlotte* wouldn't have been so fucking distracted and perhaps she would have stopped their son going into the sea on his own. And if Robert had been there, none of it would have happened.

There's a throbbing mass in Robert's head. Another in his stomach. Dark lumps of something he has not felt for years. Jealousy. Not green, but black and dense. He is jealous of this dead youth who had an affair with his wife and saved his child. Who, a long, long time ago, in a faraway land, cut off Robert's balls without him even realizing it. He wonders how many times Catherine has thought of this boy when she has been with him? How many times has she compared the sex? Does she fake it with him? Sometimes? Always? And Nicholas. Nicholas, who can't even remember the young man who saved his life — which to Robert makes *John* seem even more heroic. Unsung. A martyr. He flicks through the pages in his head. Robert barely gets a mention. He is a minor character who doesn't even merit a name. Her husband.

He sinks into himself, drooping like a stakeless plant. The words have stopped. The room is quiet. He looks up. All eyes are on him, but he cannot read them. Are they waiting for a response? Are they watching him with curiosity? What do they see?

'A lot to think about,' he says, and is reassured by the sound of his voice, deep and rich. He stands up, his authority here at least still intact. The meeting is over and everyone trickles from the room.

He will get in touch with the family — find out who they are and talk to them. The least Robert can do is let them know that he is grateful for their son's bravery and to try and make up for his wife's failings as a human being. First though, he must look after Nicholas, bring him under the protection of his wing. He picks up his phone.

'Nick? Really enjoyed seeing you the other night . . . Listen, can we do it again? Are you free tonight? There's something I want to talk to you about.'

31

Summer 2013

When Jonathan died, Nancy shattered. Her mind shrank into a small, dark thing and all she could think about was our son's absence. One step at a time, one day at a time, I kept telling her. But I couldn't reach her. I was no use to her. I remember one day, it was about two months after his death. I'd been waiting for her downstairs. I had persuaded her to come for a walk. It was an achievement even to get her to agree to that. It was mid-afternoon and she was still in her dressing gown. She went upstairs to put on some clothes and I sat in the living room, waiting for her. She was slow — everything she did then was slow. I didn't want to hurry her because I was afraid that if I went upstairs to chivvy her, she would change her mind. And anyway I could hear her moving around. I heard a drawer being opened, the wardrobe door closing. She was getting dressed; she was heading in the right direction. Then after a while I didn't hear anything, so I went up.

I expected to find her lying on the bed, but she was in the bathroom. She was fully clothed and had climbed in the bath, which, it turned out, she had run hours earlier. She was lying in freezing cold water, dressed for a walk out with me. Her head was under the water, her eyes and mouth open. I dragged her out. She was heavy, sodden. She told me she wasn't trying to kill herself. She just wanted to know what it had felt like for Jonathan. She wanted to know whether drowning had hurt. She wanted to find out for herself whether it was as painless as everyone said — whether you passed out before dying. She was angry with me for denying her this almost-shared experience, but she acknowledged the flaw in her experiment: that the fear and loneliness of being swallowed by a vast ocean cannot be replicated by submersion in an avocado-coloured plastic tub in the safety of your own home.

Acute empathy, you could say, had become Nancy's extreme sport of choice. She was the most empathic of people, and yet even she knew she was seeking the impossible. But still she tried. If anyone was capable of understanding how someone else felt, it was Nancy. There weren't as many layers between her and the world as there were with the rest of us. She had that rare ability of being able to stand in someone else's shoes and get inside their skin. There had been many a time, before Jonathan died, when she had tried to help me do the same. If I was angry or upset about something, she would coax me with: 'Try to see it from their point of view,' or 'Try to imagine what they might be feeling.' And I did try, but I never quite succeeded. Nancy felt too much though, that was the problem.

She stopped working because she couldn't face being with children any more, so I worked for both of us, to keep life ticking over. A kind of life anyway. We should have sold our house and moved out of London. I should have been tougher, made the decision to do it, but I knew I couldn't make Nancy do anything she didn't want to.

Even trying to persuade her to sort through Jonathan's things was beyond my powers.

One day, I came home from work and found her up in his bedroom, laying out his clothes on the bed. It reminded me of that day in the hotel room in Spain.

'I'm not getting rid of them,' she said sharply when she turned and saw me. I didn't say anything. 'I just want a sort-through.'

So I watched her folding and stroking his clothes and separating them into piles, which gave me hope that perhaps she was making a start on clearing out his things.

'I'll make some tea,' I said. 'Then I'll give you a hand.'

She glanced at me, nodded, and carried on going through his drawers. When I came back I saw that she had started to fill a small suitcase. I put down the tea and sat on the bed, looking round. The room still had remnants of Jonathan's boyhood: a stuffed dog, balding and scrawny, sitting on top of his bookshelf; an ornate wooden puzzle box that we'd given him one Christmas and where he kept his secret things. I remember feeling a swell of sadness mingled with happiness because I thought I was witnessing the beginning of Nancy's recovery. Until that point she had refused to touch anything in his room, wanting it left exactly as it was.

'I'm putting rubbish in here . . . ' She shook an empty black bag at me. I sipped my tea, put it down on his bedside table and opened the drawer. I smiled at the batteries and loose change; it was almost identical to my own bedside drawer, except for the packet of unopened condoms. I emptied it all into the black bag, shaking it so the condoms disappeared to the bottom. I didn't want Nancy to see them — there was something horribly poignant about the fact they were unused.

Nancy had taken over the territory of Jonathan's wardrobe and chest of drawers so I tackled the pine chest at the end of his bed. I opened the lid and saw it was a place he put things he couldn't find a place for. There were a few old toys, uneaten sweets, chocolate money left over from his Christmas stocking, some bits and pieces from camping trips, tin plates and mugs, a head-torch . . . there was even a pair of dirty old trainers. As I got nearer to the bottom I found his comics. We'd bought him a subscription to the *Beano* when he was a boy and I thought it might be nice to keep a few. I picked them up, and then saw what was hidden underneath: a collection of pornography — magazines and video tapes. Their titles and covers appalled me and I glanced over at Nancy, but she was absorbed looking through one of Jonathan's scrapbooks. I shuffled round to the other side of the bed and opened one of the magazines.

'Jesus!' The word escaped before I could stop it.

'What? What is it?' she said.

'Nothing, nothing,' I replied. 'A bit of stomach cramp, that's all.' I sat for a moment, then got up and brought the black bag over to the bed and dumped the lot into it. Nancy looked over with suspicion.

'It's got to go, darling — there are mouldy bits of old food in here. Nothing precious, I promise.' I hid the weight of the bag as I took it from the room and carried it straight out to the dustbin. Thank God it was me and not Nancy who found them. When I returned to the bedroom, Jonathan's scrapbook was still open on her lap.

'Look at these,' she said, and I went and sat down next to her on the floor. 'I didn't know they were here. They're very good.' She smiled at me with tears in her eyes. She was looking at some photographs which were loose in the back of the scrapbook. At first I wasn't sure what I was looking at.

'They were taken on a zoom,' she explained. 'Look . . . ' She held one up and I saw it was a close-up of an eye. Another showed the curve of a cheek, so close you could see the veins under skin.

'Oh yes,' I said.

'He was experimenting with his new camera,' Nancy explained. 'I bet they were the first photos he took with it.'

'Who is it?' I said. She looked through them and smiled.

'It's me,' she said, and held out the pictures, one after the other, moving from the abstract close-ups to the final revelation of her sitting in a deckchair at the end of our garden. He'd taken the pictures without Nancy even knowing he was there, and it pleased her to know he had focused so much attention on her.

There were others too: street scenes around North London; reportage of urban life. Nancy was right, they were good. He seemed to have a talent for it. Like a true photo-journalist, Jonathan had managed to keep himself out of the picture and capture something real and natural. I am sure Nancy had not had the film developed from his camera by then, but I wonder whether it was these photographs tucked into the back of his scrapbook which made her think about it. She must have assumed she'd find some beautiful images that she could have framed and shown off.

I was wrong to assume that sorting through Jonathan's things was a sign of her recovery. If anything, she got worse after that. She refused to go out. We didn't see anyone and after a year or so lost touch with all our friends. They gave up. I suppose they thought we had each other. It was about five years after Jonathan's death when she decided that she couldn't face seeing me either. For a while at least, she said. She needed time by herself, and I respected that, but I worried about her choice of Jonathan's flat as her retreat.

We'd been left some money by an aunt and we spent it on that flat in Fulham. We bought it for Jonathan the year before he went travelling. We thought it was a good idea for him to have his first taste of independence closer to home, and he moved in for a short while before he left

England. Nancy kitted it out with everything he might need: new pans, bed linen. And we donated things of our own too — things we no longer needed, like Nancy's desk. She used to go over there and give him cooking lessons: teaching him the skills he'd need to be self-sufficient. It was ready for when he came home and we hoped it would give him the space to decide what he wanted to do. We hoped he might go to university.

After he died, she still went over now and again to clean it. She didn't tell anyone in the building what had happened. Perhaps she thought that if they didn't know then she could pretend, at least in that place, that he was still alive. She lived amongst Jonathan's things, dressing the place as if it was a shrine, fresh flowers in every room. And at first she let me visit her there, then one day she asked me not to come any more. She said it didn't help her, that I was holding back her recovery. I still telephoned once a week, but after a while even that stopped. She said she would call *me* when she was ready to come home. I only agreed to her demand because she promised she wouldn't do anything to harm herself, and something in her voice made me believe her. I thought I heard a shift in it, as if she was at last beginning to find some peace. In the end it was someone from the Tenants' Association who called me, not Nancy. It's painful for me to know how useless I was to her during that time.

When I got that call I was terrified she'd broken her promise. They said that there had been complaints about the state of the common parts and a smell was coming from the flat. I cursed myself for having been so weak — for not having gone in before and forced her home. I was convinced that when I let myself in with the key I'd resisted using so often, I would find her dead. She was lying on the sofa, her eyes closed, but she was breathing. There was an unpleasant smell. The toilet had been neglected but the main stench came from a full bin liner by the front door. She had intended to take it down, but simply hadn't had the strength and so it had sat for weeks, leaking on to the floor, its rotting contents almost capable of making their own way down the stairs. She had cancer, she told me. She was matter-of-fact about it, though by then she was in pain, had been in pain for some time, endured it, relished it even. It is what she had been waiting for. The cancer filled the space which Jonathan had left. I hated that flat. When I went back and found her manuscript, it was the first time I had been there since taking her home all those years ago.

It was our separation she was referring to, I am sure, when she told Catherine Ravenscroft that she had *lost her husband*. For a while, we were lost to each other. But I had always believed that it was me who had lost her, not she who had lost me. I thought I was alone in feeling alone, so it was a comfort when I read in her notebook that she had felt as I had. She missed me as much as I had missed her.

I took her home and I cared for her and she rallied a little. She survived another two years at

186

home with me. I was still working at the private school, and I admit that I took out my pain on those children. The Macmillan nurses were wonderful. They came in while I was at work to make sure she was OK. She never complained. As I say, she embraced her suffering. It was the kind of suffering she had been searching for, something concrete to dig her nails into.

But now she is alive again — my constant companion. I hear her voice and I speak to her regularly. I told her about the phone call and the sound of fear in the whore's voice. There are no secrets between us any more. And Nancy is becoming impatient to get on with it, we both are. We want to see her fear, not just listen to it.

32

Summer 2013

Catherine sits at work, her eyes fixed on her computer screen, seeing nothing. Her head is in revolt, unable to hold a coherent thought: each one, old and new, carries its own pain. The newest, freshest memories hurt the most. Robert has moved out. She thinks he has checked into a hotel, but she is not sure. He won't speak to her. The last thing he told her was that he couldn't bear the sight of her. The words had left her gasping. What had she expected? Not that. She knew she had concealed parts of herself from Robert, but she had not realized, until now, how much of him she didn't know. When she had tried to imagine his response to the book, she had failed to conjure up this bitterness. His anger has shocked her; he has allowed it to fill every space, making him deaf to anything she might say. She sleeps in the spare room, hiding from the emptiness of their bed.

She clicks on her screen, pretending to work, but the shock she'd felt when he had confronted her with the photographs slices through her again. He wants her to be punished. He thinks she deserves it. She had tried not to look at the pictures — tried to flick them away — blinking them into fragments, but they have broken through into her head and it is a one-way street. Those images will never leave now. The photographs were used as the source material for the book, crude and base, wriggling themselves into a false projection of the real story. Unfortunately it is a story which Robert has chosen to believe. And her years of secrecy have helped him reach his verdict of guilty; her misguided belief that she had a right to silence has condemned her.

'You know the headmaster who left Rathbone College after Brigstocke was 'retired'? Well, I've found out they were friends at Cambridge. I've got a number for him — shall I give him a call?'

'Back off, Kim. There's no story. Leave it,' she snaps before she can stop herself. Fuck. She's losing control here too. She doesn't want to alienate Kim, so she reaches out, lays a hand on her arm: 'Sorry, but there's nothing there. Forget it. Forget Stephen Brigstocke.'

Kim shakes off her hand and limps away. Catherine shouldn't have spoken to her like that. She must hold it together. Work is her only refuge. She fingers the piece of paper Kim gave her a few days ago, with Stephen Brigstocke's telephone number and address, and puts it in her pocket.

'Tea?' she calls across. Kim ignores her, but Simon looks up and gives Catherine a smile.

He follows her into the kitchen, cup held out, whitened teeth gleaming.

'Everything all right, Cath?' A whine of concern in his voice. Oh fuck off. Her hate for this man is unreasonable, she knows.

189

'Yes, fine thanks.'

'Moving house is one of those things, isn't it — right up there with divorce — enough to make anyone stressed.' She keeps her back to him, hiding her fury. He must have witnessed her snap at Kim. She puts two bags in the pot, fills it with water, pours his tea without giving it time to brew, ignoring his gesture to wait, and enjoying the insipid grey she slops into his mug. Her phone beeps as she hands him the tea.

A text from Robert? She tries to hide her shaking hands: *Your recent accident could make you eligible* . . . It's an advertisement. Shit.

'You all right?'

She nods yes, but feels trapped by Simon's presence, unable to think. She stalks out, taking her phone to the ladies'. She needs privacy, some fucking privacy, to be able to think. Robert is not going to call her. She had hoped that once the first shock had settled he would find it in himself to listen to her; that she could tell him everything in her own words. Instead he has amputated her as if she were a gangrenous limb. She tries to suppress her own anger, but it is becoming harder. Doesn't she deserve a hearing? He is making her feel like a stalker, her endless texts and voicemails ignored. She calls his secretary.

'Hi, Katy. I was wondering if Robert's in at the moment. I don't need to talk to him, I just wanted to drop something by . . . ' She sounds like a woman who suspects her husband of having an affair. If he is in his office she will go there and confront him; he won't be able to run

190

away; he won't want a scene; he will have to listen.

'No, he left early,' she is told. 'He said he was going to work from home this afternoon.'

'Of course. Stupid me. I forgot.' Every day a new lie.

★ ★ ★

When she walks through the front door she trips over a holdall and her heart races. He's come home. Thank God, he's moved back in. But it is Nicholas's bag, not Robert's. It is Nicholas who is moving in. There's already a heap of dirty washing outside the kitchen. Robert is at the flat though, sitting at the kitchen table with Nick. A beer each. A smile on Robert's face, the sports pages open in front of Nicholas. Neither looks up as she walks in. There is a brief moment, a flash, when she thinks: Nicholas in the spare room, her back in bed with Robert? But when Robert looks at her she knows this is fantasy and his words confirm it.

'Nick's come to keep me company while you're away.'

What the . . . ? Nicholas turns to her and she is struck by how pale and tired he is. Does he know? But then he smiles and returns to the newspaper. She opens her mouth to speak but Robert beats her to it. Robert is in charge.

'Sounds like a big story, so I guess you'll be gone for a few weeks. I packed you a bag — I thought you'd be in a hurry to get off.'

Every sentence feels like a slap across her face.

191

He has told Nick she is going away for work. She approaches him, takes his hand: 'Robert . . . ' She wants him to go upstairs with her, to listen to her, but he pulls his hand away and picks up the phone. She hears him call a cab.

'What's the story, Mum?' Nicholas asks.

Robert answers for her. 'Oh, your mother won't even tell me.'

He sounds so glib and Nicholas isn't that interested anyway and returns to the football gossip.

'The cab's on its way. You'd better go and check I've packed what you want.' She stays where she is for a moment, wanting to scream at him how dare he, but she doesn't, in front of Nicholas.

She goes upstairs and sits on the bed. He has packed a small case, enough for a week. She looks at the folded clothes, the knickers stuffed down the side, the wash-bag zipped up and placed on top. She feels around in the case, hoping that maybe he will have slipped in a note to say he needs time to think. A little space and then they can talk. There is no note. He doesn't need to explain. She does.

'Your cab's here,' he yells up, and she closes the case and carries it downstairs. She wants Robert to look at her, to meet her eye, but he won't. He is all brisk and bright. There's supper to get ready. They can manage very well without her, thank you, she hears in her head. Nicholas gets up and shambles towards her, kicking a sock that has strayed from the pile of dirty clothes.

'See you, Mum.' She gives him a hug. No

words. She looks over his shoulder at Robert; still he refuses to look at her. Coward, she thinks, and feels Nicholas slither from her embrace. The cab is waiting.

She closes the front door and walks to the car with its engine running. The driver watches her put her case on the back seat and get in next to it.

'Where to?' he asks. So Robert hasn't decided her destination. Where to? She gives the driver an address.

33

Summer 2013

Nicholas takes his holdall up to the spare room, drops it with a bang on to the floor and launches himself backwards on to the bed: freefall, legs out, shoes on, head hitting the pillow. He closes his eyes and smells his mum. He opens his eyes. Yes, he really can smell her. He sniffs the pillow. It's definitely her. She's been sleeping in the spare room. What the fuck's going on? His dad didn't say goodbye when she left. He didn't even go to the door. That's not like him — he's a devotee. That's why Nicholas made the effort — well, someone had to. He'd felt sorry for her. He can't remember ever feeling sorry for his mum.

Seeing her leave that way reminds him of when he was little and she used to go away for work. It never bothered him. When she got home she'd fuss around him as if she'd missed him so much. He used to ignore her — it never felt real — she was putting it on. He could keep it up for days, not talking to her. She'd come home with presents — Sandy the dog was one of them. She probably bought it at the airport anyway, but he loved it — used to sleep with it every night. When she was home she was always the one who put him to bed and read to him. He'd lie there with his eyes shut, pretending to be asleep, still she'd carry on and he'd listen to the sound of her voice until eventually he did fall asleep. He'd hurt her when he told her he didn't want to keep Sandy. For fuck's sake, why would he?

If it was the other way round, she'd never have invited him to stay in their nice, new home. Dad's soft though. Mind you, it'll drive Nicholas mad if he keeps up the cheery banter: constant fucking chat about what they're going to eat. Even watching him pick away at the cellophane on their meal for two made Nicholas's skin itch; he couldn't wait to get upstairs. Still, it's good to have a few home comforts. Will he be able to stand being round his dad if he's like this the whole time? Yes, because he needs the cash. He'll sublet his room; no need for Dad to know — there's money to be made. Poor old Mum, the last thing she wants is him messing up their spanking-new spare room.

He hangs over the side of the bed and drags his bag towards him, taking out his wash-bag. He's brought his toothbrush but no soap, no shampoo. No need. He's 'home'. Mum would have a fit if she knew he'd brought drugs into their home. She'd think he was *losing control; not on top of things;* worried he was going to *slip off the edge* again. Of course he won't. Steady job. Suit. What more do they want? It's like old times — his parents knowing fuck all about what's going on. Something's going on with them though, but he can't be arsed to find out what. They can keep their secrets, he has his. Still, generous of the old man to offer to help out with a holiday. With his girlfriend. He cringes at the memory of his lie. He doesn't have a girlfriend, but it's what his dad wanted to hear.

From where he's lying he can see the tops of the trees in the garden. They fill the frame of the window. Like their old house, only smaller. It's even in the same neighbourhood, a spit from where he grew up. His dad was pleased when he said he had a girlfriend, but Nicholas doesn't want the hassle of a girlfriend — too much fucking bother. He'd like the money though, so he'll have to spin it out a bit longer — or maybe he'll say he's decided to go away with friends instead. Dad'll still cough up — he'll find it hard to back down after saying he'd help out. He laughs when he thinks what his dad would make of his friends.

Nicholas hates that word. *Friends*. What does it mean? Muckers? Mates? Companions? They're people he hangs out with, that's all. They don't bother getting to know each other. It's like being part of a shoal of fish, slipping in, dropping out, different faces all the time but all swimming in the same direction, keeping formation, floating along. The money for a holiday could keep him afloat for a whole week: close his eyes and disappear; a nice break and then back to work. He rolls a joint and sticks it in his mouth, unlit. Don't want the old man to worry. Work/life balance — that's what it's called, isn't it? And Nicholas is managing that very well: just a little something now and again to soften the edges, but never too much.

'Supper's ready,' his dad calls up. Nick rolls

his eyes and doesn't answer. Not answering. It used to drive them mad. *Supper's ready.* No answer. Eventually one of them would have to come up and get him. Had he heard? They'd been shouting for ages. It's getting cold. He rolls on to his side and buries his face in the pillow, taking in one more draught of his mother. They've never been close, yet the smell of her nearly brings tears to his eyes.

34

Summer 2013

The smell makes Catherine shrink further into herself: the smell of an old person's home. Not urine, nothing as definable as that, and yet a very particular smell. What is it? Bins left a little too long before being taken out? Years of pets? Fur merged with fabric? Fake floral scents plugged in to try and disguise all of the above?

'Hello, darling.' Her mother stands up in welcome, unsteady on her thin legs. Catherine sets down her case and moves into her arms, careful of her fragile bones as she lays her arm across her back. A gentle pat. A mother's pat, but from her, the daughter who wants to be mothered yet fears she is past it.

'Thanks, Mum, for letting me stay. It's such a mess with the builders, and Robert's away so ... ' She banks on her mother not remembering that the builders left weeks ago and Robert hasn't travelled for work for years.

'Is he in America again?'

Catherine nods, not wanting to lie to her mother more than she has to.

'Can I get you anything, darling?'

It's seven o'clock and Catherine hasn't eaten, but all she wants to do is lie down in a dark room and go to sleep. She feels sick and her head is throbbing. 'Actually, Mum, I think I've got a migraine coming on. Do you mind if I lie down? I'm sure it'll go in a bit.'

Her mother cocks her head and her smile morphs into sympathy. 'I used to get headaches at your age,' she says.

Catherine walks into the only bedroom in the flat, and puts her case by the bed her father once slept in. Two single beds pushed together. Then she remembers her mother now sleeps in her father's bed, nearer the door, nearer the loo, so she takes her mother's old bed. There's a dirty, dark patch at the end of the quilt where the cat has been sleeping. She undresses down to her underwear, gets into bed and closes her eyes. She needs to sleep. If she can sleep she might be able to think more clearly, maybe start making sense of what is happening to her life.

She hears the slow shuffle of her mother's slippers on the carpet coming closer. She hears a glass of water being put down on the bedside table, and the click of plastic and tinfoil. She opens her eyes and sees her mother standing over her, two pills in her outstretched hand. She might not know what day of the week it is, but she hasn't forgotten the impulse to care for a poorly child.

'Thanks, Mum,' Catherine whispers, and swallows the pills, closing her eyes again.

For hours Catherine lies in the dark, listening to her mother's loneliness: a small supper being prepared and eaten on a tray in front of the TV, which talks to itself. Her mother's voice answering the phone, suddenly bright and cheerful, putting on its own show:

'Oh, I'm absolutely fine. Catherine's here. Lovely surprise, yes. Robert's away. Yes, he's in America again . . . ' All plausible, until Catherine hears her tell the caller that Nicholas is fine at home with the nanny. 'Such a lovely girl . . . '

Oh we're all so good at covering up. Pretending everything's absolutely lovely. Her mother's just not as agile at it any more, slipping in and out of time-frames, giving herself away. Catherine drifts into sleep, the television chirruping away in the next room.

She wakes to silence and darkness and turns over to look at the mound of her mother's body in the next bed. She is lying on her back with her mouth open, the skin on her face hanging from its bones. It is how she will look when she is dead. Catherine studies her, overwhelmed with the sadness of things lost: her childhood, her child's childhood; her mother's strength and her belief, once, that her mother's love had given her the strength to overcome anything. Her belief that she had absorbed that strength into her bones — an armour. She needs to talk, she needs to tell someone. It is too much to hold in any more.

'Mum . . . '

Her mother stirs a little, her eyelids flicker.

'Mum, something happened . . . '

Her mother's eyes stay closed. That's when Catherine tells her everything she has been unable to tell Robert. Out it comes. Her shame, her guilt. All of it. Her mother is silent. Has she heard? Or has Catherine's story slipped into her dreams? Yes, perhaps she is dreaming Catherine's tale. She may remember some of it, who knows, and dismiss it as a dream. To have said it out loud for the first time has helped Catherine, enough at least for her to fall asleep again; a sleep so deep she doesn't feel her mother reach for her hand in the night and hold it for a while, then give it a little squeeze.

35

Summer 2013

Everything I do now is with Nancy's blessing. I feel more certain of that when I wear her cardigan; all the years she wore it have absorbed into the wool. It is a constant, although a little out of shape from where I have stretched it around me. I wear a hat of hers too, one that she knitted. There are strands of hair still in it, her DNA snuggling up against mine. It takes me back to a time when we were as close as any two people could be: how we were when we first met, before Jonathan, before she became a mother. When it was just the two of us. I feel as if it is the two of us again. Collaborators. Co-authors. Our book, not only Nancy's.

It was me who gave it a name. We always helped each other out if we were stuck for titles and I could almost hear her clap her hands together and say, 'Yes, that's it!' when I came up with *The Perfect Stranger*. The ending is mine too. Nancy had come up with a different end, a little more subtle perhaps, but I decided that for the book to make an impact on its first reader we needed something stronger. It was me who killed the mother off.

Still, it was Nancy who did the hard graft. I try not to think too often of her sitting alone in

Jonathan's flat, writing, staring at the photographs and discovering the truth about why our son was driven to save that child. She succeeded in filling in the haziness surrounding his death and making sense of its senselessness. I'm sure it kept her going, gave her a reason to get up in the morning, as it had me. It was only when she had finished that she allowed the cancer to take hold. That's why she didn't call on me during that period: the book was enough for her.

My local bookshop has sold quite a few copies, according to Geoff, and several have gone in Catherine Ravenscroft's nearest bookshop too. Not as many, but a few. It gives me a small thrill to know there are strangers out there who dislike her, that I am gathering my forces and widening the net. Softly, softly we creep up behind her. More and more of us.

36

Summer 2013

Even without looking at the numbers, Catherine
guesses which house is his. It's the house you'd
love to walk right past without stopping, but this
house meets Catherine's eye and calls to her, like
the phlegmy growl of a homeless drunk on the
Charing Cross Road.

This house is blind, its windows thick with
dirt. The paintwork, so new and pleasing on the
houses either side, is scabby and peeling. The
garden is being strangled by bindweed, though
there's one valiant rose bush, blushing pink,
rebellious, which Catherine can smell as she
walks up the path — its sweet scent defying the
savagery around it. Her knock echoes down
the street. There's no answer and there's no
bell, so she bangs again, harder this time. She
crouches down and pushes the letterbox. Its flap
stays open, no metal basket on the other side to
catch letters, straight through to the house. She
sees a pair of shoes near the door, scuffed and
dirty, and a coat hanging over a chair.

'Hello. Mr Brigstocke. Please open the door.
It's Catherine Ravenscroft.'

She is determined and yet she hears a tremor
in her voice. She tries again.

'Please. I know you're there. Open the door.

We must talk about what happened.'

The house stays exactly where it is and so does Catherine, watching for the slightest movement. He has poisoned Robert against her — driven her from her home. The least he can do is look her in the eye and listen to what she has to tell him.

'Mr Brigstocke. Please open the door. Nothing you do to me is going to bring Jonathan back. Please. I have a right to be heard.'

The door stays closed. She calls the number Kim had given her. She hears the phone ring inside. A voice answers. *We are not at home at the moment* . . . A woman's voice. Nancy Brigstocke. She can't leave a message with a dead woman. She needs to see him, needs to make him listen, needs to make him stop. She is sure he is in there. She crouches down, pushing her arm through the letterbox as far as it can go. It is slender, so, up to her elbow. She twists it, trying to reach the latch, but she can't and withdraws it. She puts her face to the letterbox again.

'I know you have my number. Call me — speak this time. I want to talk about Jonathan. I deserve to be heard, Mr Brigstocke.' She stays on all fours, her forehead resting against the door. She hears the tinny distortion of a radio coming from further up the street and glances round to see a parked van, windows wound down, two builders sitting eating their lunch. She turns back to the door and decides that perhaps he isn't in after all, so dials the number again, and this time leaves a message.

37

Summer 2013

It was as if she'd sent a sightless serpent through our letterbox. We watched its blind head sniffing the air, trying to smell us out, stretching to reach the latch — trying to break in. I should have taken an axe to her. But I'm mixing my daemons here. She is more Siren than Medusa. We heard the evil in her voice trying to lure us to the door then singing through the telephone. She wants us to listen, does she? She wants to talk, does she? She has something to say. Well, it's too late for that. We haven't got the stomach to witness her bleeding heart — or her husband's, for that matter.

He's become quite a pest, leaving messages on the site for *The Perfect Stranger*, desperate to make up for lost time, desperate to meet us. He believed we were still 'us', still Mr and Mrs, until I emailed him and broke the news that my wife had died some years ago; Jonathan was our only son; she never recovered from his loss. It's pitiful, poor man. I think he is well aware that he is an incidental character in this story. I have no interest in meeting him, but I am happy to answer his questions when I can. 'Why now?' was simple. The truth was enough. The discovery of my wife's writings and the photographs and realizing that for years she had protected me from knowing that the little boy Jonathan lost his life for was not a stranger; that my son had been intimate with his mother. Our emails have been gratifying. His reveal evidence of his disgust for his wife and the pains he is taking to distance himself from her; *unforgivable, shameful cruelty*, he is grateful for finally *knowing the truth* and he is *hoping for some kind of reconciliation*. His language is that of a committee member addressing the wrongdoings of an evil dictatorship.

I expressed my sorrow at the hurt and shock I must have caused him by sending him the book and photographs and also my regret that I had left a copy for his son at work. *I was out of my mind*, I told him. *As if I was reliving the loss of Jonathan and Nancy all over again.* I hoped he could at least try to understand my grief. And I believe he has, never questioning me over Nancy's portrayal of his wife as a sexual predator. He has joined ranks with us against her.

Nancy comes up behind me and whispers in my ear. She finds his entreaties tedious and is impatient to see Jonathan again, so I pop him back up on the screen. He is still a work-in-progress, but he is almost complete. We've enjoyed picking out photographs: Jonathan on his eighteenth birthday, the camera we gave him hanging around his neck; Jonathan with his new backpack shortly before he set off for Europe; Jonathan smiling, handsome, on a beach somewhere in England — but it could be anywhere, so we'll say it's France, the first leg of his journey. His favourite books — we still have them on our bookshelves — up they go. And music, that's important, that's a must. His taste is a bit last century, but that's 'cool' these days — shows he has depth, knows his stuff. We have kept him a teenager — we haven't allowed him to sink into middle age. He is forever young, forever on his gap year, about to start at university. He still hasn't decided where. Bristol? Manchester? All he needs are a few friends — and a best friend, we must give him that. Friends will make him appear more solid, more bona fide.

Geoff has been a great help in our project. We met up again a few weeks ago. He accompanied me to an event at our local bookshop where I had been invited to do a reading from my book. They are very keen, as Geoff said, to promote local authors. It was, I'm sorry to say, a rather pitiful affair. Me, standing by a small display of books, with only a handful of people turning up to listen to an old man who had published his first novel. The wine was cheap, the crisps were stale and I couldn't wait for it to be over. It was an ordeal. My voice cracked and I found it hard to get the words out: they lodged in my throat and tripped me up. Even though I knew I should try to make eye contact with my audience, I found myself incapable of looking up from the page. I was uncomfortable being looked at. No, I didn't like being in the spotlight.

Geoff and I escaped to the pub as soon as we could. He felt guilty for putting me through it. It was his idea, after all. I think he had under-estimated how hard it would be for an elderly man who had become unused to socializing to be on display like that.

'Geoff,' I said. 'Forget about it. *I* have.' And I picked up his empty pint and took it to the bar. When I returned with the drinks I put my hand on his, in a fatherly way. 'You have been a good friend to me,' I said. 'If it wasn't for you, my book wouldn't even have been in that bookshop. And if it wasn't for your encouragement I wouldn't have had the heart to start another novel.' This got him going.

'Stephen, that's great. What's it about?'

'I haven't worked out the story yet, but I have a character in my head. I can see him, I can hear him,' I chuckled as I tapped the side of my head. He was in there all right. 'I'm still at the research stage and I wondered whether you might be able to help me with something. I know you've already given me a lot of your time, so I don't like to ask . . .'

'No, no, it's fine. Ask away.'

So I did. I told him the character was a teenage boy and that, although I felt confident with the characterization after all my years in teaching, it was the techie stuff I was having difficulty with.

'I want to create a Facebook page for him. A real one . . .'

'You mean a fake one. A fake page? For a fictional character?'

'Ummm,' I nodded, taking a sip of my beer.

He didn't say anything. I could hear the cogs turning: old man, teenage boys, fake Facebook page. If I say it myself, I think I handled his misgivings with agility.

'He's not the main character, it's actually the grandfather I want to focus on and his relationship with this boy, but still, I need to understand a bit more about the world these kids disappear into when they go online. I mean, look . . . ' I pointed over to a table of youngsters: drinks on the table, cigarettes standing by, faces ready to break into laughter. All normal. It could have been a scene from any decade, except they weren't speaking. There was no conversation. They weren't even looking at each other. Their eyes were down, on their phones, like a bunch of old ladies checking their bingo cards.

'What are they looking at?' I shook my head, smiling in bafflement.

He nodded. 'I see what you mean.' Clunk, clunk went the cogs.

'Maybe it's a bad idea, but I feel such an imbecile around that sort of thing and I was hoping you might be able to guide me through it. An idiot's guide to Facebook and however else young people 'communicate' with each other.' I tickled that word *communicate* with my fingers. 'It's an alien world to me.'

'Me too,' he said.

'Oh well, it was only a thought.' Bugger.

'But my son's on it all the bloody time.'

'I didn't know you had a son?'

'Yeah. He's eighteen. Lives with his mother, but he comes over every other weekend. He could probably help.'

That's how it started. Sundays on the Internet

with Geoff's son. And in exchange for his expertise, I helped him out with his English essays. Geoff was delighted when his son started getting 'A's for his homework, although I think we'd both agree that I was the more enthusiastic student. I can't fault his boy's teaching though. He was extremely thorough. Fifty friends, he said. At least. And he showed me how to get them. He was a good teacher and I was the perfect pupil. At times my head felt as if it would explode with all this new information, but I was greedy for it. How on earth do you get a photograph taken in the 1990s into a laptop? How do you do it? Well, now I know. And once it's in there, spread it around. Not only on Facebook but make sure it's on Google too.

'What sort of music does he like?'

I shrugged, suddenly the dunce in the class. That afternoon he sent me home with some tracks on my laptop.

Geoff was always there, he never left us alone together. He brought us cups of tea and I would bring with me jars of Nancy's jam to have with our crumpets. It was a good arrangement and a very pleasant few weeks.

I passed with flying colours, equipped with all the tricks I needed to bring Jonathan to life again. Our son now has a future, and it feels good to hold it in our hands. This time, when he goes off on his travels, we can make sure we keep a firmer grip on his likes and dislikes, and the friends he picks up on the way. You can't have too many friends, but it's important he has one special one, a confidante, someone he can open up to.

38

Summer 2013

Catherine takes the bus to work, the simplest route from her mother's house. It's pragmatic, not cowardly. Stephen Brigstocke is the coward. She'd kept her phone on all night and he hasn't called. She sits on the bus, replaying in her head her nightly confessions to her mother, and wonders if any of them have filtered through. Her mother hasn't said anything, but does she know? Does she remember? Tears come at the thought that her mother knows and doesn't judge her. She blinks them away so she can pull down the mask the must wear to get through the day. It fits her well, no one would know it was there, and she has even got used to the way it inhibits her breathing. By the time she gets off the bus she is in her stride, marching along the stretch of road towards work like a confident woman on her way to a busy day in the office, not noticing anyone she passes. Not noticing the old man in the knitted hat who has stopped to stare at her as she sweeps past. They almost touch. He smells her as she walks by. He watches her until she disappears.

She walks into the office, unwinding her silk scarf from her throat and letting its beautiful print shiver across her chest, moving as she

212

moves. She dumps her bag on the floor and sits down in her chair, swinging round to check who else is in, but she is the first. Odd, it's ten o'clock. She takes out her diary, thinking there must be a meeting she's forgotten, and then she notices them. Piled up on her desk. Copies of *The Perfect Stranger*, spines rigid, stare back at her accusingly.

Fuck. Her hands shake as she snatches them up and shoves them in the bin under her desk. Fuck. He has been here. Thank Christ she is alone, but as she sits back in her chair and looks up, she sees she is not.

Kim and Simon are watching her. Kim and Simon are standing side by side. In Kim's hand is a copy of the book. Catherine tries to meet her eye, but she avoids meeting Catherine's. Simon walks towards her, hand held out, as if he is approaching a nervous animal. Don't speak, let him speak first.

'Cath . . . ' He imbues her name with his own sense of superiority.

She watches him come closer, her foot pressing down on the bin under her desk to stop her leg shaking.

'You OK if we have a quick chat?' And he sits down on the chair next to her. He has never been able to hide his feelings of rivalry. This is an opportunity he won't pass up. Kim stands by his side.

'Thing is, Kim came to me because she didn't know what to do.'

Kim speaks now, sounding like a nervous child: 'Stephen Brigstocke came in — he brought

213

in the books . . . his book.' One twitches in her hand. Catherine bites her cheek until she tastes blood.

'So the difficulty is,' Simon picks up, 'Kim told me that you asked her to drop the story about Mr Brigstocke, and I wondered why you were so keen to kill it off?'

'Oh, did you? Well, it has absolutely nothing to do with you.' Her voice shakes, lacking the strength of her words.

'I think it does . . . I mean, I wish it didn't, but . . . if a junior member of the team comes to me asking for advice, it becomes my business.'

'A junior member of the team? God. Who do you think you are?'

He takes the book from Kim and waves it around.

'You told Kim he was a paedophile and you asked her to track him down. Then, once she'd done that, you told her to forget all about it.' He sits back in the chair, spreading his legs and thrusting them out in front so his crotch is staring up at Catherine. 'I wonder why you did that?'

'I don't have to explain myself to you, Simon. Or to you, Kim.' She glares at her. 'This is a personal matter. It has nothing to do with work.'

'Then why did you ask me to get his address and telephone number?' Kim is on the verge of tears.

'Did you let him in here?' Catherine demands.

'Yes — reception phoned and I went down to meet him. When he told me who he was — '

Simon interrupts her: 'It's OK, Kim, I'll

handle this,' and he sends her a smile over his shoulder. 'Here's the thing. I don't know what's in this book — I haven't had time to read it yet — but a man *you* had been investigating as a paedophile turns up here with a book he has written. And he tells Kim that you're part of the story. That you are in this book. I mean, what is it? Some kind of confession?' And he fans the pages as if they'll answer his question.

'I didn't say he was a paedophile.'

'But . . . ' Kim stutters.

'I asked you to help me find Stephen Brigstocke's contact details and some background on him. I asked you, because I trusted you.' Catherine is near to tears.

'Hey, don't take it out on Kim — she's not the one who needs to defend herself.' He shuffles his chair towards Catherine's, leaning in so close she can smell his perfume. He has succeeded in making her feel like a nervous animal. She looks around the office but still no one is in.

'I told everyone we were having a meeting so they've gone to the canteen.'

'God, you're such a shit, Simon. You're enjoying yourself, aren't you? You could have done this in the meeting room, but no — you want everyone to know about this fucking charade.'

'Cath, Cath — you're the one who's created this situation. You're not being honest with us, and that worries me — it jeopardizes the reputation of the whole team.'

'What? What the fuck are you talking about?'

'Mr Brigstocke came here because he was

215

frightened. You used Kim to get his address and telephone number, then you went round to his house. He says you tried to break in and left threatening messages on his answer-machine.' He leans in even closer. She is cornered. She must get away. She picks up her bag, but Simon puts his hand on her arm.

'Cath, come on, we need to talk about — '

'Get your fucking hand off me.'

He backs off, raising both hands — one holding the book — in surrender.

'He is the one stalking me — that's why I went to his house. To talk to him . . . he is the one who is threatening me . . . '

'OK, OK. And why is he doing that? I mean, what's he threatening you with?'

She is deafened by the sound of blood pumping in her ears.

'It's private. Can't you get that through your fucking head?'

'Listen, try to stay calm.'

'Don't you fucking tell me to stay calm. You have no right to ask me anything about it and I'm not . . . ' She is about to cry and she will not do that.

'You're clearly very upset. Whatever it is you're covering up, I'm sure it would be better if you came clean about it.' He touches her again. She snatches the book out of his hand and throws it. It hits him in the face. She stares, fascinated by the burning red on his cheek and the beads of blood which appear from a cut on the side of his nose. Both of them are too shocked to speak. Kim is the only one to move, grabbing some tissues and thrusting them at Simon.

'You shouldn't have done that,' he says as he dabs at his nose, and she hears the threat in his words. His eyes flick over her shoulder and she turns to see they have an audience — small but appreciative. Her colleagues watch through a glass partition. She is the show — a one-woman show. They are shocked, but they pity her too as they sip their coffees. She has humiliated herself. Simon waits for an apology.

'You fucking asked for it,' she says as she walks out, feeling the eyes on her but refusing to meet them. She takes the lift down and imagines them all rushing to Simon. God, she looked crazy. She's really lost it. She walks past security and out through the glass doors. She keeps walking until she reaches the bus stop. She has no idea how long it takes the bus to come — two minutes? Twenty? And when it does she barely remembers getting on it, swiping her Oyster card, sitting down and staring from the window at streets that are grey and nondescript.

Summer 1993

When was the first time she saw him? Was Robert there or had he already left? Did she notice Jonathan when she, Robert and Nicholas were still a threesome? She thinks not. When Robert was there she hadn't even known Jonathan existed. And what was her first impression when she did see him? Youth, carelessness — he was carefree and she wasn't. His dark hair, tanned skin, long limbs. He was watching her and Nicholas. They were in a café near the beach. It was the day Robert left. She was trying to get Nicholas to eat his tea: one more mouthful and then he could have an ice cream, one more mouthful of rice then we can both have an ice cream. She was on the verge of tears, hating herself for not coping for one fucking day without her husband.

'Make the most of it,' Robert had said. 'It's pissing down in London.' And he'd smiled and she'd tried to smile back, only she couldn't. She didn't cry either, although she felt like it. She didn't want to make a scene or push Robert into making a choice: which was more important, work or her? She could have done that. She knows she would have won. She chose not to.

'We'll come home with you,' she'd tried instead.

'Don't be silly — why would you want to do that? It's beautiful here. The hotel's paid for — just enjoy it. No cooking, no washing, a beautiful beach.' Yes, there was a beach, there was the sea, the sun was shining, but she didn't want to be there on her own. Post-natal depression. Five years on? She hadn't owned up to it. She was lucky, that's what everyone told her. She was lucky.

Did she flirt with him? When she noticed him looking, did she flirt? Did she do something with her eyes that sent him a signal? She gave in to Nicholas and bought him an ice cream before he'd finished his rice. She had a beer. And the young man, whose name she didn't know yet, had smiled and she'd smiled back, and that little connection had given her a boost. Then she and Nicholas had returned to the hotel. He wanted to be carried, and the beer had softened her so she picked him up, even though he was too heavy and she was already carrying the beach bag with their wet towels and toys and a litre of water and her book. She remembered walking away from the café and imagining the attractive stranger watching her from behind and her being conscious of how she looked. Did he follow her to the hotel? He told her later that he was going that way anyway . . .

★ ★ ★

The bus pulls in and she opens her eyes, worried she's missed her stop. But it's the next one, then a short walk to her mother's flat. It is her only place of refuge now.

When she walks in, the carer is there and her mother is watching television, the volume turned higher than usual so she can hear it above the sound of the vacuum cleaner. Catherine would like to turn round and walk straight out again, but she has nowhere else to go. Even though it is safe here, she knows this safety is as fragile as a bubble.

There is a message from Simon on her voicemail. She hasn't bothered to listen to it. Her phone rings again. Work. She ignores that too, putting it on silent, and switching herself to cruise control: kissing her mum and saying hello to Eileen the carer; making a pot of tea and sitting down; closing her eyes and allowing the mash of noise in the flat to wash through her. When she opens her eyes again, Eileen is wearing her coat and putting on her outdoor shoes. The flat is quiet, the television switched off.

'Bye-bye,' Eileen says, 'see you next week.' She is out of the door before Catherine can reply. Her mother is fast asleep. She pictures herself and her mother, side by side, both asleep, the before and after — although Catherine wonders whether she will actually make it to where her mother is now. She stands up and goes into the bedroom.

She checks her phone. Two more messages. She listens to them: the one from Simon and then two from a woman in human resources. She sits on the bed to return the call.

'Hello, it's Catherine Ravenscroft for Sarah Fincham.' She waits, hoping that the woman will be 'in a meeting' and that she won't have to speak to her.

'Catherine, hello. Thank you for calling back.'

Catherine says nothing.

'I understand there was an incident in the office today.'

Still she says nothing.

'Simon has said that he doesn't want to make a formal complaint. Nevertheless, we are obliged to record that you physically attacked him. It will have to go on your file, although, as I say, Simon isn't pushing for any further action.'

'I see.' Catherine hears her mother stirring, the television going on again.

'And there will have to be an investigation into the allegations made by a Mr Stephen

220

Brigstocke. They are serious. I'm sure you understand that. Is there anything you'd like to say at this stage?'

'No.'

'Well. I'm going to sign you off work for a week — a week to start with, at least.' She waits. 'Catherine? Are you there?'

'Yes, I'm here.'

'I understand you've been under pressure. That you have felt under pressure with work — '

'It's not work — I haven't been under pressure at work. I'll take some leave — '

'No, there's no need for that. Save your leave — I'll sign you off sick.'

HR-speak for *you're a fucking nutcase*.

'I think we should talk again in a week, when you've had time to gather yourself. Then we can discuss next steps.'

Silence.

'I wonder whether it might be helpful for you to talk to someone about managing your anger. I'm sure they could come up with some useful coping mechanisms. We could help with that — pay for counselling. Someone independent, of course, and confidential. How does that sound?'

'Fine, that sounds fine.' Catherine chokes on the words.

'We could offer four sessions. After that, if you wanted to continue, you would have to meet the cost yourself . . . Catherine?'

'Yes, yes. OK,' is all she can manage.

The woman says her goodbyes and hangs up. Catherine lies back on the bed. It is out of control. Everything is out of her control, it is

221

sweeping her away and she closes her eyes and gives in to it.

Summer 1993

It was eight o'clock by the time Nick was tucked up and asleep. She had fooled him into thinking it was dark by closing the shutters in his room, but from her window she could see it was still light outside — too early yet for the Spanish, only a few Northern Europeans in the bar opposite. Catherine wasn't ready for bed. She put on a denim skirt and a vest and tied up her hair. She looked OK. Her skin had a light tan and she thought, what a waste, Robert not here to enjoy this peace with her. She took her book, cigarettes and key and went downstairs. The girl in reception promised she would keep an eye out in case Nicholas appeared, but Catherine knew he wouldn't. Once asleep, he stayed asleep.

She sat at a table on the terrace bar overlooking the beach. A waiter brought her smoked almonds and fresh anchovies and she ordered a small carafe of white wine. She waited until it arrived before she lit her cigarette, inhaled with relish and realized that she was relaxed. Maybe it would be OK after all. She looked at the sea. Small waves licked at the sand. A few people were still on the beach: families, Spanish she guessed, and a smattering of couples waiting to watch the sun set. That was when she noticed him.

He had a beer and was smoking. He was

222

wearing a T-shirt, pale green. He turned and looked at her and she was embarrassed that he'd caught her staring at him. Why was she staring at him? Because he stood out. Because he was the only one with his back to the sea, the only one not interested in watching the sun make an exhibition of itself. He was looking up towards the promenade and when he looked at Catherine she smiled, even though he hadn't smiled at her. She wasn't flirting, it was instinctive. She hadn't wanted to appear unfriendly. She was on holiday. So she'd smiled. He didn't return her smile, and that made him seem older. And it made her feel self-conscious, knowing that he knew she was alone.

She reached for the nuts, trying to look casual, carrying on reading, but her fingers dipped into the oily anchovies instead and she had to look up and find a napkin before smearing grease all over her book and the wine glass. And she saw he was still looking at her, then he raised his bottle of beer and almost smiled, but she pretended not to notice and wiped at her fingers with the napkin before stabbing at an anchovy with a cocktail stick. She checked the time. Eight forty-five; fifteen more minutes and she'd go up.

A flash of light caught her eye. A flash from his camera. A photo taken, but not of the beautiful salmon-coloured sun. The camera was pointing at her. She remembers being ashamed of her assumption that he'd taken a photograph of her. It was the promenade he wanted to capture, with the pink sun reflected on the buildings. And he was below her, so it would have been an odd angle to photograph her from. With his prominent zoom lens. An expensive camera for such a young man. She pulled her skirt down, trying to force it to reach her knees, and crossed her legs. It reminded her of a scene from a film, and she wondered whether to uncross them again, but thought better of it. What was the matter with her?

She remembers her discomfort. She wasn't used to being out on her own any more. She wasn't used to being looked at like that. She didn't know how to be. And she didn't know that the photograph he'd taken would find its way into her home years later and be thrown in her face by her husband. A triangle of lace and darkness, of hair and skin and shadows. All she knew at the time was the feeling his attention gave her. It made her nervous, and at the same time it excited her, she has to admit that. She felt excited. She forces herself to remember that, as she sat on the terrace with a glass of wine and an anchovy on a stick, she thought of being in bed alone later and touching herself, and that it would be that boy she would fantasize about. She punishes herself with that memory and how her thoughts of having sex with a stranger were interrupted by a phone call. It was her husband, the waiter said. He was on the phone in reception. She picked up her things, left her wine unfinished, and followed the waiter into the hotel.

While she was on the phone to Robert she saw him walk through the entrance of the hotel and her heart flipped in anxiety, not excitement. He walked through reception, right past her. She remembers wondering whether they would stop him, but they didn't. He had an expensive camera round his neck. And he had a nice face. She turned away, concentrating on Robert, telling him she missed him. He told her he loved her, which he did back then. She loved him too. Does she still love him? She won't think about that, not yet, she can't. That's not the point of this remembering. She remembers blowing a kiss into the receiver before putting it down. When she turned around she saw him sitting on a stool at the bar, looking directly at her, two drinks in front of him. His bag was on the next-door stool. Still looking at her, he removed it and put it on the floor. And then he smiled. Finally. Right at her.

★ ★ ★

'When did you get home?'

Catherine opens her eyes and looks at her mother.

'A little while ago.'

'Did they let you out early?' Her mother smiles and Catherine wonders for a moment whether she thinks she's been let out early from school, but that can't be. She's not that far gone yet.

'I finished what I needed to do.'

'Have you got another of your headaches, love?' Tears spring to Catherine's eyes. Her mother knows and doesn't know, but it doesn't matter because she knows what Catherine needs.

She needs to be cared for without being interrogated. She needs someone to trust that she isn't a terrible human being without having to tell them — without having to explain anything.

39

Summer 2013

Nick had spent most of the afternoon up in his bedroom, smoking dope: half-day, he was going to say if his dad came home early, but he didn't. It's ten p.m. and he's back up there, door shut, windows wide open. He rolls another spliff, lights up and leans out of the window. The spare room is directly above the kitchen, and when he looks down he can see his dad through the glass roof of the extension. He's clearing up after supper and Nick knows he should be helping, but his dad didn't stop him when he left the room. He leans back in case his dad looks up and sees him. Surely he can smell the smoke drifting down? Even if he could, Nick doubts he'd say anything. He won't want to risk driving Nick away. It is not easy living with a parent, but at least he's saving money. It was all he could do to stop himself screaming during supper when his dad kept asking him about work. Thank fuck for football, which got them through the rest of the meal.

He flops down on the bed, catching his reflection in the mirror on his way. He looks like death, all colour in his face washed out. He lays his laptop open on his chest and imagines the unearthly colour his skin must be with the light

227

from the screen reflecting on it. A stoned sarcophagus of an unknown young man, arms holding his book of life. He announces his return to the world and is greeted with a torrent of hellos and welcome backs. Virtual strangers, virtual friends. He gets to them all in turn, pressing the flesh, gently wafting through their outstretched hands, desperate to touch him, eager for his attention. He graces them with his presence, glad to be back in the world of the living.

He hears his dad call goodnight and Nick echoes the word, but he might as well have barked like a dog: the sound is meaningless. He is mid-conversation and won't be interrupted, his fingers chatting away, telling anyone who's out there what he thinks, what he's up to. And some of them try and tempt him out. Not far, only round the corner — a boarded-up heaven where they gather to hang out. A shit-hole of a place, but it's fine once you shut your eyes. After a while, you don't notice the smell. Not something you'd want to make a habit of — and he hasn't. He's only been a couple of times, creeping out of the house when his dad was asleep and making sure he was home in time for breakfast, beating his dad to the table, already dressed for work. Even though he was too tired to speak, his dad understood. Nick's never been good in the mornings.

Not tonight though. Tonight he is content to stay at home. He has a message he has saved till last — a private message meant only for him, from a new friend. And for once the word has a ring of truth. He gives him his full attention

— one to one, just the two of them. He's only a kid and he looks up to Nick, hangs on his every word.

How you doing? Nick asks, and the friend can't wait to tell him everything he's been up to since their last chat.

They have a lot in common. More than you'd think, given the age difference. Even a fucking book. He's read the only book Nick's picked up in years. Nick confessed he'd skipped to the end — hadn't read the whole thing, but, you know what? He has now. Fingered through the recommended chapters: the sexy stuff. Bit tame, love: try some of this, and Nick'd sent him something hot — better than he'd read in a fucking book. Nick's older, seen more of the world. Follow my lead — don't go to university, fuck Bristol or Manchester — stay in Spain — the sun's shining in Spain. He's hungry for Nick's advice and Nick has dished out plenty of it. Life's too short to waste, he says. Like he can talk — but he does. Can't stop himself, comes up with all sorts of things he'd never say out loud — never say to anyone else — and Jonathan hangs on every word that drips off Nick's fingers and asks for more, wants to know about the girls Nick's fucked and his business plans and the year he spent travelling round the States. Jonathan laps it all up and listens and learns.

40

Summer 2013

I know all about what's going on at home: she's moved out and he's on his own with Dad, who's not himself, poor man. My little delivery of books to her office seems to have unsettled things too. She is off sick, they told me when I phoned. They had no idea when she would be back. Hope it's nothing serious, I said before I hung up.

My heart has become as hard as my toenails. There was a time when I might have felt something for that boy. Once I might have tried to help him. It's touching how he's opened up to me. My teaching days taught me to spot them a mile off: the boys with the black hole at their centre. They tried swaggering nonchalance to cover it up: pretending they didn't care about anything, least of all the consequences of giving up on themselves. But I'm talking about adolescents. He's not a boy, he's twenty-five years old and however much he 'bigs' himself up to my nineteen-year-old self with his dismal little fantasies of travelling round America and whatnot, he can't hide his shivering, shrinking soul from a man with my experience.

He is desperate. Desperate to talk late into the night. He has other friends, of course, but they're as lost as he is. I've read their inane banter. And they don't know him like I do. When I go offline, off he goes to meet them in the real world, his druggy little friends, and then back he comes the following night, tongue hanging out, slathering with anticipation of my arrival, waiting to impress me with his pathetic narcotic adventures. I think it's time I started making him wait for me — just ten minutes or so, keep him keen.

It didn't take long for him to respond to my initial request — it was the photograph of his mother that got his attention. I told him I'd found it hidden in my house. Told him it had her name on the back. Told him I'd tracked him down, and I think he liked that. I think it tickled him, the idea that someone had made the effort to seek him out. It was an innocent enough photo, his mother alone on a beach, but it's given him food for thought. Let him ponder for a while whether we might be related. Did his mother have an affair? Did she have another child? Does he have a little half-brother? Could it be me? And there are more pictures to come, but he's not yet ready for those — they will need a health warning. Not that he gave me one when he sent me that filth. Still, I managed to fake my boy's appreciation well and Jonathan is such an innocent it wasn't hard to pretend he had never seen anything like that before.

He thinks I hang on his every word, and I do in a way. Poor sod — dribbling out his sorry tales to a boy six years his junior who has been dead for nearly twenty years. He may have opened his heart to Jonathan, but it is me who has marched in: me with Nancy's voice ringing in my ears, her book of words whispering to me — the source material. And with her at my side, it won't take much to nudge this feeble specimen to the brink. All I need do is feed his darkness and lead him to a point of no return, then leave him there, teetering on the edge.

41

Extract from Nancy Brigstocke's notebook — October 1998

. . . there was no feeling in her that I could see: a complete lack of empathy. I wonder whether it's ever really possible to feel another person's suffering. Perhaps I am asking too much. All the same, I'd hoped for something. Some words that might have shown an attempt to understand my loss. She said: 'Sorry. I wish he hadn't done it.' What did that mean? Did she wish that someone else had risked their life instead? Did she wish Jonathan was still alive? But she didn't say that.

I have played her words over and over in my head, trying to make sense of them. Sometimes I wonder if they slipped out from somewhere deep inside. I wonder if they were a confession: whether she wished her son had been left to drown. Is that possible? I try to imagine how a mother could want her child to lose their life. It happens, doesn't it? Mothers kill their children through neglect. They put their own needs above those of their children. They forget about their responsibilities. It happens, you read about it. And she was guilty of neglect; why else would her five-year-old son be afloat in the sea alone? Why didn't she run in to save him?

When we met, I had already discovered that

she and Jonathan had been intimate, yet she told me they had never met before that day. But hadn't they been staying in the same small holiday resort? And she repeated the lie: 'I had never seen him before.' She is a liar. I could have told her I had seen the photographs, but I didn't. I didn't have the strength for confrontation and besides, what would have been the point? It wouldn't bring him back. It took all my strength to stay upright, standing next to her at my son's grave. I was cold. I was exhausted. I had wanted her to give me something. I wanted to see her son, and I did find the strength to ask for that. I hoped that we would meet again and that the next time she would bring him with her, but she refused. There was no other meeting. I never saw her again and I never saw the child who was only alive because of my boy.

I remember how her cheeks glowed pink from the cold, shimmering with health, and I envied her that too, the heat coming off her. The sweat on her lip and her shiny skin. There was heat but no warmth. Her blood is too cold to ever understand what it feels like to have a stranger tell you your child is dead, to not be with your son at the moment he needs you most, at the moment he is crying out for you. And you cannot help him, you cannot hold him, you cannot tell him that it will be all right, that you are there. I wasn't there to hold Jonathan, to stroke his head, to kiss him and tell him I loved him. Only if that happens to you can you really understand what it is like.

Her little boy is running around above ground while mine lies rotting beneath. She didn't even look at Jonathan's stone, at the words we'd had carved into it: 'He was our Angel.' She didn't look down. She hadn't brought flowers. Why did she even bother to come? I wish her child knew that he owed his life to my son. I wish he knew that, if it wasn't for Jonathan, he wouldn't be here.

42

Summer 1993

She remembers sitting up, shouting Nicholas's name. She had fallen asleep on her towel, lying on her front, her feet facing the sea. She had been exhausted. She hadn't meant to fall asleep, but she had allowed herself to lie down with her head resting on her hands because Nicholas had been content.

She'd given in and bought him the red-and-yellow rubber dinghy he'd seen on their first day, when she and Robert had held his hands and they'd walked along the promenade. On that first afternoon she and Robert had steered Nick away from the inflatable dolphins, sharks and boats, and bought him a bucket and spade and a small truck to play with on the sand. He had cried for the dinghy, and on that last day she had given in. It would make him happy, and if he was happy, she could rest.

She looked up now and again to check he was OK and he was: sitting in the dinghy on the sand, happy at being the captain of his ship. But the next time she looked, the dingy was bobbing around in the waves. She hadn't meant to fall asleep. She stood up and called his name. The waves were starting to get frisky, and they rocked the boat, back and forth, but he was still smiling,

236

still happy. And there were others in the water, diving in and out of the waves. No one seemed worried. She marched towards the sea, her eyes never leaving Nick, calling his name, louder each time, but he didn't look up. He was lost in his own little world. Then frisky became rough, and the waves swelled and tugged at the boat.

He was out of his depth and being pulled further by the sea, out to where the ocean became dark, then black. The sun had gone and the wind had come up.

'Help!' she shouted, running now. 'Help me!' she screamed, shivering, terrified. She remembers her words with shame: 'Help me,' not 'Help my child.' 'Help *me*.' She ran into the water, up to her waist, but it wasn't her who swam out to her child. She knew she wasn't a strong enough swimmer and she was scared. She was scared of drowning. She forces herself to admit it.

She dissects that moment, sparing herself nothing. She didn't risk her own life for her child's. She knew they would both drown if she swam out. She'd always been frightened in the sea — didn't even like putting her head under. It's men who drown rescuing children and dogs, not women. Fathers, not mothers. Strange that, but she can't remember ever hearing about a woman jumping in to rescue a drowning child, though she can recall plenty of occasions when men had thrown themselves into roaring rivers or dirty canals, not thinking about themselves, driven on by blind courage. There must be women who have done it, but she can't remember reading about them. So, she is not

237

quite alone in lacking the bravery to go in after her son that day. If it had been a burning building, or a window ledge at the top of a skyscraper or a madman pointing a gun, it would have been different. Then she would have found the courage. She would have run through fire, risked falling to her death, jumped in front of a bullet for Nick . . . but the sea? The sea had thwarted her.

And then he raced in, brushing her aside as he ran past, diving like a lifeguard into the waves. Why were there no fucking lifeguards on this beach? There was not even a flag. He was the one who responded to her screams for help. 'No!' the word left her mouth before she could stop it. A howl which no one understood. She didn't want it to be him. Not him, please. She watched as he swam towards the dinghy. It was tipping back and forth wildly: Nicholas was trying to stand up. Oh God, please don't stand up, you'll fall in. She tried to gesture with her hands for Nick to sit down, but he was too far out to see her.

Others were standing with her now. A couple with a toddler and another family, English, kind, the mother's arm around Catherine. And Spanish families too, all gripped by the sight of the little boy bobbing dangerously out to sea and the young man striking out to reach him. She remembered how strong he was, and she knew he would make it to Nicholas. There would be no stopping him. And he did and the people around her smiled and the English mother squeezed her shoulder and smiled too, but she didn't smile. She felt sick as she watched.

He was swimming back, dragging Nicholas in the dinghy behind him. It was hypnotic, watching him: one-armed, one hand, keeping going. It was heroic. He was brave. She was thinking this when she heard the fear in the voices around her. A gabble of Spanish and then the English father: 'He's in trouble, they need help!' He was about to run in himself when a younger Spanish man beat him to it. Not as young as Jonathan, but still young. Late twenties? Her age? He swam out, grabbed the rope and turned, swimming towards the shore with Nicholas safely behind him. For a while it looked as if they weren't moving, the waves beating them back, the current pulling them away from the shore, but he managed it, this other Spanish man. He moved closer and closer to the shore and to safety. And everyone looked at him and Nick, not Jonathan. They all assumed he was OK.

And at last Nicholas was on the beach and she scooped him out of the dinghy, wrapped him in a towel and held him close. He was shivering from cold, his chattering teeth rendering him speech-less. He buried his head in his mother's chest and she pulled the towel right up over his head, like a hood, protecting him, holding him. Only then did she turn and see the young Spanish man and the English dad swim out to Jonathan, who had been left behind. He didn't seem to be making any effort to get to shore. He was flapping his arms, pushing down at the sea. It was all in slow motion.

239

People were speaking to her in Spanish, kind voices, smiling, stroking Nicholas's head, happy at the rescue of this little boy. Then the English mother pressed against her ear and whispered:

'Don't let him see. He mustn't see.' And people gathered round to screen Nicholas's view of the beach. Catherine turned to see Jonathan's body being carried from a boat. A speed boat had come, but too late. She watched as Jonathan's body was laid out on the sand. Then she looked away and shielded Nicholas.

'You're hurting me,' were his first words.

She hadn't realized how hard she had been pressing her son against her. Other mothers had formed a barrier to protect the child from seeing the body of the man who had saved him.

'You should take him back to your hotel,' said the English woman, her hand on Catherine's arm. 'Where's your stuff?'

She had pointed to her towel and bag, and the woman went and gathered them up. Hurriedly, Catherine had put a T-shirt on Nicholas, then taken his hand.

'Shall we go and see if the hotel will do you a hot chocolate?' She was shocked by the calm in her voice.

'Yeah,' he said brightly, and he picked up the rope to take the dinghy with them.

'Let's leave it here, Nick. We're going home tomorrow. We won't be able to take it on the plane. Someone else can play with it.'

She had braced herself for tears, but he was fine about it. Forgotten already. The novelty worn off. He didn't mention it or the incident

240

again. Ever. She waited for it. For the memory of his fear, of the realization that he was too far out and she wasn't with him, that the sea was too rough, that he had been rescued, yet it never came. He never said a word about it. He was freezing, he had said that, but he never said that he thought he would drown. He never said he was scared. Perhaps he hadn't been. He'd been cold and he'd wanted to get back to the beach, then someone came and got him. Simple as that. He had never really feared for his life.

As they walked up the steps from the beach, Catherine looked over her shoulder one last time and saw Jonathan lying on the sand, covered in two towels. Dead. She knew he was dead. And what did she feel? She presses herself. *What did you feel?*

43

Summer 2013

A story has been playing on the news all day: a story of children who have died of shame, unable to tell their parents about pictures they have posted on the Internet to predatory adults who pretended to be their friends. Some of these children are as young as eight. This has been the soundtrack as I have pored through photographs of Jonathan as a child, the news story running through my head as I search for the picture which best captures my son — the one which shows him as I wish him to be remembered. If Jonathan were a child today, I don't believe he would have become a victim of those monsters. He would never have died of shame, because he knew he could always talk to his mother. He knew he could tell her anything and she would never love him any less. They were as close as a mother and son could be.

So close that it was Nancy, not me, who was the one to tell him the facts of life.

His mother, not his father. You'd think it would have been easier for me, but it was Nancy he listened to, Nancy he talked to. When I tried to tackle the subject with him he'd stuck his fingers in his ears and la-la-la'd so loudly he'd drowned me out. Nancy and I had laughed about it afterwards: how funny he was, how silly. He'd hit puberty early, he was only eleven, but he needed to know what was what so she said she'd do it. I remember thinking, good luck, he'll be even more embarrassed listening to his mum talk about sex. He wasn't.

She'd sat him down and made him look her in the eye and told him there was nothing to be frightened or shy about. It was natural. One day he would meet the right person and then his uncomfortable urges would make sense. There was nothing to be ashamed of, he should feel free to explore his own body. In fact she encouraged him to do so and told him that if he was ever worried about anything he could always talk to her. I remember a few occasions when I walked past his closed bedroom door and heard the murmur of their voices. He knew he could trust her and I knew not to intrude on them. Jonathan could be sure that, no matter what he did, his mother would always understand. Our son would have been safe from Internet predators like me.

I have lied about my age to lure someone younger than me into being my friend. I have pretended to be someone I am not.

Last night I posted up the rest of the photographs. No child should have to see their mother like that. What would it do to you, seeing your own mother exposed like that, everything on show: the shame, the filth? I doubt whether he'll ever be able to erase those images from his mind. But there's no going back now. We are on a mission.

Little Nick. He is waiting for me — he wants

243

to know more about the photos. Who took them? And so I tell him. Then I post up the picture I have chosen of Jonathan. A little boy aged ten, wearing the sweater his grandmother knitted him for Christmas. He looks as pleased as punch, chest out, showing off the Ninja Turtle she'd stitched into the front. And I add the words:

Jonathan Brigstocke
26 June 1974 — 14 August 1993
A perfect stranger who died saving your life

It will take him a while to get his head around Jonathan's death — his young friend who never was — to get his head around everything I have posted up for him. The book will help him; I have given him page numbers so this time there'll be no chance of him failing to recognize her or himself. Nancy must have her say too. Perhaps he can come up with some answers to her questions.

Why didn't she help her child? How could a mother turn her back on her child and leave him alone in the sea? A child who couldn't swim. No armbands, no rubber ring. How could any mother in their right mind do that? Was she out of her mind?

She would have watched her child drown — she said that she'd wished Jonathan hadn't done it. Those were her actual words. Was her passion for Jonathan greater than her love for her child? Little Nick. Is he such a devil of a child that even his own mother didn't think him worth saving?

244

Up it all goes, the extract from Nancy's notebook, my last post. I feel as if I have stuffed a kitten into a sack and dropped it in the canal. I can hear it mewing, but there's nothing I can do to save it now. Sink or swim: it is up to him.

44

Summer 2013

Somebody grabs his arm and pulls him to the door. Finish up now, finish up. Somebody pushes him out on to the street, bolts the door, locks him out. He starts to walk but trips. Is pushed? No, trips. Better sit down. Sit it out. And he sits on the ground, leaning against the wall. He's still holding the book. Flicks to the end. Wants to read his mother's death. He laughs. Pure fucking fantasy. Good luck to them, trying to get her under a train. Go back, go back, go back further. Find the sex. Mum sucking the nineteen-year-old's cock. How fucking weird is that? Shit. It's working on him too, can't have that. He stands up, drops the book on the ground and pisses on it. Greasy, cold beads of sweat ooze from his pores as he urinates; his piss spits back at him. He presses his hands against the wall, steadying himself, and kicks the book as hard as he can; watches it scuttle along the pavement. He slides down the wall, sits. Shuts his eyes. No good: it's in there. It's in his head and he can't get it out. He digs his fingers into his scalp, wanting to prise the images out of his brain, but he can see them so clearly.

Mummy's love. Lost at sea. She watched him die. Poor old Mummy. A flip of a coin, and Nick won the toss. Saved when he should've been lost. Someone should help her; give her a hand throwing herself under a train. He closes his eyes and a red-and-yellow dinghy bobs by: a little speck in the distance; a little speck bouncing off the edge of the world.

Numbers swim in front of him. A two or a seven . . . no, two. Two twos: twenty-two. Then nothing. A blank house. Boards instead of windows. There is a bell and his fingers scrabble for it, his ear presses the door. He's hot, cold, nauseous. He can't remember getting here, yet here he is. This is where he wants to be. Hasn't been for a while, has resisted the urge. It's where he needs to be. A buzz, a distant buzz. The door opens and he falls through. Aah, the familiar smell of dog shit. He's sick into his hands — tries to catch it. He's tried that trick before — it never works, bits escape. His cupped hands overfloweth, and no one cares. Clean yourself up, mate. He is inside, makes it up the stairs. Just needs to close his eyes for a minute, he'll be all right. He curls up on the floor, a giant foetus, and listens to their low murmur. He doesn't need to know what they're saying, all he wants is to hear the sound. It's enough to know he is in their midst — a fellow traveller.

He imagines a different story for his mother: a tragic heroine who lost her only child in an accident at sea. She would have made a full recovery from that loss; she would have played that part well — it would have suited her better than being the mother of a low-key, low-energy, under-achieving worthless shit.

He rolls on to his back and opens his eyes, staring at the ceiling. A face peers down at him and smiles. 'You all right?' He smiles up at them. He feels better. A bit better. Makes it to the bathroom. Washes the sick off his hands, washes his face, swills his mouth with water, spits. His phone vibrates in his pocket. Dad. Fuck off. But he calls his mum. Is that his voice? Is he leaving a message? Something comes out.

'You OK?' A voice from outside the door.

'Yeah,' he croaks, staring at his lips moving in the mirror. He tears himself away and opens the door. A girl is standing there. A pretty girl.

'You all right?' She looks over his shoulder into the bathroom. 'Who's in there with you?'

He stands to one side and she looks in.

'Who were you talking to?'

'No one.'

'You were crying.'

'I was being sick.' He grabs her hand, wanting her to come with him, but she pulls away. He stumbles on into the main room and sits down on the sofa. It stinks, someone's pissed on it and springs dig into his spine. But he doesn't want to move. He never wants to leave this place. This is where he can be his best self.

45

Summer 1993

She remembers the questions from the Spanish police: did she know him? Had she ever met him before? She'd never seen him before that day, she'd said, and they'd accepted that and allowed her and Nicholas to catch their flight home the following day. The police had his bag; they knew where he'd been staying; they would inform the British authorities; they would contact the young man's family. A tragic accident. She was free to go home. There were no more questions.

That evening she packed their suitcase. The next morning she and Nicholas took a taxi to the airport and caught their flight home. An easy flight, she had told Robert when he'd come home that evening. She'd brought back a bottle of duty-free whisky and they drank a couple of glasses before going up to bed. She remembers closing the bathroom door and looking at the bite on her neck in the mirror: patting more make-up on to cover it up and then turning off the light when she got into bed. And he had reached for her, kissing her mouth, moving down and kissing her stomach. He was so gentle. They had made love, even though she hadn't really wanted to. But she felt she needed to, that it was a necessary act to help erase what had happened.

He had stroked her body; he had missed her, he said. He had been thoughtful, gentle. And she concealed for weeks, until it faded, the tell-tale mark on her neck. And the bruise on her thigh was already a yellowy green, easily missed. She could keep her secret, burying it in her head; gradually, over the years, she succeeded in chewing on it like a piece of gristle until she could finally swallow it down without choking.

There had been moments when she'd nearly told Robert, but she thought it would have been selfish. If Jonathan hadn't died, things would have been different. If he had swum to shore with Nicholas in tow, everything would have been different. It was her secret. It belonged to her. She had chosen not to share it.

Catherine's phone buzzes on the bedside table. She grabs it, not wanting to wake her mother who has just gone back to sleep after another trip to the loo. It is four a.m. Her heart thumps. It is Nicholas. She gets out of bed and rushes from her mother's room, gently closing the door behind her, trying not to wake her.

'Hello? Nick?' She isn't quick enough. His call has gone to voicemail. She hopes he'll leave a message. He does. She listens to it and it is as if she has been swept back twenty years. The same rush of adrenalin which begins in the groin, so fierce it actually hurts. A mother's basic instinct, when her child is running too close to the edge. She feels it now as she listens to Nick's message: no words, just choking sobs, heaving down the phone to her.

She is freezing as she dials his number, over

250

and over. All she hears is another Nick, telling her to leave a message. A bird is singing outside, but it's not dawn and it sounds wrong. Like her, it's been squeezed out of its nest too soon. She grabs her coat and bag and leaves the flat. She has no car, so runs to the local mini-cab company and waits. Five minutes, that's all, for a sleepy man to pull up and drive her to her home. A twenty-minute journey at this time of day, with no traffic. She pays him and runs to the front door and lets herself in.

46

Summer 2013

How could Nancy possibly have known what went on between Jonathan and the whore? How could she describe their intimacy in such detail? She had the photographs with their gruesome detail and she used her imagination: it's what writers do. She played around with some of the facts — I doubt very much whether Jonathan would have been interested in pursuing Orwell, Bowles or Kerouac. Wishful thinking? Artistic licence. Of course she changed names. To protect the innocent? Perhaps I should have changed them back again. It was a work of fiction, but still, I like to believe that it released the truth from its ballast: it allowed it to float up to the surface. It's the substance of a story that is important, after all.

Jonathan had travelled out to Europe with his girlfriend, a fact Nancy left intact, though she changed the reason for Sasha's early return. Her father hadn't been taken ill, that's not why she came home. She and Jonathan had had a row and Sasha had stormed home. That's a fact. But it's not an important one. What is important is that Jonathan continued his travels alone. He was a nineteen-year-old boy, alone in a foreign country. He was vulnerable. I remember how

252

Nancy worried about him being on his own. I didn't. I suspected he'd have a much better time without his girlfriend. I thought he might meet someone more fun.

When we'd returned from Spain after identifying Jonathan's body, Sasha was the first person Nancy called. She didn't want her to hear about his death from anyone else. It was Sasha's mother who answered the phone. She said that Sasha was out, but that she would tell her what had happened. We never knew whether she did or not, because we never heard from Sasha again. Nancy always sent her cards on her birthday and at Christmas, but we never heard back from her. I was furious and upset about it, but Nancy was more generous. She said she understood. Sasha was young, it was too much to expect of her, and certainly her mother would not have encouraged her to stay in touch. Relations with Sasha's mother had never been easy.

When Sasha had returned home from Europe, I remember Nancy taking a call from her mother. Though I only heard Nancy's end of the conversation, I was struck by her patience as she listened to the woman's rant. She stayed calm, repeating over and over that it was up to the two young people to sort out their differences, it was not right for parents to interfere. She managed to end the call with civility, but when she put down the receiver I could see she was white with anger. Yet she had not lost her temper, and I admired her for that. She maintains that same even tone in her notebooks. They whisper, they don't rant.

She wishes for things, she doesn't demand them.

I wish her child knew that he owed his life to my son. I wish he knew that, if it wasn't for Jonathan, he wouldn't be here.

47

Summer 2013

Catherine puts her key in the door and turns it, almost expecting it to no longer fit, but it does. She lets herself in and runs straight up to the spare room. She takes in the empty bed, the mess on the floor, the state of abandonment. Then she opens the door to her bedroom and stands over Robert. He is fast asleep. On the bedside table is a packet of sleeping pills, and next to them, a much-handled copy of *The Perfect Stranger*. Once this would have shocked her, but now it sickens her that he is keeping it next to the bed. That he has brought it back into their bedroom. She wonders where the photographs are. Does he keep those in his bedside drawer or has he destroyed them?

'Robert, wake up.' His sleep is so deep he hasn't heard her run up the stairs, doesn't sense her presence looming over him, doesn't hear her voice in his ear. She reaches down and shakes him. 'Wake up.'

He groans and turns away. His eyes stay shut.

'Robert!' she shouts, angry now. 'Wake up!' She picks up his phone and checks for calls from Nick, but there are none, only missed calls from her. How dare he sleep? She grabs the glass of water next to the bed and pours it over his head.

Justified, needed, excusable. He splutters and shrivels. He looks pathetic. Her anger and dislike take her by surprise.

'Robert, for fuck's sake — wake up. Where is Nick?'

When at last he opens his eyes he is confused, useless.

'What are you — ?'

'Where is Nick?'

Still he looks blank, trying to drag himself back from sleep. She waves the book in his face.

'Have you told him?'

He slides to the other side of the bed, then gets out and looks at her. He is naked and she turns away.

'Have you told him?' she yells.

He walks to the bathroom, returning in ankle-length towelling. He is calm, not at all worried.

'I haven't told him anything,' he says. 'But I'm going to — '

'Well it's a bit late for that. The father has beaten you to it. Nick called me at four this morning and now I can't get hold of him. He won't pick up, hasn't answered any of my calls. He left me a message' — she shakes her phone at him — 'he was in a terrible state.' And she starts to cry. 'He knows. Where is he? We need to find him.'

'I don't know where he is. Probably with a friend.' He refuses to join in her panic. 'He went off to work this morning — he didn't come home for supper, so what? He's twenty-five.' He is defensive. 'I'm sure he's fine . . . What do you mean, he was in a state?'

'He was crying — he didn't say anything. All I

could hear were his sobs.'

Pain washes across Robert's face: 'Oh Jesus, I wish to God I'd told him. He should never have had to hear it from someone else.' He pushes past her to get downstairs.

'I've never heard him like this, Robert . . . I'm scared.'

He turns on her. 'Well, what did you expect?' He looks her up and down until it seems he can no longer bear to look at her. 'I should have been the one to tell him . . . and now he's had to hear it from a stranger. Can you imagine how shocked he must be?' he says.

'That crazy fucking bastard has got to him — '

'What?' he interrupts. 'You mean the father of the boy who drowned saving Nick's life? The father of the young man you fucked and then denied you'd ever met? After he had died saving our child? You mean *that* crazy fucking bastard? You are unbelievable.' God how he hates her. He is consumed by it. *The young man she fucked.* He should be worrying about Nick, not attacking her. She despises him for not being able to focus on their son, not working with her to find him.

'Don't you get it? Our son is in danger. That man has got to him.' She holds out her phone and plays Nick's message. It is heartbreaking. Tears come to Robert's eyes.

'This is your fault. You have done this!' He spits the words at her and she turns away, but he carries on. 'I don't recognize you any more. What did you expect?' He pulls her round so she is facing him.

'Are you surprised he's upset? The lies, all the

257

lies over the years. It was inevitable he would find out in the end — I just wish it had been me who had told him. You didn't care about him, did you? You were so caught up with your lover that you left our child alone in the sea when he couldn't swim. What is he supposed to make of that? He was a kid — you were the adult. You were his mother. You were the one who should have saved him, but you've never put him first, have you? It's always about you!'

She pulls away from him, turning her back, refusing to defend herself. She needs to concentrate on Nick. She can feel Robert's eyes on her, despising her. She had never expected it to come to this, but she can't think of that and instead goes through her phone, searching for the number of the local hospital. She calls it, waits for an answer.

'Hello, I'm trying to track down my son — I'm worried something may have happened to him . . . he called me very upset . . . he's twenty-five . . . yes, but he has a history of drug problems and he was in a terrible state on the phone . . . he may have done something to himself . . . Nicholas Ravenscroft . . . ' She can tell they're not interested. A twenty-five-year-old man with a mum phoning to check where he is. It sounds absurd.

She runs upstairs to the spare room. He could be anywhere — any hospital in London — on any train out of London — on any railway line . . . She calls the police, but they brush her off. Her son is twenty-five. She heard from him two hours ago. Did he say he was going to harm himself? No, she has to admit that he didn't.

258

She starts searching through his things. His laptop reveals nothing. She finds his wash-bag with tell-tale signs of his drug-taking. Please, no. She runs to the top of the stairs and screams down:

'Did you know he was taking drugs again? Did you?'

Robert comes to the bottom of the stairs and screams up at her: 'Don't start trying to tell me how to parent our son!' But she can see she has got to him.

She goes back into the spare room, gets down on her hands and knees and crawls through Nick's mess, sifting through it for God knows what. She finds a letter from John Lewis. A letter of dismissal, dated two weeks ago. She snatches it up in triumph and rushes down the stairs with it.

'He's lost his job. So where's he been every day when you thought he was at work?'

Robert can't answer that. Now he is as shocked and frightened as Catherine and she feels ashamed. How could she have felt triumphant? She looks down at him and says in quiet desperation, 'Don't you have any idea who he might be with? Hasn't he mentioned anyone?'

Robert doesn't answer. He doesn't know. Neither of them do. What a state of parenthood, she thinks. Neither of them knowing who to call — neither of them knowing who their son might be with. Does he have friends? There are none left from his teenage years, she is pretty sure of that.

'He mentioned a girlfriend, but I've never met

her, I don't know her name. I'm not sure whether she even exists . . . ' He tries Nick's number but it goes straight to voicemail: 'Hi, mate. Give us a call when you wake up. Let me know you're OK . . . Love you . . . '

Then Catherine's phone rings; she doesn't recognize the number. Her fingers shake as she presses *Answer*.

48

Summer 2013

It's time to begin tidying up — to wipe our fingerprints away. I have closed down Jonathan's Facebook page. Nancy had wanted me to leave it up, but I felt it best to take it down. She is feeling frustrated, I can tell. She doubts that my softly, softly approach, as she calls it, will achieve the outcome she desires. I ask her to be patient. Look, I say. Look at little Nick's Facebook page. He hasn't touched it. That means something. There has been nothing new on his page for twenty-four hours. That is unusual for him. He can't keep his mitts off his page. Status. What a very grand word. His status hasn't changed. How good that must make these young people feel. To have status. Jonathan never had any doubt about his — he didn't need Facebook to endorse him. He never had to doubt his importance in his mother's life.

I can say it now. I was sometimes jealous of Nancy's devotion to Jonathan. Our relationship changed after he was born, of course it did. Not at first. At first it was us and our new baby, but as he grew, as he became more defined, I felt at times that it became me and them. They had a special bond and there were occasions when I found myself competing with him for her

261

attention. I must have seemed needy to her, weak. Naturally Jonathan needed her more, and it was unfair of me to ever try and pull her away from him. The only times we ever rowed were over Jonathan: over how best to manage him. We didn't row often; less and less, in fact, the older he became. I started to back away from decisions about him. Nancy was unwavering in her belief that what he needed was unconditional love and support. That's what every child needs, she said, and it was hard to disagree with that.

Oh, Nancy, how brave our son was. When I heard how he had died, saving a child, I was surprised. How shameful is that? I didn't know he had it in him to save another life. And you suspected me of that, didn't you? Although you never accused me of doubting his courage, you knew that I would have had a problem matching his death with his life. I am sorry it has been left until after your death for me to try and make amends. When I discovered that the little boy he saved was his lover's son, it made more sense to me. He wanted to please her; he wanted to show her how brave he was. He was in love.

I leave the computer open on Nicholas Ravenscroft's Facebook page and go into the garden. I have already started building the bonfire. It was something Jonathan and I used to do together when he was a boy. He loved Bonfire Night, staying up in the dark, throwing things on to the fire, writing his name with a sparkler. It is dark now and I flick through a notebook, not reading it, watching Nancy's handwriting dance before me, and then I place it on the pile of wood, along with the others. I light a taper and hold it against the firelighter; watch it catch with a satisfying flicker and lick. The leather smells and curls as it burns, darkens and smoulders, the paper hungry to swallow the flames.

When I go inside I see Nancy. She is sitting in front of the laptop and she turns to me and smiles and I think it's because the smell of the bonfire has conjured up happy memories of Jonathan and I together on Bonfire Night, but I am wrong. There is a message from the father on Nicholas's Facebook page.

49

Summer 2013

Nicholas was left outside St George's Hospital in South London. A body dumped in the entrance-way. The doctor told Catherine and Robert their son had had a stroke. Cocaine, probably injected. Too early to say how much damage had been done. They'd know more over the next twenty-four hours. Catherine and Robert stood side by side at their son's bed. Opposite them, on the other side, were the machines that were keeping him alive: helping him breathe; checking his heart; vital liquids dripping into him, trying to restore the balance. The Intensive Care Unit was quiet, almost silent. Rows of bodies on beds, wired-up eyes closed, frozen, waiting to be reborn. Or not.

Catherine stares at her boy, whom she failed to protect. The doctor was wrong. It has been more than twenty-four hours, two days in fact, and they still don't know how much damage Nicholas has done to himself. She and Robert are no longer able to stand next to each other, so they take it in turns to sit with their son. Robert won't allow Catherine to be there at the same time as him and so she has to wait for him to leave before taking up her position. She resents the time Robert is there, denying her those hours she could be with her son, but she doesn't fight

264

him. In a way she is relieved not to see him. She has no room to think about him, all she wants is to be with Nicholas. She is with him now and every moment is precious.

She finds herself wondering if her son has always been vulnerable to an early death. He has been saved once already, but she is frightened that this time they will not be so lucky. When she looks at him, helpless like a premature baby whose system is not able to function independently, it is as if she is newly born too. Her mind and body are raw. Strangely, it feels good: good to feel the outside world touch her at last. She is able to look at her son and really see him as she had seen him when he was first theirs: those first few years before his presence became tangled up with the mess and filth that she deposited on him. Yes, she must accept her part in how they came to be where they are now. She cannot push it away, it must be thought about. And when — if — Nicholas is strong enough to bear it, she will tell him what she should have told him years before. She touches his cheek, gets down on her knees and kisses his forehead, resting her head on the side of his bed.

Catherine has told her mother that Nicholas is in hospital and her mother was distressed at first, but immediately neatened up the information, tucked in its corners and reassured Catherine that people rarely die from measles these days. Better that he has it as a child. She is almost envious of the way her mother's mind works. It is deteriorating and yet with it comes a determination to put a positive spin on nasty intruders.

Her mother seems content: she is creating, for the time being at least, a much nicer world for herself.

'Why don't you go and get a cup of tea, something to eat? I'll sit with him for a bit.' A nurse puts a hand on her shoulder. Her kindness brings tears to Catherine's eyes. She is grateful, but she cannot leave Nicholas.

'I'm fine, really.'

'Go on. I'll be here. You look exhausted. You should have something to eat. Get some air.'

And she is persuaded, getting up from the floor. There is a chair she could have sat on, but it wouldn't have allowed her to rest her head so close to her son's. She needs to be as close to him as she can get.

She leaves the ICU and walks towards the hospital entrance, passing the darkened café, bookshop, newsagent's. She buys a coffee and some chocolate from a vending machine and takes them outside.

It's four in the morning but there are a few people outside smoking. One patient, a couple of visitors like her. She sits on a bench, the cold seeping through her jeans. This is where Nicholas was dumped, washed up on the doorstep of the hospital. They still don't know who dropped him there: strangers who cared only enough to get him to hospital.

She can't face the chocolate and puts it in her pocket, taking out her cigarettes instead. One with her coffee. A few minutes to smoke it. She looks at her phone. There's a text from Kim. It sits among a couple from friends, female friends who've been in touch since they heard that Nick was in hospital. Catherine had telephoned work and told them, letting them know she was taking extended leave. And she had called one friend, asking her to pass on the news, but she didn't want to see anyone. They send messages now and again, telling her they are thinking of her, letting her know they are there if she wants to talk. She doesn't. She wants to keep them all at a distance. She reads Kim's text: *I'm so sorry. Let me know if there's anything I can do. Thinking of you all. Kx.* Catherine stubs out her cigarette, and sips her coffee. It tastes of plastic and is of no comfort or sustenance. Kim's message gives her some though. There is no blame in it. She has read the book, but it doesn't matter any more. Whatever happens, that part at least is over. If Nick survives, and she believes he will, there will be no secrets. He will know everything. And Robert? She pushes him to the back of her mind.

She gets up and drops her cup into the bin, returning to the inside world. The low throb and buzz of the heat, the light, the monitors, the machinery that keeps this place, and those within it, ticking over. As she walks towards the ICU she studies the pattern on the glossy linoleum floor. Even the black scratches have been buffed and she imagines someone sitting on yet another machine, whizzing up and down the corridors. She thinks she has seen this image, but can't remember whether it was real or on the television.

She presses the buzzer and the nurse looks up,

267

sees her, and lets her in.

'Your father's here,' she whispers, smiling. Catherine's tired eyes follow the nurse's. She looks at the skinny figure hunched over Nicholas's bed. Her father has been dead for ten years. She doesn't scream: she yells, running at him. She grabs him, pulling him away, digging her fingers into his bony shoulders. He is so light. She turns him round to face her and pushes him as hard as she can until he falls, banging against a chair, landing on the floor where he stays and looks up at her. But then she is grabbed from behind and held. The nurse who had been so concerned before for Catherine is now concerned only for the old man lying in front of her. She crouches over him, talking to him, checking he is able to stand. She helps him to his feet as Catherine watches, a second nurse restraining her. This isn't right. She struggles against her.

'He shouldn't be in here! Get him out of here!' she shouts. 'He is not my father. You shouldn't have let him in. Get him out. Get him out of here!' Her hysteria makes the nurse tighten her grip.

'If you don't calm down, I'll call security.'

'It's OK, I'll go. I'm so sorry . . . ' The old man trembles, his voice shaking as he says: 'I only wanted to see how Nicholas was. I'm so sorry.' He is in control. Catherine is not. He has a small cut on his head, but he doesn't want a fuss. She watches him being helped to the door, the nurse compelled to support this frail, injured old man. Catherine hears him playing a part, stuttering out more apologies. All he wanted was to see Nicholas. The doors hiss shut behind him and Catherine cowers down on her knees, her head resting on Nicholas's bed.

She is being watched now. The second nurse stays near by. Catherine cannot be trusted. She begins to cry, tries to explain through her tears:

'She shouldn't have let him in. He mustn't be allowed in — he wants to hurt my son — '

'You're upsetting the other visitors. We can talk about this outside. I can call someone for you to talk to . . . '

Catherine shakes her head.

'No, no.' She doesn't want to leave. She can't leave Nick alone in here. It isn't safe. 'I'm sorry,' she says. 'But it can only be Robert or me; no one else can come in.' The nurse walks away.

* * *

Robert arrives earlier than usual and Catherine rushes over to him in relief.

'He was here. The father. He was trying to get to Nicholas. He was going to hurt him.'

He shakes her off. 'The hospital called me. I know what happened. I told him he could come. I invited him. He has every right to see Nick — '

'You asked him to come? Are you mad?'

'No, I'm not mad.'

'Why on earth would you do that?'

He looks at her as if he can't believe her question.

'He knows what it's like to lose a son.'

'Have you met him?' Her voice rises, while his stays quiet.

'No, not yet. If I'd known what his son had done for ours, I'd have been in touch with him and his wife years ago. I would have thanked them. It's too late for me to thank Jonathan's mother, but I can at least try and make it up to his father.'

It is the first time she has heard him say Jonathan's name.

'How could you, Robert? How could you ask him here?' He ignores her question and walks past her to Nicholas's bedside. She follows him, hissing in his ear. 'Why do you think he chose four in the morning? Don't you see that he wanted to come when he thought no one would be around?' He turns and grabs her, his fingers digging into the tops of her arms.

'I saw him leaning over Nicholas. He was — ' she starts to protest.

'He was what? The nurse told me exactly what happened. She told me what you did . . . ' He is pushing her towards the door.

'Please, Mr Ravenscroft . . . ' A nurse marches up. 'We can't have this in here . . . '

'I'm sorry, I'm so sorry,' Robert says. 'My wife is leaving now.' He turns his back on Catherine and takes up his place at Nicholas's bedside.

50

Summer 2013

A little nudge, that's all it would have taken. I had to clean myself up, make myself look presentable. I spent longer in front of the mirror this morning than usual. I wanted to look as good as it is possible to do at my age. I am missing a few teeth, but luckily they're not at the front and if I manage my smile carefully the gaps are not too noticeable. I practised smiling in front of the mirror. My eyes were a problem though. They didn't catch my smile and the whites were the colour of spit with a trace of tobacco. I opened the bathroom cabinet and found a bottle of eye drops. Probably not a sensible thing to do, as they were long out of date, but I administered them anyway. It stung, and for a moment I feared I'd done myself serious damage, but after frantic blinking they recovered and looked slightly more wholesome than they had before.

Dressing was altogether more straightforward. I have one decent jacket, and a shirt I've always been fond of. Not too jazzy. Soft cotton, white with a faint check in it. Neither fits as well as they used to, but with Nancy's cardigan underneath to fill me out, it worked I think. I haven't completely lost it, you know. I do have

271

some sense of how I need to appear to the outside world. It's all very well, wearing comfortable old clothes at home when only your loved one can see you, but a degree of effort must be made for strangers.

If the father had been there, I'm sure things would have gone to plan. He would have welcomed me, even fetched me tea. An elderly man, parched, exhausted by the two hours it has taken me to get to the hospital. Public transport . . .

' . . . yes, it's a long way, but I had to see Nicholas. I know it's what my wife would have wanted. She was wonderful with young people, you know . . . she would have loved the chance to get to know Nicholas . . . it would have meant a lot to her . . . No, no, of course, I understand. I understand. It's not your fault. Oh, thank you, that is thoughtful. Yes, a cup of tea would be very nice.' And I would have watched him leave and then I would have flicked a switch, pulled out a tube, and left. All over. Finished. The boy wouldn't have known anything about it. Quite a nice way to go, really. He wouldn't have felt a thing. Quicker than drowning. And he's halfway there already — probably more than halfway. Took himself there; I didn't touch him. I didn't lay a finger on him. And the consequences? What do I care for the consequences? I don't. I couldn't care less. But that's not what happened.

When I looked into the ward and saw the rows of beds I worried that I wouldn't find him, but a nurse kindly pointed him out. And smiled. I smelled right. I looked unthreatening. All I had to say was 'Nicholas Ravenscroft' in a whisper, and the poor, tired nurse assumed I was a grandparent. No need to correct her. But then in flew the mother. The Fury. Stupid of me. I had counted on her being as negligent with her son now as she was when he was a child. I thought she would have been safely tucked up in her bed at that time of night.

There was fear in her eyes when she looked down at me. I recognized it straight away because I've seen it before, although I'm not used to seeing it in an adult. I've never been the type of man who strikes fear in those his own size. Yes, she looked frightened, although not for herself. She was frightened for her son, and that surprised me because it was not what I was expecting. I expected anger, fury and righteousness, not that instinctive protection for her child. But then I became distracted by the nurse touching me. It's been such a long time since a woman has shown me concern. I liked feeling her hands on me, taking care not to hurt me, being careful with my pain. And her voice was gentle too. It was real, her concern for me, and so was my response. I was grateful for her kindness.

Now it has become more complicated. I thought I'd be able to slip in and out, job done; instead I will have to pay another visit. What is the alternative? To rely on fate to finish him off? It is possible that he will slip away all by himself with no need for intervention. A stroke, the nurse said. He's had a stroke. He may survive, but he may be 'severely impaired'. Will that do,

Nancy? No? Severely impaired not enough? I am tired and I ache from the fall and the journey home.

The phone rings. Nancy answers. A man's voice leaves a message, but I interrupt.

'Hello?'

'Hello, Mr Brigstocke, it's Robert Ravenscroft here.'

I wait. Why should I help him?

'I hope you don't mind me calling. I wanted to say how sorry I am about what happened. About my wife. I'm so, so sorry.'

'It's not your fault, Mr Ravenscroft — '

'Robert, please call me Robert.'

'She was shocked, I suppose, to see me there. You didn't tell her you had invited me?'

He doesn't answer. I wait again.

'We don't really speak. It's stupid, I know, with Nicholas so ill, but . . . I'm finding it hard to understand what she did . . . why she didn't tell me . . . '

'I'm sure it is difficult for you.'

'Sorry, I didn't mean to sound self-pitying. I'm phoning to apologize for her and to say I hope you will come again. I am sure Nicholas would want you there. Perhaps we could meet. I can understand if you feel nervous about that, but . . . '

'Yes, perhaps we can,' I say. 'But I'm afraid I must go now. I'm very tired and a bit shaken, to be honest. I was on my way up to bed when you rang . . . '

'Yes, of course. I'm so sorry again. I just wanted to make sure you got home safely.'

'Quite safely, thank you, Robert.' And I hang up.

I rather regret giving him my number. I can see he might become a nuisance. I hold on to the banister, dragging myself up the stairs. The nurse said the base of my spine may be bruised, but I suppose it could have been worse, I could have broken something. On second thoughts, perhaps that would have been useful. I would have had to stay in hospital, planted on a ward, perhaps just down the corridor from the boy. Never mind, I have an invitation from the father himself. We will stand together over his gravely ill son's bed.

I reach for the glass of water on the bedside table. It is half empty, but there is enough for me to take the pills. Two for pain, two for sleep. A little something for anxiety. The water tastes stale, it's been there for a while. Dusty and stale. Sleep will come easily, I can feel it on its way, I only hope it won't be so deep that I miss the phone if the husband calls. He has promised to let me know of any change in Nicholas's condition. Nancy will answer though. He will hear her touchingly, hesitant voice: *We are not at home at the moment. Please leave us a message so that we may call you back.* I drift off for a while, but then I wake too soon and it is not Nancy's voice that has woken me, I am sure of that.

The house is silent, yet something has pulled me back to consciousness because I am still thick with sleep. I had been dreaming that I'd fallen through a window, crashed through a huge pane of glass. The glass had gone before me and was waiting, hovering above the ground, its edges pointing upwards, ready to slice me like wafer-thin ham. That is what woke me. The sound of breaking glass. Someone is downstairs.

And then I hear the door close. It is impossible to shut our front door silently: the catch is positioned a little off-kilter so it always clicks when opening or closing. Has someone arrived or have they left? I imagine gloved hands. I imagine the police, but this is silly. A twinge of guilt, perhaps. Silly, though. The police would knock, they would have no need to break in. I heard the front door, but now nothing. I pull on my trousers and take the cardigan from the back of the chair. I creak, the floorboards creak, the stairs creak. There is no hiding my descent and I don't try to. I am fearless, no longer a coward.

I stand at the bottom of the stairs and look around. Light is shooting through the bottom of the curtains. The pane of glass in the front door has been smashed. I look around the room, half waiting for something to hit me on the back of the head. Nothing happens. And the room is empty. I walk through to the kitchen, slowly, still stiff and sore. The house is empty. Then I see that I am mistaken. The house is empty but I am not alone. She is standing in our garden, looking at the bonfire which still smoulders. I walk to the back door and she turns and looks at me. This is the moment I have been waiting for. Here she is. She is destroyed. Nicholas is dead? What will she do? Will she try and kill me? I wait. Neither of us says a word. Then she walks towards me and I stand aside, letting her come back into the

276

house. She sits down at the kitchen table and puts her head in her hands. She rubs at her eyes so hard I fear they will pop from her head. When she looks up they are red and dry. There are no tears. Red-rimmed, but not wet. I wait for her to speak.

'Sit down.'

So I do. Why not?

And then she spits at me. Covers me with it. It seems as if she cannot stop. It keeps coming until I am awash with thick, clogging mucus which pours out of her, and settles on me. I am an insect again, trapped by the spittle of my predator who is planning to eat me alive. I am being eaten alive.

51

Summer 2013

Catherine has blood on her hands. Mixed with her sweat, the inside of both her palms are a filmy red. But it is her blood, from a cut on the heel of her right hand where she broke the glass and reached through to open his front door. She sits in her car outside Stephen Brigstocke's house and wipes it off on to her jeans.

She hadn't bothered to knock. She simply broke in and closed the door behind her. The curtains were drawn and in the dim light it took her a few moments to recognize that she was walking through the wasteland of a life. Dirty cups, plates, empty tins of beans still with the fork in them littered the table. The floor was strewn with bits of paper; an old Welsh dresser recoiling in humiliation: its drawers hanging out, its doors flung open. Her eyes gravitated to the only tranquil spot in the room: a desk, neat and tidy, with a silver-framed photograph of a young couple from the sixties and a laptop: open, but sleeping. She woke it up with a stab of her finger and then flinched as Nicholas's Facebook page blinked back at her. There is a message on it from Robert giving an update on Nicholas's condition.

She walked on through the filth and stink of the kitchen to the window at the back of the house.

278

She knew he must have heard her; knew he was probably upstairs, but she was in no hurry. She looked out at an apple tree laden with fruit; a garden neglected, yet beautiful still. Wildflowers tickled through the unmown grass and mature shrubs stood proud against the weeds that threatened to strangle them. A bonfire smouldered and she went outside, peering down at the remains of the things he had tried to destroy.

She felt him before she saw him: a shrunken figure, hugging a woman's cardigan around his scrawny, bare torso, standing at the open back door. He didn't protest, barely blinked, when it poured out of her, but she saw him wilt and shrivel under her words.

Catherine remembers more than she told him. Unspoken words swam around her head, but she held them there, not wanting them to clutter up her story. Get to the heart of it. And she had. When she finished he was silent, looking down into his lap, his hands gripping the edge of his stool.

'I'm sorry.' The words surprised her. They came from her, not him. She hadn't planned on saying them, they just came out. She left them there, got up and walked out.

And now she allows herself to cry. Years and years of tears pour out of her.

Summer 1993

When Jonathan smiled at Catherine sitting on that bar stool, after her phone call with Robert, she smiled back. It was instinctive, yet it embarrassed her and she ignored his gesture inviting her to join him and hurried instead to the lift up to her room. She locked the door and moved over to the bed, checking on Nicholas. He was fast asleep, spread-eagled in her bed. She opened the door into the adjoining room and carried him through to his own bed. Then she had a shower before going to bed herself. Nothing had happened that night. Nothing.

The following day she and Nicholas went to the beach. It was early, Nicholas had been up since seven, so they were there by about eight thirty. She remembers feeling lonely, but she remembers too the brilliance of the sun, not too hot, and the miles of sandy beach. A beach all to themselves, she remembers telling Nick. There were endless trips to the sea and back with buckets of water. They were building a town, or at least Catherine was. Nick hadn't quite got the hang of it, and thought the buckets of sand she emptied out for the shops and the houses were there to be knocked down. She remembers her patience, and also the twinge of guilt she had at being conscious of her patience. It hadn't come naturally. She went with it though, went with him. And as he flattened down the buildings, she started on the roads, dragging a spade through the sand, creating winding streets through the heaps of sand he trashed.

After a couple of hours other people started arriving and by lunchtime the beach was full. By lunchtime too, Nicholas was hot and tired. They went to a café for lunch, leaving their towels but nothing valuable behind. They were hand in hand, and Catherine remembers being happy. She remembers the pleasure of Nick's pudgy little hand in hers and giving it a squeeze, and him squeezing back. They were leaving the day after tomorrow and for the first time she found she had the heart to make the most of the time they had left in the sun.

Nick ate his lunch without a fuss and after, she bought them ice creams. She had strawberry, he vanilla, and they shared them as they walked back to the beach, each taking a lick of the other's. She remembers the blob of strawberry ice cream on the end of Nick's nose where he lunged for hers at the same time as she held it out to him. He giggled, enjoying the cold on his face and then daubed his cheeks and chin with vanilla. He tried to stretch his tongue round to lick his nose and chin, but it didn't reach and Catherine used the edge of her beach dress to clean him up and stop the wasps homing in on his sweetness.

When they got to their towels, they flopped down, hot from the walk. She remembers taking off her sundress and sitting with her legs apart, and Nick snuggling up between them and leaning against her bare stomach as she read to him. His body became heavier, and his head lolled against her arm. He had fallen asleep, and she carefully lifted him from between her legs and lay him on his side, draping her sundress over him to protect him from the sun. He slept for over an hour and she read her book, happy. Really happy. She fell asleep herself for a bit, curling around him, spooning her son.

When Nick woke, she woke. When she sat up, she saw Jonathan. There were people between them. He was closer to the sea than she and Nick, but he had a clear view of them. He was lying on his stomach facing in their direction. She wondered how long he'd been there. She pretended she hadn't seen him and turned her attention to Nick, getting a drink out of the bag. He must have taken some photographs of them then. She doesn't remember him doing it, but she has seen the photographs. The snap of her and Nick sitting on their towel and her handing Nick his drink. The plastic bottle was warm and the drink must have tasted disgusting, but Nick didn't complain. She remembers feeling self-conscious about her near-nakedness. She was exposing no more flesh than anyone else on the beach, and yet she felt exposed and moved her legs closer together and pulled up the straps of her bikini top when they slipped from her shoulders.

By about three, Catherine and Nick left the beach and returned to the hotel. She can't remember what they did in the next couple of hours there, but the time passed peacefully. Then they took a taxi into the town. Catherine would have preferred to walk, but it was too far for Nick, so the hotel ordered them a taxi. They ate pizza in a café, and afterwards they walked hand in hand around the small streets until they came to a square and she remembers Nick's squeak of excitement when he saw the carousel. It was as if it had appeared straight out of the pages of a children's book. He wanted to go on his own horse and for Catherine to sit on the one behind. She remembers putting her hands over his, making sure he held on to the pole thrust through his horse, and then she mounted her own, right behind him, just as he'd asked. She felt queasy as the horse went up and down, round and round, and she worried every time Nick turned round to look at her that he might let go, but he didn't, and he loved it. He had a wonderful time.

After the carousel was the helter-skelter. Not too high, just right for a child his size. She didn't follow him up, certain she'd get wedged in the narrow slide, so she watched him go up the steps, carrying his mat while she stood at the bottom, smiling as he shot towards her, his face shiny and golden. He flew off the end into a heap of giggles. A soft landing. Safe. And then it was time to return to the hotel so they went in search of a taxi rank, Nick tired now and complaining. He wanted to be carried but she held his hand firmly and told him it wasn't far. She promised they'd come again tomorrow, on their last night. They did do that. They returned to the little fair, but it wasn't the same. She tried to make it the same, but she couldn't.

They found a taxi rank. There were no taxis, only a sign with the word *Taxi* and a picture of one. They were the only ones waiting, but there were lots of people around, in cafés, looking into shops, walking out in the early evening. She picked Nick up and he snuggled into her, sleepy and smelling of sugar. And then she saw him,

Jonathan, whose name she still didn't know. He was sitting next to a girl in a café across the road. The girl was studying a map and he leaned over and looked with her. The girl seemed surprised, and Catherine remembers wondering whether they knew each other, or whether they had just met. He glanced up suddenly and caught Catherine staring and she squirmed, turning away and looking up the road for a taxi. She remembers her relief when one came, three in fact, all at once. She put Nick down and leaned in to tell the driver where they were going. She remembers looking out of the window as they pulled away and seeing Jonathan watching.

She picked up the key from reception and went to the room. Nick brushed his teeth, put on his pyjamas and then she closed his shutters and sat on the edge of his bed and read him a story. He was happy to sleep in his own bed as long as she kept the door open between them and she promised she would. That way he could see her from his bed if he woke up. He was asleep before she'd finished reading, and she kissed him, and went into her own room and lay on the bed. Her shutters were open and she could hear the street outside, busier now in anticipation of the night. She closed her eyes for a moment and felt a swell of happiness. One last treat, she had thought, and decided to finish her evening with a glass of wine and a cigarette on her balcony.

She went downstairs, locking the door after her, and ordered a large glass of white wine. The bar was empty, which wasn't surprising. Why would anyone want to sit inside in this rather soulless hotel bar? She signed for her drink and took it upstairs, struggling not to spill it as she unlocked the door. She checked on Nick. He had kicked off his sheet and was lying with his arms up, hands against the pillow, in the way he had as a baby. They had had a special day together, she and Nick. Robert hadn't been there, but she hadn't missed him. She had forgotten that. Only now does she remember that, actually, she hadn't missed Robert that day. She had relaxed into being with Nick and she had enjoyed it. The slight dread she'd felt when she'd woken in the morning, of a long day ahead trying to keep Nicholas happy, trying not to get irritated, had passed without her even noticing and she had slipped into just being with him, as she had always hoped she would. Only now does she remember thinking that perhaps it had been a good thing that Robert had gone. She had completely forgotten that. It had been wiped out. When she'd yelled at Robert recently, a few weeks ago, that he shouldn't have left her and Nick alone, that she had been depressed and hadn't wanted him to leave them, she had thought it was true. In a way it was, but she had forgotten how nourished, how satisfied, she'd felt, from a day of simple pleasure with her son. Yes, she only remembers that now. It had been wiped out.

She took her glass of wine and cigarettes on to the small balcony, sat down, and looked at the world passing by, for once not wanting to be part of it. She was happy. She recognizes now, as she sits in her car outside Stephen Brigstocke's house, that she had been happy at that moment.

Her eyes brim up, and the tears begin again as she wonders whether, in truth, that was the last time she had been truly happy. Has all the 'happiness' after that been a pretence? Not quite, not quite. But that happy feeling, she hadn't told the old man about that. That wasn't part of the story he needed to hear. She didn't want to confuse things. She had got to the meat of it with him.

She finished her wine and went back into the room, closing the doors and shutters behind her. It was still early, but she was tired. Shower, book, bed. Her feet were already bare and she was taking off her top when she saw something out of the corner of her eye. She had pulled her top over her head and she turned to look, her arms half in, half out of the sleeves, held in front of her like a straitjacket. It was dark with the shutters closed, but she could see someone standing in front of the door. Tall, broad. She could smell him. Maybe she smelled him before she saw him. That was possible because his aftershave was thick and sickly. The door was shut and she could hear the jangle of a key in his hand. She must have left it in the door when she was trying not to spill her wine. Her fucking wine. She pulled her arms out of the sleeves and held her top in front of her, trying to cover herself. Before she could shout, tell him to get out, his hand was over her mouth. His large, hot hand. She could taste the sweat on it. She can still taste it. She told the old man that. That she can still taste the fear, or was it excitement, on his son's hand all these years later. Taste and smell: senses imbedded in the memory. Impossible to shake off. How sick that she had forgotten the happy memory so easily but remembered so clearly the foul ones.

His other hand grabbed hers when she tried to hit him, and her top fell to the floor. He looked down at her body and she struggled, trying to pull her hands away, and he let go and put his finger to his lips, glancing at the open door through to Nick. Then he reached into his pocket and took out a penknife. He pulled out the blade and rested the point on her left nipple. Pushed it down under the cup of her bra and pressed, lightly. His other hand grabbed her by the throat, and he dragged her with him as he went over and closed the door to Nicholas's room and locked it with the hand holding the penknife, his other still on her throat.

'If you make a sound, I will slash your face and then your son's.'

He didn't threaten to kill her. Maybe if he had she would have fought more. Perhaps she wouldn't have believed him, but she did believe that he would cut up her face and her child's. He took the knife and ran it down the inside of his arm — a straight line, followed by another, forming a cross, clean and red. He was showing her how efficient his blade was. He held his arm out to her and made her lick off the blood.

She was surprised when she heard him speak. She was shocked by the hatred in his voice. Before that moment, in the days before when she had been aware of him looking at her, when he had raised his bottle of beer to her from the beach, when he had smiled at her from his stool in the hotel bar, she had imagined other words coming from his mouth. And she had imagined his voice differently too. She'd thought it would be gentle. Stupid bitch. The shame of that: the shame of assuming that she was being admired. Why hadn't she recognized that to him she was not human? To him she was nothing more than a small animal to be tormented; something to take his frustration and hate out on. She had assumed his desire was harmless, playful. She forced herself to remember these details, but she hadn't told them all to the old man, to his father. She is the one who must remember the minutiae; she must excavate these details and blow away the dust before examining them, seeing them for what they are. She must spare herself nothing.

He turned on the light next to the bed so he could see her better and leaned against the door into Nick's room and told her to undress. He had a small rucksack over his shoulder and he took it off and put it on the floor at his feet. Then he took out his camera and hung it round his neck, his eyes never leaving her. Watching her. Making sure she stayed where she was. She remembers wondering whether he was planning on blackmail. He moved away from the door and walked across the room. She could see the key to Nicholas's room in the lock.

'Take it off,' he said, pointing to her bra with the knife. She pulled down the straps, pulled the bra around and unhooked it. She could have easily reached behind and undone it, but she was delaying. And she thought her pathetic tactic had

288

worked. She thought it gave her enough time to lunge for Nick's door, unlock it, get to the other side, lock it again, lock him out. But she fumbled, couldn't get the key out of the lock before he grabbed her by the shoulder, turned her round and slapped her hard across the face. She had never been hit like that before, only the occasional slap on the back of her legs from her mother when she was a child. Her ears rang, her teeth crunched against each other.

'Mummy? Mummy?' A small voice from the other side of the door.

He held the knife, point up, under her chin.

'You better get him back to sleep.'

'It's OK, darling. Ssh now, there's a good boy.'

Her voice must have sounded strange to Nick, not right. He said he wanted to see her.

'You promised to keep the door open, Mummy . . . ' He was getting upset.

'So open the door,' he hissed in her ear. 'Then shut him up.'

And she did, hoping she could close it behind her, but he was too quick and jammed his foot in the doorway. He'd concealed himself in the shadows, but she could feel him watching as she sat down on Nick's bed and stroked his hair. Watching them both.

'What's that smell?' Nick said.

The smell was his aftershave.

'Oh, just some smelly stuff from the hotel. I had a shower,' she said, kissing his forehead.

'Pooh. Stinks,' he said, and she tried to smile.

'Go to sleep, darling. I'm here. I'm going to bed now too,' she lied.

'You said you'd keep the door open,' he said, trying not to let his eyes close, but they were fighting him.

'Yes I know. I'm sorry. Look. It's open. Shh, ssh, sweetheart, go back to sleep,' and she carried on stroking his hair until his eyes won, and closed. It only took a few minutes. She heard him move behind her. She felt him standing over her and Nick. She saw him look down at Nick, then take his knife and move it over Nick's sleeping eyes. From left to right, the blade hovered over her little boy's lashes. She held her breath as she stood up and moved towards the door. She needed to get him out of Nick's room. Thank God he followed her. If Nick had woken . . . What would he have done?

Back in her room she told him to lock the door, and he smiled as if he thought she didn't want them to be disturbed again.

'That's better,' he said. 'Now where were we?'

She'd put her T-shirt on again when she'd gone in to Nick, and so she peeled it off once more. Slowly this time. She wanted to win him over. She didn't want him to hurt her or Nick and she hoped that maybe he only wanted to look. She heard the click of the camera as she pulled the T-shirt over her head. She didn't know what to do. Should she pose? What should she do?

He looked at her, standing there in her knickers. They were plain, white. Decent. Modest. He was disappointed. He went over to the chest of drawers and opened the top drawer and riffled through. He found the underwear

Robert had bought for the holiday and he held it out to her.

'Put these on,' he said. So she did.

'Sit down on the bed.' She sat down on the bed.

'Sit back a bit. Relax.' She tried to. She put her arms behind her, leaning back a little.

'Open your legs,' he said. She did.

He sat down on a chair and looked at her.

'Put your hand in your knickers.' Oh fuck, she thought. She took a deep breath and put her hand in her pants.

'Be nice to yourself,' he said. 'Make yourself come.'

How could she? She couldn't. But she had to. Her fingers began to move and he put his eye to his camera and waited. She was dry. Nothing there. She moved her fingers faster and then she heard the click, click, click begin, the whine of the zoom as he came in closer and closer, and she shut her eyes and tilted her head back. She parted her lips, gasped, faked, bit her top lip, moved her fingers, groaned and she knew she would never get there but he would never know and then a final groan, a sigh. And she waited. She kept her hand there, not daring to move, wondering if that was all he wanted. Would he touch her? Or had her touching herself been enough? Click, click, fucking click. Slowly she took her hand away. Slowly she turned to look at him. He was sitting down. He looked relaxed, the camera hanging round his neck. No sign of the knife.

'Please. Please go now,' she said. 'Please.' And

suddenly he wasn't relaxed and there was the knife again. She'd made a mistake. She shouldn't have said that. She should've pretended it was what she'd wanted too. He took his knife and cut her pants and then he grabbed her hand and shoved it down the front of his jeans, his pants. Wet. She could smell it, the pungent smell of his spunk. And her hand felt him getting hard and her heart raced and her throat clenched and she knew it wasn't over. She felt sick with terror. Panic. Fear for herself, fear for her little boy. Her hand gripped his penis and she wanted to rip it from his body. He pulled her hand away.

'Not yet,' he'd said, as if she was impatient for him. 'Turn over.'

'No, please don't . . . ' She'd started to cry, hoping that somewhere he would feel pity for her. Instead he walked over to the door adjoining Nick's room.

'Shall we show him what Mummy likes doing?' And she imagined, for a moment, what it would do to her son if he saw what had happened, and what might happen. What would that do to him?

'OK, I'm sorry, I'm sorry.'

He looked at her.

'Please, come back,' she said. He came back and she got on all fours and he pulled her pants off, which were only hanging by a thread.

'Smile,' he said. She did.

'So I can see you,' he said, and she turned her head and smiled.

'Do it again,' he said and he snapped away as she reached her hand back, taking herself from behind. She closed her eyes. She was hiding herself from him, and trying to think. What should she do? She had to get him out of there. She had to get him away from Nick. Maybe she could leave the hotel with him . . .

'Why have you stopped?' She hadn't realized she had. She started again, faster, faster again, her wrist aching, and then he grabbed her, and pushed into her, the pain, blood, then he turned her over, kissed her, his teeth, his spit, she could taste his aftershave, bitter on her tongue. She couldn't make a sound. He didn't have to put his hand over her mouth to keep her quiet. How could she scream with Nicholas there? What? Was he going to come and rescue her? She had to take it. And hope to God it would soon be over and he would leave. He pressed his knee into her thigh and pushed into her again, hard, hard, hard. But quick. It was over. Over quick, but he was young and ready to go again. And again. And then finally he had had enough. How long? Hours. It felt like hours and hours. It was three and a half. It lasted for three and a half hours. And she had let him brutalize her. She hadn't fought, she hadn't screamed. She had thought of Nick. Don't scream. Don't cry. He lay next to her on the bed and took her hand and turned to her and smiled.

'Thank you,' he said. 'That was nice.' And she wanted him to die. She would have given anything to watch him die. She did tell his father that. She felt he needed to know that. She couldn't pretend to be sorry for that. It was real. It's what she had felt.

He reached into his rucksack, took out a pack of cigarettes and offered her one. She shook her head. He was about to light it.

'Not in here,' she said. Nick would smell it, but she didn't want to say that. She didn't want to remind him about Nick. She pointed to the balcony. He opened the shutters and the doors and went out.

'Sure?' he said, turning back and offering her the pack again, and she thought she'd better and took one and followed him out, closing the door behind them. They stood side by side on the balcony, looking down at the party people, the happy people, the normal people enjoying a night out. Someone glanced up as they walked past. Saw them, standing side by side smoking. Companionably. No idea they were looking up at a rapist and his victim. She remembers finishing the cigarette. He kissed her when he left, one more assault, as if he had no idea what he'd done.

52

Late summer 2013

The door gives its familiar stutter as it closes behind her. When she had finished speaking, she had looked at me and said 'sorry'. And then she had got up and walked out. I didn't reply. I had only interrupted her once to ask a question and she'd answered it. I didn't get up and see her to the door or thank her for coming. I stayed where I was. I wish I hadn't burned Nancy's notebooks — I would do anything to have them back. I need the comfort of her words but the house is silent. Except it isn't. I am trembling so much that the chair I'm sitting on is banging against the table and I have to grip the seat to steady it and me. Why did I destroy Nancy's note-books and keep the photographs? What a fool.

I feel raw, as if my skin has been licked off by a cat's rough tongue, removing my protective layer, and I am not sure I can survive without it. I flail around for something to cling to and grab at the nearest thing. She is a liar. She has been lying for years — everyone knows that. She is lying again now. And I listen out for Nancy's voice to echo mine, but I can't hear it. All I hear are Catherine Ravenscroft's words describing how Jonathan cut a cross on to his arm and made her lick his blood, and I remember the purple marks I saw when we identified his body. Scarring from an injury sustained in the accident, they told us. But so neat and perfectly drawn? I try Nancy again:

'Why didn't you ask her about the photographs? Why didn't you confront her when she said she had never met Jonathan?' But Nancy remains silent.

'She has no proof,' I howl.

I cannot stand the silence and put on my jacket and leave the house. The bus stop is at the end of the road and I march to it: left-right, left-right, eyes front. I can hear the low hum of the bus and turn to see it coming down the road behind me. I quicken my pace, turning round to try and catch the driver's eye. I put out my hand. I am still twenty yards from the stop. He overtakes me, pulls in and waits. A youth gets off. I am nearly there, but the bus pulls out before I reach it. Didn't he see me? He must have seen me. How cruel. He didn't have the decency to wait, a minute, three at the most. I give the rear of the bus a salute as it disappears round the corner and wait for the next.

Time passes without me noticing. I have emptied my head. When the next bus comes I get on and sit behind the driver. An elderly woman sits opposite. She tries to catch my eye but I look past her through the window.

'It's going to be a lovely afternoon. They said it'll clear up later,' she says. I look at her. I want to reply but I cannot speak, so I nod and turn away. A woman with two small children gets on at the next stop and the elderly lady pats the seat next to her for one of the children to sit down. The child looks nervous, she doesn't seem to recognize the old woman, but the mother smiles, picks her up and pops her on the seat, then picks up the other child, a little boy, and carries him. They are about two years old; I think they must be twins. Now the little girl is staring at me too. I stare back. The two women chat about nothing, but it fills the space nicely between me and them.

She is right, by the time I get off the bus the grey has shifted and the sky is blue, the sun bright, but low. It shines directly in my sight-line and I have to squint. Even then all I see ahead are dark, ill-defined shapes. I turn left through the gate and now the sun is to my right and my vision clears.

This is where Catherine Ravenscroft and Nancy met: the place where Jonathan and Nancy are buried. I used to come regularly to tend their graves but I haven't been for a while. With Nancy back at home, I haven't felt the need. We bought our plot when Jonathan died, deciding to settle down with him when it was our turn. For some reason dog walkers seem to think this is an appropriate place for their dogs to stretch their legs and defecate. It usually annoys me but today I sit on a bench and watch them. Jonathan and Nancy are on a rise behind me.

The dog walkers here are good sorts, they always pick up after their animals. I watch a man scoop up his dog's mess with impressive efficiency. One smooth move, hand in black bag, a swoop down, pick up and then straight into the bin, the lid already raised by his other free hand. I smile and nod as he walks on. I watch him until he is out of sight. I look the other way. A jogger enters the gates but he takes another path, away from my bench. I get up and open the doggy bin and reach in and take out the black bag. Holding it between finger and thumb I walk up to my son's grave. I untie the bag and the reek makes me gag.

'You fucking little shit!' I shout and hurl it at Jonathan's grave. Some of it flicks out, sticking to his headstone and I am immediately ashamed. Nancy lies next to Jonathan: *Devoted mother, beloved wife, forever missed.*

I look round to see if anyone has seen me, but they haven't. I go to the tap and fill a watering can and bring it back, throwing water over Jonathan's headstone. It takes three trips to clean it all off, and then I pick up the black bag and drop it into the bin. I return to the graves and kneel down between them and weep.

'Did you know, Nancy? Did you suspect?' And my weeping turns to sobs and I am on all fours, prostrate at their feet. I feel a hand on my shoulder.

'Are you OK?'

I look up at the man I had seen earlier with his dog. He reads the headstones.

'Your wife and son?'

I nod, expecting another pat before he walks away, but he stays with me.

'How did your son die?' There is no prurience; it is a gentle question. My mouth is full of spit and tears and I struggle to get the words out. He offers me his hand and helps me up.

'He drowned,' I manage.

'How terrible,' he says. I want more.

'He was trying to save a child.' I hear him catch his breath.

'That's incredibly brave,' he says, and nods as if he understands now who Jonathan was. 'And did he? Save the child?'

'Yes, he did.'

'What a brave young man he must have been.' He puts his hand on my shoulder, then walks away.

Yes, he was. Whatever else he may or may not have done, Jonathan was brave to have saved that child, no one can deny that. On that afternoon he had shown courage. He was the first to run in. That's what the police said. He swam in without a thought for himself. If he hadn't acted so quickly, Nicholas Ravenscroft would have been swept out too far for anyone to reach. The young Spaniard may have been the one to drag Nicholas on to the beach, but it was Jonathan who really saved him. I would have been too frightened, most people would have been too frightened, but in that moment Jonathan forgot himself and found the courage to do the right thing. 'He was a very brave young man,' is how witnesses had described him to the police and how they had then described him to us. 'He sacrificed himself,' was their dramatic translation from Spanish into English.

I know that I have never felt as proud of Jonathan as I should have. It shames me to recognize that I never quite believed in his courage. Was it bravery or recklessness? I try but fail to recall a single time, in the nineteen years he was with us, when he did not put himself before another human being. Not once. So why then? And why couldn't he swim to shore? Was the sea really too strong?

'Why did the Spaniard make it back and not Jonathan?' I had once burst out to Nancy and she gave me the answer I wanted to hear.

'He was too far out by then. He was exhausted. He had done the hard work. The Spaniard only had the last leg.'

* * *

When I get home, I start to shiver again. The temperature in the house is colder than outside. I sit down at my desk and open the drawer where I keep the photographs. I look through them. Pictures of a mother and son on a beach; in a café, her coaxing a spoon into his mouth; eating ice cream together. They look so natural. She smiles, he smiles. They are on holiday. In one photograph she is looking straight into the camera. You could believe the photographer was sitting with them at the same table, but I don't believe that any more. She didn't know she was being photographed, like Nancy didn't know when Jonathan captured her sitting in the garden in the deckchair. He was good. He had a talent for photography. They are the sort of photographs you would see in a celebrity magazine taken by a member of the paparazzi. Up close and personal, but from a safe distance. A delusion of intimacy. We had bought our son the most expensive zoom lens we could afford.

The photographs in the hotel room are different. There is nothing natural about them. They are posed, I see that now. And as I look at them, horror is added to my shock. I see something I had chosen to miss before. It is fear.

If it had been me and not Nancy who had developed the film from Jonathan's camera, and if I had sat alone looking at those photographs as she did, would I have seen what she saw? Or would I have remembered the collection of porn I found in Jonathan's bedroom? Or perhaps I would have had the film developed first and found the porn later? Then would I have made a connection? I threw the magazines away so Nancy could remain innocent of her boy's appetites. But I made myself an innocent too. I dismissed them at the time, and then failed to recall them when I came across the photographs all those years later. I saw what I wanted to see. I wonder about Nancy though. I wonder whether perhaps she did see something else. And I wonder whether that was what compelled her to write the book. She wrote it for herself, no one else.

Did she construct that story so she could lay her son to rest in peace? Not my son though. My son is in an altogether less restful place. I say a prayer for Nicholas Ravenscroft's recovery and think how Nancy would laugh at me, but I cannot conjure her up and I realize I am grateful for the silence. I return the photographs to their envelope.

I asked Catherine Ravenscroft why she hadn't told Nancy when they met. Why didn't she tell her she had been raped? She looked at me in surprise.

'I haven't told anyone,' she said. 'And I didn't want to cause her any more pain.' I was the first person she had told. And she told me because she had been forced to. She had been forced again, against her will. I think she actually meant it when she said sorry. She pitied me, but I don't want her pity. I want her to hate me. I need someone to hate me more than I hate myself. I need to tell her what I did to her son. That I am the reason he is where he is now.

I dial her number. I have dialled it before, but never spoken. She picks up.

'Hello?' She must be driving — her voice sounds small against the hum of traffic in the background.

'I showed your son the photographs of you.' I wait for a response but none comes, so I go on. 'My wife wanted you to suffer as she had . . . ' I tell her about my contact with Nicholas. 'I led him to believe you were in love with Jonathan; that Jonathan's life was worth more to you than his.' I hear her breathing above the sound of the road, short little gasps, but she says nothing. I expect her to hang up. She doesn't.

'You should tell your husband,' I say, as gently as I can.

'You fucking tell him,' she whispers, and her words give me hope that at last she has found it in her heart to hate me.

53

End of summer 2013

It is Robert who is at Nicholas's bedside when he opens his eyes and it is Robert who tells Catherine the news. He sends her a text and she receives it during her second session with the therapist she had agreed to see through work. She had almost not gone, but she had a feeble hope that maybe it would help her. The therapist frowns when the text comes in. Her phone should have been turned off. Catherine stands up and says she has to leave. The young woman cocks her head and says nothing. The therapeutic experience feels to Catherine as if she is having her teeth individually pulled out with great earnestness and super care, and that the new dentures she will eventually be fitted with will make her feel a whole lot better. In the meantime though, it is important for her to get used to the gaping, bloody holes in her mouth.

'It's my son. He's just opened his eyes.'

The head cocks the other way.

'He's in intensive care.'

A look first of surprise, then of enlightenment as if the therapist suddenly understands what this is all about. She doesn't, but it's not her fault. Catherine hasn't told her. She hadn't asked. She hadn't asked any of the right questions and Catherine had only responded directly to questions, not volunteering anything herself. She is an uncooperative patient: a patient who seems unwilling or unable to help herself.

★ ★ ★

When Catherine arrives at the hospital a nurse tells her Robert left five minutes ago. He is careful to time his arrivals and departures so he doesn't have to see her, but she is not sure she cares any more. She sinks to her knees, leaning into Nicholas, telling him that she is there, telling him everything is going to be all right, telling him he is safe now, telling him she loves him more than anybody — more than she has ever loved anybody. Nicholas has opened his eyes but he doesn't focus on anything. He stares at nothing, unresponsive; still the doctor is hopeful. Patience. It will take time. They will carry out more tests; in the meantime the signs are good. He is likely to make a slow but possibly full recovery. It is good news. If the good news had not come, Catherine had decided she would kill herself. She'd thought about how she might do it. Throwing herself under a Tube train was not an option: pills and alcohol were her preferred choice of death.

Robert still doesn't know she was raped. She is waiting for the moment when he will be told. She hopes it will come soon. Surely Stephen Brigstocke will find the courage to do this one thing for her? If he doesn't, she will have to tell Robert herself and she feels sick at the thought

304

that he might not believe her. She shouldn't have to persuade him; she shouldn't have to convince him that she is telling the truth, yet she fears that that is exactly what she would have to do. His contempt for her is so solid now that he is more likely to believe Stephen Brigstocke than her. Even so, it would be cruel to leave him in ignorance much longer. She is punishing him by delaying the revelation, but it was Robert who was so quick to allow a wall to come between them, Robert who slammed the door shut on her.

She will not hesitate to tell Nicholas. Now she knows they are both going to live, he must hear it from her and no one else. However painful it is for both of them, he must know. But he is not strong enough yet; it will be a while before he is ready. She strokes his hand. His fingernails are too long. She will bring in some clippers and tidy them up. She has a sudden memory of the tiny clippers she'd used on his nails when he was little. How soft his nails were. In the end she'd used her teeth to gently nibble them down so he wouldn't scratch himself in the night. She checks the time, Robert should have been here by now but she is glad that he is not. She catches the eye of a nurse. She saw Catherine look at her watch; she disapproves. They all disapprove of Catherine. They prefer Robert. The poor husband. The devoted father. She is a hysterical, unstable mother. The woman who attacked that frail old man. Once she would have cared what they thought; not any more. She lays her head on the bed and closes her eyes, grateful for this extra time alone with her son.

54

End of summer 2013

'My son raped your wife. She told me and I believe her. I'm sorry. I'm sorry about everything . . . '

Poor man. It is a lot to take in. I have been too abrupt. We are sitting in the café at the hospital. He has brought me a cup of tea. Insisted on it. I tried to stop him, I said I didn't want one, but he was trying to put me at ease — to make me feel welcome. He said he was getting one for himself anyway. He misread my nervous state — he thought I was anxious because of what had happened the last time I was here. He had only just put the cup down when I told him. I say it again more slowly.

'My son raped your wife. She told me what happened and I believe her. I am ashamed to say it, but I believe my son was capable of that . . . I'm so sorry.'

I want to say more, but I make myself stop. He needs time to digest. He will have questions, and I will answer them.

'My wife told you that?'

'Yes.'

'Catherine?'

'Yes.'

'And you believe her?'

I nod. He looks beyond me, over my shoulder. There are people sitting near by, but we have a table to ourselves. We look like a father and son. People will assume that my wife, his mother, is in a ward and that we are there to comfort each other.

'I am sure she was telling the truth.' I repeat myself: 'Your wife was raped by my son.'

'When did she tell you?' His voice is flat as if he is speaking under hypnosis.

'Yesterday. She came to my house . . .'

He takes this in, his eyes avoiding mine. They graze my shoulder as they move down to look into his tea, both hands wrapped around the cheap china.

'Yesterday?'

'Yes. She came to my house yesterday morning.'

Then he looks up at me and I see his exhaustion. His eyes are blue and his hair, once blond, is washed out with grey.

'Why didn't she tell me? She should have told *me*, not you.'

I cannot answer that. Ask me something else. Ask me something I can answer. The silence grows, chewing at the air between us, and I see anger build inside him. He is waking up . . . four, three, two, one.

'Why didn't you tell me before? You must have known. You bastard! Why didn't you say anything before?'

'I didn't know. I didn't know until yesterday. I hadn't met your wife before. But when she sat down in front of me and told me what

307

happened, I knew she was telling the truth. No one wants to believe their son is capable of such a thing.' He is grasping around, searching for something. He is mind-fucked. Now I know what that means. We have both been mind-fucked.

'He raped her?'

I nod.

'You think he was capable of that and you didn't say anything . . . He'd done it before — '

'No, no, I'm sure he hadn't,' I protest. 'It was hearing her describe to me what happened: the details, the knife and . . . I know she was telling the truth.'

'The knife?' He closes his eyes, imagining. 'But the photographs . . . '

I watch the guilt begin its descent on him. He reaches over and grabs me by the coat, spilling scalding tea on my legs. A woman at the next table turns to look. She must wonder why I don't move or make a sound, but I don't feel a thing.

'I felt sorry for you,' he says. 'I was grateful to your fucking son . . . '

Then he pushes me away and sinks his face into his hands.

'I needed to tell you face to face — I couldn't do it over the phone.'

And oh, shrivelling creep that I am, I remind him that it was my wife who wrote the book, not me. I see revulsion crawl on to his face. I sound as if I am blaming her, but I am not. I believed what she wrote and I felt I owed it to her to make it known. It was her book, her words.

'She never meant anyone else to read it. I should have left it where it — '

'You sent it to my wife. And my son. You sent me those photographs. Jesus Christ! How could you not know? You've admitted you thought him capable of it, so why didn't you question it?'

'Why didn't you?' And I squirm under the pain my question inflicts on him.

'Why didn't I question it?' His face sags into his hands. I watch his shoulders shake and I want to put my hand out and touch him, but I can't. I can't comfort him, there is nothing I can say that will ease his guilt or take away the image of his wife reading that vile book and feeling as if she was being raped all over again. I have no business here any more. It is done. He knows. I leave him there and go up to the ICU. I don't go in, I just look through the window, hoping for a glimpse of Nicholas, and I see her on her knees at her son's bedside. She looks as if she is asleep.

55

End of summer 2013

He kneels down beside her and she feels his arm across her shoulders. She keeps her eyes closed. His face is close to her neck. It is wet. He is shaking.

'Forgive me, Cath. I am so sorry. Please forgive me. I know what happened. He told me what his son did . . . ' These last words are buried in her neck. Still, her eyes remain closed. She is dizzy. He takes her hand and she opens her eyes, but it is Nick's eyes that meet hers, not Robert's. Nick, who is looking right at her, seeing her. It had happened before Robert came, not opening his eyes, but being able to focus. Catherine was holding his hand at the time and his head shifted a little and then he looked at her and she knew he could see her, recognize her, and a wave of happiness swept through her and she smiled and cried.

'Hello, my darling,' she said. He hadn't answered, just looked at her. She had texted Robert. She hadn't known he was in the hospital café with Stephen Brigstocke. A nurse had been with her and for the first time in a while, Catherine received a smile from her. Then the doctor came and confirmed what they already knew. This was real progress. If he keeps this up, he could be out of the ICU within a week.

Nick closed his eyes again, and she closed hers. And then Robert came in.

'Dad's here,' she whispers to Nick. Robert had been too busy looking at Catherine to notice his son open his eyes, but she hears him gasp and feels the joy pulse through him like the low hum from electric pylons.

'Nick,' he says. 'We're here. We're both here. It's going to be OK.' And he squeezes Catherine closer to him.

Nicholas looks at his parents smiling down at him. There is bafflement in his eyes as they move from one to the other.

'I'll call the doctor,' Robert whispers to her.

'He knows,' she says, and tells him the good news.

They stay there until late into the night. Side by side, occasionally one of them going off to fetch something to eat and drink. They dare not leave Nick's side in case he speaks. It is possible. And they don't want to miss his first words. By one a.m. they decide it is time to go. Part of Catherine dreads it. They will have to speak now and she is too tired.

Robert drives them home. It is late and she feels a sting of guilt that she won't be with her mother tonight, but she called her and thinks she understood that Nick is on the mend and Catherine is going home with Robert. Catherine is drained. All she wants is to be taken home and put to bed. She's so exhausted she doesn't say much; her quiet is calm and peaceful and there's a stillness in the car, as if she and Robert have been vacuum-packed inside it. He is in no hurry to talk either — he is as shattered as she is. They go upstairs and Catherine showers and washes the hospital smell away. She goes to bed with wet hair, relishing the cold on her head, keeping the heat away. Robert lies down next to her and reaches for her hand, but there is nothing searching about it, he just wants to hold it and she lets him. She stays facing him, although she would like to turn away. She sleeps more comfortably on her right side, still she stays on her left, careful of his feelings.

'Cath,' he whispers.

She makes a sound in reply, not quite a word, as she drifts into sleep.

'Cath, I am so sorry. I'll never be able to forgive myself . . . '

She puts her hand on his cheek, her eyes still closed. It's not his fault. He didn't know, she didn't tell him. But she is too exhausted for this now. She turns over, pulling the duvet up to her chin, breathing in its familiar smell.

'Why didn't you tell me?' he whispers into her neck. She is drained by his need for her to justify herself. It is his need, not hers, and she pretends not to hear him. All she wants is to be able to sleep at last, with the knowledge that finally the truth has broken free.

★   ★   ★

The next few days and evenings are spent together at the hospital — both of them concentrating on Nick's recovery. It is coming,

312

they can see it. He is awake and fully conscious. He has started to speak. His words are a little slurred, but they will come back. Therapy will sort it out. He still looks confused by his parents. He knows who they are yet he looks at them with suspicion. It breaks Catherine's heart when she sees in his eyes that he doesn't quite trust her, but he is nowhere near ready for the truth yet; it wouldn't be fair, and so she pretends she doesn't notice his reserve and busies herself putting fresh fruit, peeled and cut by her that morning, on to his table. Making sure his cup is full of water. Wiping his hands and face with baby wipes. Trimming his nails. Rubbing cream into his hands and feet. He allows her to do it. He is as weak as a baby. He needs someone to do it.

Catherine is prepared to give him time, but Robert is in a hurry.

'It wasn't true, Nick, any of it. It was all a lie. Mum loves you. She loves me. It didn't happen, not like — '

'Not now.' She stops him. What was he about to say? The man who saved your life raped your mother? She feels a tinge of resentment towards him. This is her story. She has been sole owner of it for years. It is not his to tell, it is hers, and she is the only one who will be able to help Nick understand why she chose never to speak of it.

★ ★ ★

It is slow, but Nicholas does progress. He is sore from the tube which ran down his throat, but words start coming gradually. Though his skin

313

remains grey and he is thin, he will make it. He will be fine. Catherine thanks God. Well, she thanks someone, and she calls him God though she can't quite place him. Still she is so grateful that Nicholas has been saved again. And through all the time that Nicholas is progressing, so do Catherine and Robert, slowly working their way back to a place where they can be easy with each other again. Robert wishes Stephen Brigstocke was dead. He wants to punish him for what he has done to his family. It stops him sleeping, this sick, fucked-up man's malevolence bumping around in his head. Catherine sleeps well for the first time in ages.

When she thinks of Stephen Brigstocke, it is with sorrow. She had watched him swallow an unbearable truth. He could have fought it, she expected him to call her a liar, but he didn't. He knew the truth when he saw it and she respects that — it's not something many people are capable of: denial is so much easier. Most parents would have found what she said about his son, his dead son, inedible. She feels guilty for causing Robert pain — guilty that she allowed him to be told that way. He should have heard it from her, and she has tried to explain to him why she wasn't able to do it. When she watched Jonathan Brigstocke die, she saw him being punished for what he had done to her. He would never be able to do it to anyone else; she would never have to stand up in a court of law and prove her own innocence. She saw it as a sign that she was being given the chance to wipe away something that, she knew, would pollute

314

their lives. And the fact that Nicholas had been spared had made her believe that even more.

She was mistaken, she knows now, to think that she could carry it alone; that it wouldn't affect her. Of course it did. She knows it affected her relationship with Nicholas. She thought she was protecting them all by preventing it from entering their lives.

'But it did enter our lives . . . with the book. Why didn't you tell me then?' He is pleading.

'I don't know. I wanted to . . . I tried to . . . '

He looks at her, waiting, waiting for her to explain how she tried to tell him but didn't.

'There were times when I nearly did. I don't know, Robert. When you have kept something like that — never said it — never told anyone — it becomes more and more difficult to.'

She finds these conversations too painful. They leave her crying, shamed, guilty. And she wants him to say, 'Was it me? Did I stop you?' But he doesn't. He never asks himself that and she never pushes him. There is no fight left in Catherine. She doesn't challenge Robert and ask him what was it about 'Charlotte' that convinced him so easily it was her? She doesn't tell him how painful it was to see his anger and hatred. Instead she cries and he apologizes. He is sorry for upsetting her. He doesn't want to do that — it's the last thing he wants, and so he stops asking, leaves her be. And she is relieved. She fears the resentment these conversations arouse in her; the pressure she feels from them.

★ ★ ★

315

Nick has been back at home for two weeks. Catherine and Robert had gone together to collect him. It felt like when they'd brought Nick home from hospital as a newborn: they had both been so careful around him, new parents, a little uncertain. When he was a baby she had dreaded Robert returning to work; now she can't wait.

Today is the first day she has had Nick to herself. He is ready. And she tells him she was raped. There was no affair. She didn't love Jonathan Brigstocke. She didn't know him. She tells Nick that he was asleep in the next room. She tells him how she feared Jonathan Brigstocke would hurt him. She tells him about the knife. She makes no excuses for why she hasn't told Nick any of this before. She says she hadn't told anyone.

'Did he save my life?'

'Yes he did.'

'Why?'

'I don't know. We'll never know. Perhaps he felt guilty?'

Nick's face is pale, it has lost its grey pallor, but she can see he is getting tired. They have had lunch and he will want to nap soon, but he wants to know everything. He wants to keep talking.

'Guilty?'

'I don't know, darling.' She pauses, wondering how much more he can take. 'Maybe. We'll never know why, but he did save your life. That was deliberate — he went in after you. He didn't have to. He wanted to save you.' She rests a hand on his shoulder and his head droops and she sees a tear fall down his cheek. She reaches over to

316

pull him towards her, but he stiffens.

'I'm OK,' he says.

She kisses the top of his head, smelling the shampoo from his morning shower. She wants to hold him, but he is not ready and she turns away before she begins to cry herself.

'You're tired,' she says. 'You should sleep now. We can talk later.'

He nods, getting to his feet, and she stands up too, watching him make his way to the stairs.

'I'm sorry I've been a useless mother,' she says.

He turns and shrugs, then shakes his head. No words, but at least he shakes his head.

When Nick goes upstairs, Catherine lies on the sofa and closes her eyes. *If only*s fill her head. If only she had called the police the night it had happened. If only she had phoned Robert. He would have come out to be with them, wouldn't he? But she had been sleep-walking. Nick woke early the next day and came running through to her room and bounced on her bed. She hadn't slept at all. The night before she had emptied out a travel-size pot of cream and cleaned it out, then she had pressed it against her vagina and pushed his semen down, out of her. The small amount that hadn't trickled down her leg. A cloudy gob. She screwed on the lid and put it in her wash-bag. She remembers wondering what would happen if her luggage was checked — if some unsuspecting uniform had stuck his nose into that particular pot of cream. She had taken photographs: the bruise on her thigh; the bite on her neck. The police would want evidence, so she gathered it for them.

Would they have believed her though? She had left the keys to her room in the door. She knew that, however much evidence she produced, someone, some man probably, would stand up in court and call her a liar: would tell her that she'd enticed this young man into her room. That she had known him. He'd bought two drinks in the bar of the hotel she was staying in — would anyone remember that she hadn't joined him there?

But then he died. Thank God, she had thought. He is dead. And she knew she wouldn't have to prove herself innocent, so when she had the film of their holiday developed she destroyed the photographs of her injuries and kept the snaps of her and Nicholas and Robert.

When Nick had bounced on her bed, she had lain there pretending to smile, pretending to watch him. Every action, every word that morning was disembodied. It hadn't come from her. They had breakfast. Nick ate, she didn't. She even remembers him telling her to eat up. He was desperate to go to the beach. She didn't want to, but what else would they do? She did try to change their flights. Nicholas was impatient as they hung around the hotel, waiting for an answer. It was no. So they went to the beach. And on the way she bought him the dinghy. A life-saver, she thought at the time. Keep him happy, keep her upright. It did keep him happy. In, out, in, out, he jumped, chatting to himself; playing the part of every member of the crew. And the heat and the shock suffocated her and she lay her head down and she closed her eyes and she fell asleep. She didn't watch her little boy. He nearly drowned. It was a perfect stranger who saved him.

Robert stops asking why she didn't tell him and it makes her feel forgiven. He knows she didn't have an affair; he knows she didn't betray him. And he has a new role now. He is no longer the aggrieved husband, he is the supportive one. He is there to help her and he urges her to talk to someone, a professional, who will be able to guide her back to the past and then lead her out again, but Catherine is sickened by the past. She is not going back there. She should have gone back there a long time ago, but it's no place for her now. It is the present she wants to concentrate on.

56

Autumn 2013

I have been spending a lot of time thinking about Jonathan, trying to understand what sort of person he was. It is hard to admit that you do not know your own child, that you never really knew your own child.

I said once that Jonathan would never have died of shame because of his mother's love, that whatever he did, she would always forgive him. But in a way I think he did die of shame. The Spanish used the right word: *sacrifice*. When he raped Catherine Ravenscroft, I think he knew he had started down a road from which he could not return. He had lost himself. He didn't risk his life, he deliberately gave it. Perhaps I am grasping for something to comfort me, but why else would he have done something so out of character? I believe Jonathan looked himself in the eye and had the courage not to flinch. He saw himself for who he was. Very few of us are willing to do that. I am only now beginning to find that strength and I suspect Nancy never did. That takes courage, doesn't it? To look beneath the mask and see the real you?

I cannot be certain that he had not raped before, but I don't believe he had. I do know though that something sent his girlfriend, Sasha, running home to her parents. We called her his girlfriend, though in reality they hadn't known each other very long and I remember being surprised when he told us that she was going with him on his travels. I was less surprised when she came home early. If he had raped her, her parents would have pressed charges I am sure. On the other hand, something happened to cause her mother to make that angry phone call. Nancy knew, but she never told me, and to my shame I never asked her for details. All I knew was that Nancy took up her default position as Jonathan's defender. She had been doing it for years, ever since he was little.

I recognize Nancy's voice now for what it was: the voice of a woman demented by grief; a voice I kept alive for years, allowing it to spin out its desperate yarn while I sat back and listened. Nancy dressed up our son into someone he wasn't and, long before he died, I had colluded with her in covering up all the clues that should have made us uneasy about our boy. Little things when he was a child that grew as he grew into bigger and bigger denials of who he was. I had stood by and let it happen. My son was a rapist. Nancy's son, no. But mine, yes. Did Nancy ever suspect? If she did, she showed no sign of it. Even if she had, she would not have allowed herself to believe it. She rewrote Jonathan just as I rewrote her. I am as guilty of delusion as Nancy was. I turned my wife into someone she was not. I wasn't brave enough to recognize that, long before Jonathan died, she had lost her way. For years I had helped stoke up her fantasy, joined in her blind devotion, never once confronting her, never once challenging her. I rubbed along with them both: the made-up Jonathan and the made-up Nancy. My only defence is that I did it from love. We both did. But it isn't much of a defence.

Even when he was a small boy, people didn't warm to Jonathan. He was only at nursery for a month before Nancy took him out and said she wanted to keep him home with her. She said he wasn't ready for it yet. And when he had to go to school she took a job there, so she could stay close to him. He had friends who came round to play at the house, but he was never invited back. I noticed, though I pretended not to. I think the children liked coming because of Nancy — she was wonderful with them. It was easier to pretend all was well when he was little, but when he hit adolescence, her influence faltered. Still, she was always there to defend him. I should have taken her on, but I knew if I had I would be joining the other side, the enemy, all those who didn't understand Jonathan. I would have had to do battle with her, my wife the anti-Medea.

Instead, I disappeared into my own fantasy. I used to imagine what it would be like to have one of the boys I taught as a son. A boy I could talk to. A boy who, when you spoke, listened and who perhaps was rude or cheeky at times but at least looked you in the eye, made a connection. After Jonathan died I allowed this fantasy to take hold. I went to pieces.

There had been a boy I taught at GCSE and A level. I pretended for a while he was my son. He wasn't as clever as Jonathan. Jonathan passed his exams with no effort and an unpleasant scorn for those who struggled. He couldn't have cared less and looked into his future with the same indifference, which is why Nancy suggested we pay for his trip around Europe. He needed time to find himself, she said.

The boy I 'adopted' could not have been more different. When he went up to university, I followed him there. I took the train to Bristol and told anyone who'd listen that I was going to visit my son at university. My wife and I had children very late, I said when I saw them wondering whether it was possible for me to have a son of university age. I spent a fortune getting the train up and down to Bristol. Nancy never knew. I'd taken time off work, but she thought I was going into school each morning. I stopped going after the beating. I was glad for it. It knocked some sense into me.

It is not Nancy's fault, any of this. It is mine. My love took root in our first twenty years together and I had neither the desire nor the will to undo it, then or now. I still see so clearly the woman I fell in love with; the woman I married and lived with. But now I also see the woman she became after Jonathan was born. An initial blooming, followed by an uncontrolled growth of suckers, branches, straggling unkempt shoots, taking off as she tried to reach out and hold on to him — to keep him safe — to turn him into something he wasn't. She had to distort herself to do that: she had to become a thorny, knotty creature. I should have taken my pruning shears

323

and cut back the suckers before they got out of control; before they drained the life out of what had been good. You have to be cruel to be kind. Cut back, just so, in the right place, so the plant isn't starved of nourishment, so it is able to flower.

I have started gardening again: pulling up the weeds, sweeping the leaves into piles ready to burn. The neighbours have complained about the smell. I'm not considerate, they say; they've had their washing out. I'm afraid their complaints encourage rather than deter me. I like fires. I like the smell of the smoke on my clothes and in my hair. I relished throwing the photographs on to the fire, took pleasure in witnessing their destruction. The yellow envelope with Kodak on the front turned brown then black and I imagined the negatives inside, shrivelling into nothing. I had looked through them one more time, in case I had missed Jonathan caught on camera. Perhaps his reflection in a mirror or his shadow on the wall, but he wasn't there. I will burn my son's belongings next. There is nothing I wish to keep. I have already started chopping wood to rebuild the fire.

Yesterday I took the laptop to Geoff. A present, I said. He was surprised, but I told him that I had my eye on a new one. A lie, of course.

'How's the new book coming along?' he asked.

'Oh, I abandoned it,' I said, giving him a cheery wave so he wouldn't worry. Today I am off to see the ladies in the charity shop.

'I found a few more things,' I say, opening up a carrier bag containing Nancy's evening bag,

324

knitted hat and cardigan. I've practically worn the cardigan to death. There are holes under each arm and the top button is missing. I decline their offer of coffee and watch them peer into the bag, reluctant to touch its contents. I wonder whether the cardigan will outlive me after all, or whether those nice ladies will put it out of its misery.

When I get home someone is leaving a message with Nancy. I haven't been able to bring myself to erase her voice. The message confirms an appointment. It is for a week's time. Time enough for me to finish what I need do. I sit down at my desk and take out a pen and paper.

57

Autumn 2013

Catherine is shedding layers too. She has told work that she is not coming back. She cannot face it — for the moment at least, it seems pointless to her. She has given up on her therapist too, not bothering to return after that second session, though perhaps she will try again with someone else. She probably should.

She glances over at her mother. They sit in twin armchairs, side by side: Catherine in the one her mother used to sit in before her father died; her mother in Dad's chair. They are watching some antique jamboree, jolly, carefree, warm TV, both with a cup of tea in their hands. The doorbell rings and Catherine answers. It's Nick. He said he might pop over and see Granny, but Catherine hadn't been sure he meant it. The fact that he did and is standing there makes her heart leap.

'Mum, Nick's here,' she calls, and her mother struggles out of her chair and totters over to her grandson.

'Hello, darling,' she says and reaches up to kiss his cheek. 'Are you all better now?'

'Yes, Gran, I'm fine,' he says, but he isn't. He is depressed. He is lonely. He is a drug addict. He needs help. Seeing Granny helps though. She has always adored Nick and Catherine watches her take his hand and hold it between hers, fuelling him with her clean love. He relaxes a little and sits down in Catherine's chair, taking a handful of sweets from a bowl on the coffee table.

Catherine goes to fill the kettle, hovering on the threshold between kitchen and sitting room while she waits for it to boil. She studies the back of her mother's and son's heads; how they move constantly — her mother's from the tremor which afflicts her now and Nick's from his manic chewing of sweets. Perhaps she and Nick should have therapy together? She dismisses the thought as soon as she has it: he is already seeing someone as part of his rehab and she doesn't want to interfere with his progress. She tops up the teapot and takes it in, sitting down on the floor and leaning against Nick's chair.

'Do you want to sit here?' he asks.

'No, no, I'm fine,' she says, patting his leg.

She wonders how different it would be for Nick if she and Robert had had more children — if he'd had a younger sister or brother to deflect some of the scrutiny. She was an only child and a very happy one — that had always been her argument to Robert whenever he tip-toed into the arena of whether they should have more children. Nick had almost had a brother, or perhaps it was a sister — she will never know.

Catherine was pregnant when she came home from Spain. She didn't know it at the time. Her periods were pretty irregular so she left it over a month before she did a pregnancy test. She had been back at work for a week and went out in her lunch hour to buy a kit from Boots, then she locked herself in the toilet. Of course she knew it was a possibility, but she had convinced herself the test would be negative. She deserved one bit of fucking luck, didn't she? Evidently not, because there it was. A baby inside her. She put the loo seat down and sat for a while, gently rocking to and fro, thinking. It could be Robert's baby. They had had sex during the holiday. Once. Despite the effort he'd made with her underwear, it was still only the once. Maybe a baby would help. A baby might be the distraction she needed. Not work, but a baby. Whose baby though? What if it looked like him? What if it had dark hair and dark eyes? She didn't cry and she didn't make a decision right away. She needed more time. She unlocked the cubicle and dropped the test in the bin, then stood and looked at herself in the mirror.

'Good news, I hope?'

She jumped. She hadn't noticed anyone else come in. A colleague was standing next to her, smiling.

'Your meeting with Tony — did you get the commission?'

'Oh yes — yes — well, he seemed to like the idea, anyway. Said he'll let me know tomorrow.' She smiled and grabbed some paper towel, giving her hands a cursory wipe before dropping the paper in the bin, making sure the pregnancy test was buried. She felt slightly mad, the way she could pretend so easily — make people believe what she wanted them to believe. She'd had no idea she was so good at it.

The more she thought about having another baby, the more she realized it was an impossibility. So she booked herself into a clinic and told Robert she was going to her friend in the country for the weekend. But she didn't leave London. It was like a sleepover with a bunch of girls in a boarding school. A few of them had come from Ireland. All of them were relieved when it was over — and they sat up in their pyjamas, eating biscuits and drinking tea and joking with a nurse who came in to discuss contraception with them. To make sure that there wouldn't be any more unwanted pregnancies. And she joined in. It was nice to be with these women, be part of their gallows humour. She didn't tell them about the rape — she didn't want to spoil the mood, but she wondered if she was the only one. She was tired and pale when she got home on Sunday evening. It was only then it hit her. It had been a pretty ghastly weekend, she'd said to Robert.

Be with you by 7. She reads the text from Robert, texts back *Great, see you then.*

He is coming to pick them all up and take them out to supper. She looks at the time. It is quarter to six.

'Mum? Do you want me to help you do your hair before we go out? I could wash and dry it for you.'

'Yes please, darling.' Her mother pushes herself out of her chair. 'Your mum is good to me,' she says to Nick as she makes her way to the bathroom.

'You will come with us, won't you?' Catherine whispers to Nick.

'Well . . . ' he sighs.

'Oh please, love, Granny'd love having you there. We'll be home by nine.'

'Yeah, OK. Oh, by the way, a letter came for you as I was leaving the flat. I had to sign for it.' He hands her an envelope. There is a stamp from a solicitor's office in the corner and she rips it open with a frown, wondering what fine it is she has forgotten to pay. She reads the letter twice, then folds it up and puts it in her bag.

Winter 2013

'Are you OK?'

She nods, letting Robert's hand rest on hers. He leaves it for as long as he can before taking it away to flick the indicator. They take the next left then slow to a crawl, dragging along until they find a space to park. He stops the car and Catherine releases her seat belt. Robert leaves his on and puts out his hand in gentle restraint.

'Are you sure you want to do this?'

'Yes,' she says, failing to conceal her irritation. It is the fourth time he has asked her. She opens the door and gets out.

The pane of glass in the front door is still broken, but this time Catherine uses the key to let herself in. It is hers now. The house and everything in it. She walks through, looking around, taking stock. It is even more of a mess than when she was last here.

'Jesus,' Robert says.

She goes upstairs, peering over the banister at him standing in the middle of the sitting room, open-mouthed with horror.

'Disgusting,' she hears him mutter. Yes, it is. It is all disgusting. She opens the first door at the top of the stairs and looks into Stephen and Nancy Brigstocke's bedroom: a double bed, dressing table, chest of drawers, wardrobe. The bed is still as it was the last time Stephen Brigstocke lay in it. Catherine will not be the one to drag his dirty sheets from the bed: she has organized others to come in and clear the house in a few days. She hears Robert's feet on the stairs and within seconds his arm is around her, but she is restless and turns on her heels, marching on to the next room.

It is the only other bedroom. It must have been Jonathan's. The walls are pale green and there are marks where pictures, or perhaps posters, have been ripped down — clean rectangles of missing things. She walks out, passing Robert, who hovers in the doorway, not knowing whether to go in or to follow her. She wishes he hadn't come. He looks like a husband whose wife is dragging him around a house he has no intention of buying while the owner looks on. She peers into the last door upstairs. A relic from the seventies. A bathroom with an avocado suite. She closes the door on it and goes down. Robert follows.

They walk through the sitting room to the kitchen and look out at the garden. Since Catherine was last here, someone has been at the plants. They have been hacked at, and their branches thrown, probably, on to the blackened hole in the middle of the lawn. It must have been quite a fire. He was the last thing to go on to it. The neighbours really complained about the smell then. They'd got on the phone to the council when they smelled that other, sickening smell. Catherine heard one of them on the local news.

'He didn't make a sound,' the neighbour said. 'He didn't cry out. We didn't hear a thing.' Naturally if he had they would have phoned an ambulance, not the council. But nobody had seen. They'd kept their windows shut, after he'd started with his bonfires.

Catherine had been watching television with her mother when they saw the story on the local news. Her mother had tutted at the horror of it. An elderly man, living alone, burned to death. The police did not treat it as suspicious. A can of petrol was found near the body. She hadn't realized it was Stephen Brigstocke until she met his solicitor and he told her what happened. He had made Catherine his sole beneficiary. This house and the flat in Fulham.

'Come on, darling, let's go,' Robert says.

'No, you wait in the car if you like, I'm not ready yet.'

Reluctant to leave her, he stays, opening kitchen cupboards and recoiling at the filth. He kicks at a broken cup which has been left where it fell on the greasy linoleum floor. She watches him wander into the sitting room, his hand holding his coat away from the doorway,

332

protecting it from picking up any dirt. He looks around for somewhere to sit, but thinks better of it.

'Why don't you wait in the car?' she says. 'I'm happy to be on my own for a bit.' He looks at her, not understanding.

'I want you to. I'd like to be on my own. Please.'

'Are you sure?'

She nods.

'I've booked a table for lunch,' he says. 'One thirty, Pier Luigi's — I'm not going back to work this afternoon.'

He is a thoughtful man. He is trying so hard. He leaves the house and she goes to the sitting-room window and watches him get into the car. He takes out his phone and makes a call. It will be to work and she is glad because it means he is not thinking of her, and that gives her a breath of freedom. She has decided to leave Robert. She hasn't told him yet. She has been thinking about it for weeks, wrestling with herself: stay or go. Now she is clear.

She needs to forgive, but she cannot. She cannot forgive him because she has watched him over the last few weeks manage the idea of her being raped so much more easily than he had managed the idea of her having an affair. Of course he was upset and angry: he felt impotent; he hadn't been there to protect her. Yet it seems to Catherine that the new truth he was offered was easier for him to swallow than adultery. When she is at her most brutal she thinks that, given the choice, he would rather she had suffered than to have enjoyed a burst of illicit pleasure. He was so hurt. He was so betrayed. He was so angry. He said his anger was because he felt he didn't know her: that she became a stranger to him. Now he believes he has his old Catherine back. He is wrong: she can never be that woman again. Robert's Catherine was the one who couldn't tell him the truth. The Catherine who preferred to strap the burden to her own back rather than share it with him. She was a self-sufficient, independent woman — a Catherine he could be proud of. Not his fault, more hers than his.

She remembers an evening soon after Nicholas came out of hospital when Robert grabbed her hands and said, 'I'll never forgive myself, Cath — how could I have believed you would have done that to us? I'll never forgive myself . . . ' And every word he said had buried her love for him a little more. He cried, and she cried too, but their tears were travelling in parallel lines. It was too late. They should have cried together years ago.

And there was anger mixed in Catherine's tears. Robert had looked at those photographs of her being tortured and seen pleasure. He had missed the savagery and seen only lust. He had been too caught up in his own jealousy to see her. She could never forgive him for that. She thought when Jonathan died she would never have to tell anyone; she would never have to prove her innocence. Robert had made her feel that she had had to.

She opens the back door and goes out into the

garden. It is drizzling; a soft grey damp that she breathes in as she walks across the patio, putting her hands in her pockets and looking down at the crooked grey slabs, wondering whether Stephen Brigstocke had laid them himself. She steps on to the grass, trimmed now into a lawn, and walks towards the blackened pit in its middle. A flutter of yellow catches her eye, a scrap of tape caught on a bush: a remnant from the short police investigation. A few charred remains have been dragged from the fire and left there: relics which perhaps the police thought would give them some idea of what had happened. But they learned little and concluded that it was an act of desperation by a lonely old man. By the time the police arrived there was hardly anything left of him and what there was had been taken away for examination. She dips the toe of her shoe into the black pulpy mess. Robert had told her Stephen Brigstocke blamed the book on his wife. Was that true? Did she write it? Perhaps; perhaps not. Does it matter? Not really, not any more.

She looks at the house and tries to imagine how it must have been once. A young couple, a small child, their first home together. A cared-for garden, sunshine. A paddling pool? A picnic on the lawn? But this is her memory. It does not belong to this house. She is remembering her and Robert with Nick when he was little, when he was very little. Before that trip to Spain. Nick jumping in and out of a paddling pool, her crouching down by his side, him naked, gleeful, wielding a wooden spoon and Tupperware,

335

which he banged like a drum. Her memory. She imagines that Stephen and Nancy Brigstocke had moments like that in this garden with their little boy. Poor them, poor them, she thinks. She has no anger for either of them any more. God knows, they suffered. She is even grateful to Stephen Brigstocke. He sat opposite her and listened to her story. He didn't call her a liar. He didn't make her prove her innocence.

She went alone to meet Stephen Brigstocke's solicitor; she didn't tell Robert about the will until later. It was an odd meeting: the solicitor lacked curiosity, didn't ask anything about her relationship with his client, even though the will had been changed only a few months before. All quite straightforward, he said, going on to summarize Stephen Brigstocke's last wishes. She said nothing. It wasn't until she stood up to go that he handed her the letter. He told her his client had asked him to put it directly into her hand. She didn't open it then — it took her a few days to pluck up the courage to read it.

It was a faltering, awkward letter: hard to imagine it had been written by a man who'd had a career teaching English. He didn't want his *gesture to feel like another assault*. He didn't want her to be *burdened by my legacy*. He assumed she would sell both properties, and his hope was that the *money could be used to make your life and your family's easier*. He was careful not to use the words *compensate* or *compensation*. He finished up by saying that, by the time she received this, his *pain would be over*; but he wanted her to know: *I am aware that you and your family must continue to live with the pain I inflicted on you.* He ended: *I hope you can forgive my lack of courage.* She puzzled over this. Was he calling himself a coward for killing himself? Or because of the negative he enclosed in the letter which he should have been brave enough to give her in person? A negative which had never been developed, he explained. Dismissed as a dud by both him and his wife. It was folded into the heart of his letter: . . . *I enclose it for you now.*

She holds the small brown square up to the light: shades of darkness with Catherine, a smudge in the foreground, an unrecognizable blur. The feeble winter sun moves behind a cloud, denying her enough light to see the ghost in the frame, but she knows he is there. Stephen Brigstocke searched through the negatives for his own son — instead he found hers.

He would have seen and heard everything from his position in the open doorway. The door which she thought had stayed closed. The door behind which she'd believed he was asleep. But he had got out of bed and opened the door. He was standing looking into the room. The only light in the negative; a small white figure, unmistakable once you know he is there. A little ghost who appeared, then disappeared again without anyone knowing.

She has studied it over and over, securing it on a light box, squinting at it through a magnifying glass, to be sure. He would have heard everything too: her fake groans of pleasure. He didn't say a word. He didn't call out to her. He

337

closed the door again and went back to bed, too frightened and shocked to speak. Perhaps he lay there for a while, hiding under the bedclothes, trying to make sense of what he had seen. Perhaps he woke the next morning and thought he had dreamed it. His child's brain erased the memory of what he saw and heard that night. But it has always been there, this image and memory of his mother. An alien mother whom he could never quite trust, never quite believe in. In that hotel room in Spain all those years ago she had tried to imagine what it would do to her son if he had seen what was happening to her. He *had* seen, and heard. And all through his growing up the signs were there, but she had failed to recognize them.

Yesterday Nick saw the negative for the first time. Catherine feared she'd made a mistake and wished she hadn't shown him.

'I don't remember it . . . I don't remember anything,' he said. He shook his head and studied his small self, but he couldn't get back into that child's head. She put her hand over his as tears gathered along his eyelashes. He tried hard not to cry, holding his breath and swallowing down a sob. She reached over, expecting him to resist, but he came into her arms and rested his head against her chest, allowing his tears to fall. He allowed her to stroke his back and hold his head, and she was overcome with gratitude for the chance he was giving her to get to know him at last.

Acknowledgements

The following people are my 'without whoms' — thank you all.

Richard Skinner of the Faber Academy for his brilliant guidance, and my fellow Faberites of 2012 for unstinting support; brave friends Nic Allsop, Meera Bedi, Claire Calman and Beth Holgate, who read and encouraged; Tiana Brooke for her inspiration; everyone at Transworld for ensuring the book is as good as it could be; Felicity Blunt for her kindness and unstoppable energy, and all those who work with her at Curtis Brown; and finally my husband, Greg Brenman, for popping me in the shed with a laptop and suggesting I get on with it . . .

We do hope that you have enjoyed reading this large print book.

Did you know that all of our titles are available for purchase?

We publish a wide range of high quality large print books including:
Romances, Mysteries, Classics
General Fiction
Non Fiction and Westerns

Special interest titles available in large print are:
The Little Oxford Dictionary
Music Book
Song Book
Hymn Book
Service Book

Also available from us courtesy of Oxford University Press:
Young Readers' Dictionary
(large print edition)
Young Readers' Thesaurus
(large print edition)

For further information or a free brochure, please contact us at:
Ulverscroft Large Print Books Ltd.,
The Green, Bradgate Road, Anstey,
Leicester, LE7 7FU, England.
Tel: (00 44) 0116 236 4325
Fax: (00 44) 0116 234 0205

Other titles published by Ulverscroft:

PERSONAL

Lee Child

You can leave the army, but the army doesn't leave you, notes Jack Reacher. Sure enough, the retired military cop is soon pulled back into service, this time for the State Department and the CIA. Someone has taken a shot at the president of France in Paris. The bullet was American — and how many snipers can shoot from three-quarters of a mile with total confidence? Very few, but John Kott, an American marksman gone bad, is one of them. If anyone can stop him, it's the man who beat him before: Reacher. Though he'd rather work alone, Reacher is teamed with Casey Nice, a rookie analyst who keeps her cool with Zoloft. They're facing a rough road full of ruthless mobsters, close calls, double-crosses — and no backup if they're caught . . .

FIRST ONE MISSING

Tammy Cohen

There are three things no one can prepare you for when your daughter is murdered: you are haunted by her memory day and night; even close friends can't understand what you are going through; only in a group with mothers of other victims can you find real comfort. But as the bereaved parents gather to offer support in the wake of another killing, a crack appears in the group that threatens to rock their lives all over again. Welcome to the club no one wants to join.

BEFORE IT'S TOO LATE

Jane Isaac

Following an argument with her British boy-friend, Chinese student Min Li is abducted whilst walking the dark streets of picturesque Stratford-upon-Avon alone. Trapped in a dark pit, Min is at the mercy of her captor. Detective Inspector Will Jackman is tasked with solving the case, and in his search for answers discovers that the truth is buried deeper than he ever expected. But as another student vanishes and Min grows ever weaker, time is running out. Can Jackman track down the kidnapper, before it's too late?

HER

Harriet Lane

Emma is a struggling mum, faintly resentful of her husband and children and their domestic needs; she misses her career and feels she has lost herself. Nina is a successful painter in a second marriage with a teenage daughter; she is sophisticated, independent, and entirely in control. When the two women meet, Nina generously draws Emma into her life. But this isn't the first time their paths have crossed. Nina remembers Emma, and she remembers what Emma did . . . A seemingly innocent friendship slowly develops into a dangerous game of cat and mouse as Nina eases her way into Emma's life. Soon, it becomes clear that Nina wants something from her unwitting companion — something that might just destroy Emma completely . . .